Totally Bound Publishing books by Antonia Church

Single Books

American Royalty

AMERICAN ROYALTY

ANTONIA CHURCH

American Royalty
ISBN # 978-1-83943-742-7

Interior text design by Claire Siemaszkiewicz
Totally Bound Publishing

Published in 2021 by Totally Bound Publishing, United Kingdom.

Totally Bound Publishing is an imprint of Totally Entwined Group Limited.

AMERICAN ROYALTY

Dedication

To my partner, who is both a perfect angel and an exquisite little devil.

Chapter One

"What's your pleasure, Princess?"

"The name isn't *Princess*. It's Kane. And I'm good, thanks."

Kane Liberty took another sip of her Long Island Iced Tea and sighed. The last place she wanted to be was out in public. The last place she ought to be was home alone. So here she was at a bar, trying to beat her feelings back with a club—a bustling club with bangin' beats. The lively dance music was the opposite of her gloomy mood.

She looked sideways at the stranger a couple of seats beside her at the bar, a mountain of a man not so easily dismissed. He loomed next to her, about six foot six, a mass of muscle and masculinity. His skin was the color of her Long Island Iced Tea, warm and pleasant. The stranger possessed a sort of human gravity that was hard to ignore.

"Let me get you something," he tried again.

"I've already have enough," Kane said.

Despite looking like the kind of man who didn't give up easily, he didn't bother Kane again.

That was good. Kane wasn't at the bar to meet a man. She was there to forget one. His name was Dilly. Dillon Durfee. He was supposed to be The One. They had been together for three years. Kane had been waiting for him to give her a ring. Instead, he had packed one bag and given her his key to the apartment they'd shared—then he was gone. He had disappeared before Kane had even realized it wasn't just some cruel practical joke.

That had been on Monday. This was Friday. Kane was still a wreck. Work had distracted her for the last few days, but the weekend had arrived and she faced two free days without a boyfriend for the first time in years. Kane had texted her girlfriends after work and Lani and Sora had promised they would meet her…at seven. It was only six-thirty and Kane had her first drink already half gone.

She looked around the bar, avoiding eye contact with the stranger who had offered to buy her a drink so as not to encourage further flirtation. Kane might be browsing, but she wasn't ready to buy. She was a long way from even taking something off the shelf. It had been quite some time since she'd even bothered to look at the selection. Like going to the grocery store when you were already full, Kane had only given a perfunctory glance at the men available in places like this while she'd been dating Dillon. Now that she was free, she looked harder at the merchandise than she had in the last three years.

Men had changed while Kane had been off the market. They looked softer, more scared, less aggressive than the boys who had always hit on her before—before Dilly. Boys at the bar in designer jeans and too-tight T-shirts sported look-but-don't-touch smirks. Middle-aged men moped like pets trained to beg for treats and know their place. The gaze of old geezers skittered across the floor and ceiling, as if they only had interest in shoes and scalps.

With the exception of the beefy bull beside her, no one had tried to even make eye contact since she'd walked in. The new rules in society likely made for a more cautious climate in the dating scene. Disrespectful interactions were no longer tolerated, and maybe this put guys on the defensive. The modern dating pool felt like swimming with hungry sharks that were all afraid to bite. She wasn't ready to get nibbled yet, anyway.

"So what happened?" Kane asked the big man beside her.

Her Long Island Iced Tea was almost gone, and the alcohol made her bolder than she'd been in a long time.

"What happened to what?"

"Men."

"There are plenty of men all around us." The big guy had a sexy British accent. Kane wasn't in the mood for sexy…or foreign. She missed humdrum and familiar.

"These aren't men," Kane complained.

The big Brit shrugged.

Butterflies flitted about in Kane's stomach, a mixture of excitement and nervousness. Over the course of the last three years, Kane had become *chill*. Complacent. Content. She'd believed Dillon was her one and only. She hadn't expected to ever have to start again. Kane had been relieved that she was done with first encounters—first dates, first kisses, first fucks. Kane thought she was closer to endless instances of 'only' with Dillon—her *only* wedding, her *only* family home, her *only* child. Now she couldn't stop thinking about her lasts—the *last* kiss, the *last* time they'd made love, the *last* fight, the *last* words Dilly had said to her.

Kane took another drink until the glass was empty.

Even the bars had changed. They weren't as loud, as if meaningful conversation had replaced bass-beat flirtation. The place was bright and clean instead of smelly and dirty. Screens were everywhere—twenty TVs playing sports on every wall, phones in hands like candles flickering all across the room, terminals advertising games for money at every table. LED lights ran along the underside of the bar, trimmed windows and doorways, glowed under the floor and illuminated the deejay stand. There wasn't a shadow to hide in in any corner at all. Mirrors covered the rest of the surfaces, either reflecting everyone's sin or a reflection of this modern generation's endless vanity.

"You started without us," Lani scolded as she approached the bar while Kane sipped her second drink.

"She needed a head start," Sora said, waiting back as Lani ordered from the bartender. "This girl needs to get numb."

"What're you having?" Lani asked Kane.

"This is already my second tea. Maybe I shouldn't have another."

"Maybe you should grow a set of balls," Lani said. "I'm getting you a fucking drink."

"Whatever you're having," Kane conceded.

"In that case, you might be in for a threesome with that hot-ass deejay."

Lani had been married since they were kids and was always too much talk about a whole lot of action.

The bartender brought two shots of something bright and pink, like liquid candy.

Lani took the empty stool beside Kane and put her arm over Kane's shoulder, giving her a side hug. The three girls had known each other since elementary school and Kane laid her head on Lani's bare shoulder. Lani had three kids and patted Kane on her temple like she was a toddler with sniffles instead of a grown-ass woman with a broken heart.

Lelani 'Lani' Travers was blonde and busty, with double-barreled weapons that could get her a free drink in any bar in America. Her curves should come with road signs to warn eager eyes of the dangers of each turn. She wore makeup as a mask and a costume as colorful as Supergirl, like some kind of superhero of sex with boots more appropriate for a prostitute than Powerwoman.

Sora Chan took the stool on the other side of Lani. Sora was half as wide, twice as terse and doubly dressed, every inch of her covered from chin to toe. She wore glasses to make her look smarter, which would put her in the company of Einstein or Faraday. Kane wasn't sure if Sora had come right from work or if dressing in a pantsuit and putting her hair in a bun was her idea of 'loosening up'.

Back in high school, Missouri Lewis had nicknamed the three of them 'Neapolitan' because Kane's skin was medium mocha, Lani was white—or orange if she had recently spray-tanned—and Sora was all Asian. None of them were quite sure how Sora equaled pink instead of butterscotch. Lani had explained politely to Missouri that Neapolitan *"is chocolate, vanilla and fucking strawberry. I'm not sure what kind of shitty ice cream you were eating."* Still, the name stuck. Sometimes they would still share a serving of Neapolitan as dessert and laugh about it. Kane preferred the strawberry.

"You can do better than Dillon Durfee," Sora said.

Sora had said that for the last three years. Maybe she was right. Kane hated him right now, and yet she still loved him so much. He'd been Dillon, her Dilly, for so long now. He'd been her everything, and now there was nothing. He might not have been movie-star material, but Dilly had been her heart. Now he'd broken free, leaving it in shambles. And Kane didn't want to hear that she could do better. It was like when people offered condolences when they discovered Kane was an orphan. Many would offer empty expressions about her deceased parents, like *"They're in a better place."* or *"God must have wanted more angels."* None of those words had helped the fact that her parents weren't there.

Kane grabbed the pink drink and took the shot in one big gulp.

"You look dressed to slay, sweetheart," Lani said.

Kane had stopped by their apartment—*her* apartment—and put on her shortest red dress and highest spiked heels. She'd puffed her head of black curls out into a nimbus cloud that floated around her face, like a thunderhead preceding the storm. She wore the bracelet Dillon had given her for her birthday and the necklace she had gotten for a Christmas gift, but Kane had left behind the promise ring that didn't mean anything anymore. Maybe she had inadvertently lured the British man who had tried to buy her a drink. Her bare hands hadn't indicated an affiliation.

"Would you rather I had on a sweatshirt and yoga pants?" Kane asked.

"I so would not," Lani said. "You and me, we could snag any guy in this place."

"I'm sure your husband would love to hear that, La."

"Do you think Chase would rather have a wife who couldn't attract anyone?" Lani asked.

"Not *couldn't*. Maybe *wouldn't*."

"Kane's not ready to start all over with another relationship so soon, Lani," Sora warned.

"Who said anything about a relationship? She just needs to find a hunk of man who can take her mind off that creep who dumped her, even if only for one night." Lani gave Kane a big wink.

Kane looked back over her shoulder for the big guy who had offered her a drink, but he was gone. She didn't want to start anything with anyone, anyway—not even something as meaningless as casual sex. She just wanted to drink a little and wallow in some dance club depression here among her girlfriends.

"How are the kids, La?" Kane asked, already tired of talking about Dillon and her damage.

"Nonexistent," Lani said. "Don't try to change the damn subject. We're here for you, Kane. This night is all about forgetting the past. No crazy kids. No bad relationships. No miserable yesterdays. Just right now."

Kane wasn't sure if Lani had said that for Kane's benefit or for her own. Lani wore a top cut dangerously low, as if the twins might spill out if she made any sudden movements. Her exposed midriff was flat and impressive for a mother of three. Daily yoga with her personal instructor paid off. Lani's jeans looked as tight as a pair of spandex, showing off every bulge and crevice. Lani might be thirty, but she could pass for a coed.

Asian and elegant, Sora had short hair chopped right below her ears, straight and black. Her pants were a dark navy color, pressed and perfect. She had sensible shoes that would be comfortable even after an entire day on her feet. CEO of her own business, Sora always looked like the adult in the room.

"So, what happened?" Kane asked, looking around at the men who were just looking back. It felt like a junior high prom where everyone was afraid to ask each other to dance. "The last time we went out on the town without any boys in our group, we got hit on by every guy in the club."

"That was when we were on the other side of thirty," Sora said.

"Hey," Lani snapped. "Who said anyone was over thirty?"

"Well, you graduated the same year I did," Sora replied.

"Keep it down when you're spreading your version of the truth, Sora," Lani hissed, looking around. She preferred that everyone believe she was ten years younger. Lani dressed like she was on a collegiate soccer team instead of as a soccer mom. Lani's outfit was tighter than the sports bra Kane wore for Tuesday night cardio.

"The last time we went out without any of the boys was the night I met Dillon," Kane said.

"He's such a dee-bag," Lani said.

"Not now, La," Kane sighed. "I'm not ready to be angry."

"You aren't pissed that he gets to be a heartless son of a bitch while your heart is just *broken*?"

Sora flashed a warning look at Lani and Kane picked up on it. There was something Kane didn't know—something about Dilly, something that her girlfriends didn't think Kane was ready to learn. There was more to the story. But wasn't there always? And didn't it bring more hurt with it, every time?

"Love is like my beer," Lani said, holding up a bottle freshly delivered by the bartender. "All fizzy and fun and cool at the beginning. But by the end, it gets as flat and warm as a puddle of piss."

"You should write for Hallmark," Sora said dryly.

Kane didn't ask what Lani had been talking about before Sora shut her down. She wasn't drunk enough for more truth…more hurt. She wasn't drunk enough to ask what Lani had hinted around.

Not yet.

* * * *

Kane had served as a bridesmaid when Lani had married Chase Travers ten years prior. Lani and Chase had been high school sweethearts, and both attended the same local community college. When Lani had found out she was pregnant the week after she'd turned twenty-one, they did as so many young lovers and got married…quick. The ceremony had been perfunctory, and the reception was epic. Lani was four months along at the time and couldn't drink a sip. Chase had made up for her abstinence by getting as drunk as Kane had ever seen a man. Before the night had ended, Chase had streaked through a nunnery, pissed all over the front porch of Goober Stanhope's brownstone and made out with his best man.

Sora had gotten married about five years after Lani, and Kane was a bridesmaid again. Lani served as the Matron of Honor, and Kane had wondered if it was because Lani was already married and brought some clout to the composition of the wedding party. Sora had already owned her own business and Sevin Chan was an ambitious young executive uptown. Their wedding had cost more than Kane made in a whole year. The affair had been stodgy and proper. The only unscripted moment had been when an inebriated Matron of Honor bobbed in the punchbowl for apples that hadn't existed. Lani had been as drunk as Kane had ever seen a woman.

So just recently, Kane had found herself at an impasse. Over the last couple of years, in those romantic moments where she'd imagined walking down the aisle with Dilly, she had wondered who she would pick for her Matron of Honor? Lani or Sora? She finally settled on having them both. Dual Matrons. *Dueling Matrons?* They didn't always get along. But Kane could never choose between them.

Now all those fantasies had become just bitter memories. Wasted time. Kane wondered as the men passed by without even stopping for a lame pick-up line or an asshole comment on Lani's ass whether she had wasted too much time on Dilly. The endless men who had flirted when she was younger had now moved along, drifting by without interaction or indicating any interest. Maybe Kane was lucky Dillon had ended it when he had, before forty was closer than thirty.

"Let's dance," Lani said. "This deejay is banging these beats."

"Are we supposed to ask the guys nowadays?" Kane asked. *How has everything changed in just three short years?*

"Not unless you want to encourage groping and slobbering," Lani said. "Every horny bastard in this place is afraid to make the first move on a woman in this day and age, but once you talk to one of them, it's like an open invitation."

"Afraid?"

"It's a woman's world, Kane," Sora said. "*Finally.* #MeToo revolutionized the dating scene. The guys leave the driving to the girls. You get some if you want some. Otherwise, they leave you in peace."

"Unless you're looking for a piece," Lani added with a wink.

"Is it like that everywhere?" Kane asked. She had never been the outgoing type. Sora had an intellectual confidence and Lani was absolutely fearless, but Kane was content to remain relatively introverted. She'd rather play the prey than act as attacker.

"Not everywhere. But a lot of places like this even have safety words. Some creep comes on to you, and you order a certain drink from the bartender using a code word."

"Yep," Lani added. "If I order an Angie on the Rocks, it means that I have some asshole who needs to be taken care of. The bouncers tend to be pretty rough on those kind of guys."

"So, we won't get asked to dance," Kane summarized. "And if *we* ask, they think it means we want to sleep with them."

The girls nodded.

"So we dance with each other?"

They both smiled and nodded again. Kane shrugged and followed them onto the dance floor. It was a club mix of a song she might've heard on the radio, but Kane wasn't the right generation to name either the song or the singer—if it was even considered singing or if the sound was even a song anymore. It was just rhythmic noises, booms and whistles to a beat, but it was enough to dance to.

The men in the club were domesticated dogs, trained to sit and obey and wait for the attention of the owner. The girls were their masters. Kane caught a dozen eyes on her as she moved to the music. She felt like a fish in a bowl while the pets watched and licked their chops. Kane was a terrible dancer, but the men weren't judging her on her moves. They might have become trained like dogs, but they were still mostly pigs. Kane tried to keep Sora and Lani between her and the drooling beasts along the perimeter of the dance floor.

"That deejay is so watching me," Lani said, her ass competing with her boobs for the shakiest shake. "I feel his eyes all over my body."

"That's probably because you have more of your tits hanging out than tucked in," Kane said.

"Three kids and a ten-year anniversary in two weeks and I've still got it," Lani sang, infinitely more musical than the sound coming out of the speakers.

Kane smiled. "He hardly looks old enough to even get into this club, La."

"Yet he appreciates some prime MILF," Lani bragged.

So Lani could still make the guys take a good, long look. *More power to her*. Kane hoped she would be so fit after three kids. Then the wave of sadness washed across her, flooding over the buzzed part of her boozy brain. She had to start all over again. Kids were a long way off. First, dating again. A new relationship. Engagement. Marriage. Kids were years away. Kane would certainly be sneaking up on forty before she even started a family. Having three kids was likely a fairy tale.

Kane Liberty didn't believe in fairy tales.

"What's with that guy who has been looking at you all night, Kane?" Sora asked.

Lani wasn't listening. She had moved closer to the deejay booth, gyrating to a rhythm that had nothing to do with the song. Kane wondered what Lani's husband was in for when she got home tonight. Hormones radiated off the married woman in palpable waves.

Kane looked around and the tall, dark stranger who'd offered her a drink now sat at a table, still alone, now nursing a beer. His gaze scanned the whole club, but his eyes lingered on Kane every time they passed over her. He knew that she'd noticed, but that didn't stop him. Perhaps he was unaware of the new rules of social interaction.

"He asked if I wanted a drink earlier," Kane told Sora. "I told him to take a hike."

"He's cute," Sora said. She wasn't usually prone to commenting on appearances. He must've been attractive indeed.

"Too soon," Kane said, "isn't it?"

Sora nodded. "Of course it is."

But Sora sported that look again—that she knew something that she wasn't telling. But Kane still wasn't drunk enough to ask what it meant. *Not quite. Getting closer.*

Kane left the dance floor and went back to her drink. Sora followed. Kane gulped the rest of the alcohol in two big swallows. As she set the glass down, her head started swimming. The British stranger watched her from across the room. His eyes were dark and mysterious and daring.

Too soon.

Isn't it?

Lani finally noticed that Kane and Sora had returned to the table. She danced away from the deejay, her backside bouncing to the bass. The deejay watched her ass like it was the pendulum of a pocket-watch, hypnotized by the sway. He pushed the beat harder, faster, making Lani move like sound was a hand and he could guide her every action. The rules may have changed, but some guys always found ways to cheat. The deejay flirted without saying a word.

"God, Lani, take it down a few levels," Sora said. "You have a husband to get home to tonight."

"Jesus, I'm just having some fun, Sora," Lani snapped. "Might do you some good to loosen up a bit. Get a little sexy yourself. Maybe Sevin would show you some interest once in a while."

"You don't have to be a witch, you know," Sora said.

"She meant *bitch*, you know," Kane added, coming to Sora's defense.

"Yeah, but Lani gotta be Lani," Lani said.

Kane wondered what Lani meant about Sevin's waning interest in Sora. And why was Lani flirting so overtly with the deejay? Kane worried that her own relationship was not the only one in crisis among the trio of girlfriends. But Kane couldn't worry about Lani and Sora. Not tonight. Tonight was for wallowing in her own woes.

"Don't make this about me, Lani," Sora said. "Let's keep focused on Kane. She needs both of us."

Lani's eyes had fogged over with booze and desire, but they cleared up when Sora said those words. This was about Kane. But this was about more than just Kane's broken heart. There was some secret that Lani and Sora shared about Dilly, something they wanted to tell Kane.

"So what is it?" Kane asked. "Out with it."

She was finally drunk enough to hear what they had to tell her.

Sora looked reluctant, but Lani was inebriated enough to weaken the dam between being sensitive and not giving a damn. "It's Dillon," she said. "He's already shacking up with some whore."

The words stabbed Kane right in the chest like a knife. She even looked down to see if someone had really plunged a blade into her heart. What was already broken could apparently be further destroyed. Dillon really wasn't going to rest until Kane was shattered, sliced, smote, reduced to ash and scattered to the winds.

"I just spoke with Jon Ryder this morning," Kane said, catching her breath for a moment. "He said Dillon was staying with him."

"One dog lying for another," Sora said.

"My cousin Cheryl has a friend who knows a guy who works with this bitch," Lani added. She showed Kane a stranger's social media page on her phone. It was Dilly and his new woman—a whole lot of new woman. Her tank top barely contained her boobs. Platinum blonde, she looked more like a ghost of an old girlfriend—a very substantial ghost, with a backside twice as wide as Kane's. And she had a tattoo on her face. On her *face*. Her name was Wendy, and her status was *Just moved in with my man!*

"She looks like she could kick my husband's ass in a fight," Lani said.

"It looks like it was going on for a while, Kane," Sora said softly.

"What?" Kane stammered.

She didn't understand. Dilly had said it wasn't working out. He'd said they should both see what else the world had to offer. But he had apparently already taken his own advice when he'd said that. Dillon had cheated on her…with Wendy. With wide and white Wendy, who was the opposite of Kane in every apparent way—except Dillon. They had that in common for an unknown, overlapping amount of time.

Kane shuddered. She thought she might be sick.

Sora took her hand. "You didn't deserve this," she said. "He's a pig."

"He's a man," Lani said. "Fry them up, and they all smell like bacon."

Kane's head whirled and she felt like she couldn't get her bearings. The last three years were an anchor to everything that was supposed to be ahead of her, but all those months slid out from under her like mud sloughing down a hillside, threatening to take her into the dirt and grime. She wanted to post the nastiest thing she could think of on Wendy's page. Kane was ready to get an Uber to Wendy's place and scream at Dillon at the top of her lungs from the street. She wanted to get drunk, pass out and not wake up until next year.

"You want us to take you home, sweetie?" Sora asked.

"No," Kane managed, looking across the club at the British stranger who had offered to buy her a drink. He was still looking at her—not creepy, just calm—like she was a painting at an art museum. "Let's fucking dance."

* * * *

Sora had gone home after ten. Lani stood on-stage, too close to the deejay for a woman who had a husband and a family. The deejay looked dirty, a smattering of wispy whiskers just fuzzy evidence of avoiding a razor, acne still spotting his plaid face and a stocking cap covering hair as greasy as anything Kane could have ordered off the bar menu. Sweat ran down his temples like tears. Lani kept touching her blonde locks and her face and his arm in endless flirtation. *Where is that going? Where will it end?* Did Kane even care tonight? She was a drink or two past caring about anything.

Dilly was a cheater.

Kane started to lift her hand to the bartender to order another drink. The dark and handsome stranger suddenly appeared between her and the bar. He was big and blocked out everything beyond, taking up all the space in Kane's immediate vicinity. She looked up and up, and when she thought she was looking at his face, her blurry vision resolved into a view of his broad chest. A little higher and he was staring at her with his smoldering eyes. His gaze felt intense and interested.

"Are you going to offer to buy me a drink again?"

The stranger shrugged.

"My answer hasn't changed," Kane said, and he started to turn around. "But maybe I don't want to drink alone."

Kane leaned around the mountain of a man and waved at the bartender, who nodded and sent over another drink. Kane pushed it across the table in front of the chair Lani had left empty for the last hour now. The stranger sat down opposite Kane.

"Whiskey," he observed with a sniff. "Straight up?"

"I'm not playing around with my drinks tonight," Kane said.

"No, I guess you're not."

"So, what's your name, anyway?"

"Gade Williams. Short for 'Renegade'. It was my call sign when I was in the Air Force."

He looked ex-military. However, he was so big and strong that he seemed built for physical combat on the battlefield rather than wedged into the canopy of a jet. His shirt was casual and breezy, but it couldn't conceal a chest that was as thick as a slab of beef and biceps that looked like twin guns that were heavily loaded. His skin was dark and yet seemed to shine.

"You sound more 007 than *Top Gun*."

"My father was also Air Force, stationed at Lakenheath in Great Britain. I went to a private school in London."

"How posh," Kane said.

Gade shrugged.

"You've been watching me all night," Kane said.

"You're kind of hard not to notice."

"There are dozens of other girls in this club—younger and prettier and probably a hell of a lot nicer if you offered them a drink. A guy like you in a place like this could score any cheap hookup he wanted."

"I'm not interested in a cheap hookup. You just looked like you could use someone keeping an eye out for you."

"Keeping an eye *on* me, maybe," Kane teased.

"It isn't difficult to stare," he admitted. His whiskey was almost gone. Kane called for another tumbler and the waitress had it in Gade's hand before the first one was empty. "I can't recall a time a woman ever bought me a drink."

"I bought you *two* drinks," Kane reminded him with a little smile. *Is this flirting?* She couldn't remember what that was exactly like, but this *was* a distraction. She needed a distraction.

"You did," he said. "I'm not used to drinking this much. In the Air Force, I didn't have a whole lot of time for alcohol."

"You keep using the past tense," Kane said, leaning forward. Her dress was cut low and she knew she was giving him quite the view, but she didn't feel as shy as she normally did—not tonight, not after damned Dilly and a dozen drinks. Now this guy… A distraction, indeed. "You're not in the Air Force anymore?"

"I went into private business after my last tour," Gade said, then tried to change the subject. "Your drink is empty. Can I get you another?"

"I've had enough," Kane said. Her head was swimming. Thoughts of Dilly were swept away on waves of alcohol. "Maybe I should be heading home."

Gade looked at her with his dark eyes. They were intense and unblinking and didn't tell her a damn thing about him. They were wide and open and full of mystery. She couldn't see what was right in front of her. That seemed to be a chronic condition.

Gade sighed. "You're going to let me drink alone?"

His tumbler was already half-gone again. "You're almost done."

He finished the whiskey in a single gulp. "Turns out I'm still a little thirsty."

"I think you're a lot thirsty," Kane slurred.

So Kane ordered him another. The lights, the music and the people on the dance floor as well as the smells and the everywhere insinuation of sex were as intoxicating as one more drink. Gade kept talking and Kane listened and sometimes replied, but the words danced off as soon as they escaped her lips, twirling away on the beats and the bass. Gade's deep voice gradually grew bleary, his pronunciation fuzzy, his accent almost unintelligible. One more whiskey was one more 'one more' than he could obviously handle.

"So what's your story?" Gade asked.

"Same as everyone's." Kane sighed. "Life sucks."

"Is it a guy?"

"That obvious?"

"Must've ended badly."

"My brother says all love ends badly," Kane whispered. She paused, losing grip on her disintegrating thoughts. She collected herself enough to forge forward without sounding like a total lush. "Mark thinks the only way love stays true is if it ends before it starts to curdle."

"Like bad milk?"

"The worst milk."

"That doesn't sound like a fairy-tale ending," Gade said.

"Does life seem like a fairy tale to you?"

Gade didn't reply. He just sipped his drink like it was grandma's tea.

"Mark likes to talk about my parents…my *real* parents. I call him my big brother, but he's really my cousin. We were raised together. See… My father and mother died when I was very young. Mark says they died before their love did. He thinks it's all very romantic. I think it's morbid and sad."

"Do you think he's right?" Gade asked. "About true love?"

"How many people do you know who have been in love longer than just a short time?"

"My parents have been married for almost forty years."

"And are they happy?" Kane asked.

"They're still together," Gade replied. "I'd call that love."

"I love my friends. I love my Aunt Polly," Kane said. "Loving someone is different from being in love with someone."

Gade looked off into the distance, not focused on anything at all. Then his focus came back, and he looked at Kane. Looked *at* her. Looked *into* her. "I guess I choose to believe in the possibility. Better to look on the bright side than to sit your whole life in the dark."

"Pollyanna," Kane teased.

Then something happened. It was the way Gade gazed at her. Kane could see it in his dark brown eyes. He was into her. He wanted something more than she could have given just a week ago. But that was a week ago. Now she could give whatever she wanted, because the decision was hers and hers alone. Kane was a little surprised that she was entertaining the option at all.

"Time to go," she finally said, because if she didn't leave then she wouldn't get home. She would end up somewhere else, with someone else—with this Renegade.

"Let me get you a cab," Gade offered.

"My friend will take care of it," Kane said. "Her uncle has an Uber."

"Your friend left with the deejay a half-hour ago," Gade said.

No, Kane thought. *Lani wouldn't. Lani couldn't!*

Lani had.

Kane scanned the whole bar for Lani. Indeed, she wasn't in the deejay booth. Kane tried to call her phone, but it went right to voicemail. Lani's phone was off. *What is she doing? Is she crazy? She's married! A mother!* Leave it to Lani to make the night about herself after all.

But this night wasn't about Lani. It was about Kane and Dillon. *That son of a bitch Dilly*. She didn't want to think about it. Kane wanted it to swim away. One more drink and she would be sick in the morning. Alcohol wasn't the best option for further distraction.

Maybe she needed something…stronger. Kane looked Gade up and down. His arms were like pythons, his chest like Superman's. His face was carved from some dark wood, like mahogany. He looked like six and a half feet of pure muscle. The closest Dilly had ever gotten to being a soldier was ranking at the top of his *Call of Duty* league. Gade was military all the way from top to… Well, maybe Kane wanted to find out.

"All right," Kane agreed. *Is this a good idea?* "Let's get a cab."

Suddenly, Gade looked like he wasn't so sure about it. "As in *we*?"

"Aren't you a big, strong soldier? You think a young woman such as myself should stumble home drunk at this hour?" Kane asked. "Alone?"

"Of course not," he answered, a reaction as automatic as a Boy Scout volunteering to escort grandma across the street.

Kane certainly wasn't feeling very grandmotherly.

She waved her hand for the tab.

"I'll get it," Gade offered.

"This isn't a date," Kane replied. *Is it? No, certainly not a* date. *But maybe something else?* "I'll pay my tab. You get yours."

Kane paid cash. Gade used a card.

Kane got up, using the table to steady herself. Gade stood, *almost* unwavering. He started toward the door, parting the people crowded in the club like an ocean liner plowing through stormy seas. Kane laced her fingers through his and he looked back. That expression crossed his face again, like a kid caught with his hand in the cookie jar. His hand hadn't even gotten close to Kane's cookie jar. *Not yet.*

Outside, it was warm. The night was nice. A little breeze stirred in her black curls and made Gade's shirt snug against his chest, thin enough to show the sculpted lines of his pecs and abs. He might not be military anymore, but he was still built like a soldier. His scalp was even buzzed close like he was fresh out of boot camp.

He flagged a cab then held the door while she slipped inside. Gade got in beside her. The cab driver asked the address. Kane suddenly thought of being home, back in the apartment she had shared with Dilly these last three years. His ghost was everywhere. Everything still smelled like him. Half of the things in the apartment were items they'd bought together. Kane would roam the rooms wondering what they had acquired after the point that Dilly had already been screwing around with Wendy.

"I don't remember," she said, so softly only Gade could hear.

"What's that, ma'am?" the driver asked.

Gade looked at Kane, and Kane looked at Gade, like it was a contest on who would blink first. But this wasn't about closing her eyes. It was about opening them, seeing something new. If Kane could imagine someone actually falling into another person's gaze, she would swear that Gade fell into hers.

Gade gave the driver his own address. Kane smiled. She wasn't going home tonight. And she wouldn't be thinking about Dillon. For tonight, Dilly was in the past. Gade was her present—a present she couldn't wait to unwrap. Gade was strong and dark and beautiful, and he looked at Kane like she hadn't been looked at in a long time. There'd be no thinking about Dilly—not for the next few hours, at least.

Chapter Two

Kane woke up in an unfamiliar place with a strange light coming from an unidentified source. The bed was king-sizes, the sheets were as Egyptian as a pharaoh and she remembered being called 'Princess' in the murmurs of passion. She felt around for her phone and found it bedside. It was not her bed—and it was ten o'clock in the morning.

The strange light was the sun, seeping in between the cracks of vertical blinds covering a patio door off the large bedroom. Kane's gaze swept across the room, spying a weight set, a handsome dresser, her little red dress, a silver military medal in an ornate display case hanging on the wall, her spiked heels kicked askew underneath, a plant in a large pot adjacent to the patio door, her bra hanging over a leafy frond, a desk that was immaculately organized and her satin underwear dangling off the doorknob to the en suite bathroom.

Gade slept silently beside her. Like large objects detected in the dark, she was aware he was there. His body-heat was against her back. Scenes from the previous night flashed through her memory like highlights in a preview of upcoming attractions at the movies. It was a lot of action…certainly some romance. She wondered if a little was special effects. Parts of it had seemed like magic.

Kane slipped out of bed silently. She'd had three years of practice. Dillon had been a late sleeper with odd hours, and she'd always worked a nine-to-five job. So she would sneak out of bed every morning without waking him. The thought of Dilly was both worse without the effects of alcohol and slightly less barbed after the night of something strange. Kane moved like a ghost across the bedroom and closed the door of the master bathroom without making a sound.

A T-shirt hung on the back of the bathroom door, and Kane pulled it over her naked body. The front said *Air Force Fighting Falcons*. It hung to halfway between her hips and her knees. She checked herself in the mirror and her hair was like a black cloud that had been stirred up by the exhaust of a jet plane. She expected her eyes to be puffy and bloodshot, but they were clear and bright and chestnut brown. Her light brown skin seemed to glow from within. It seemed late-night exercise was great for staving off the after-effects of last night's drinking.

Kane sat on the lid of the toilet and called Lani first, but the call just went to voicemail. She called Sora next. Sora answered on the first ring. Sora could stay up till five and she would still be up by six, even on a Saturday. By ten a.m., she was probably already at the office, putting in a few extra hours.

"How are you feeling?" Sora asked. She didn't have a clue as to all the adventure that had happened after she'd left early for the night. "Hung over?"

"I'm at some guy's house," Kane said.

"Say *what*?" Sora screeched, a woman prone to neither outbursts of exclamation nor grammatically suspect phrasing.

"It's the big guy who was watching me all night—the one who you said was cute."

"I guess a lot happened after I left," Sora said with a smile in her voice. "You little vixen. We have to meet for lunch. I want *all* the details."

"I really don't know if there are words to describe some of the things we did," Kane said with a flush heating her cheeks. "He was physically up to any kind of challenge, I can tell you that."

"Stop," Sora interrupted. "I want to hear about it in person. Two o'clock. O'Malley's. Unless you are delayed by the sequel to last night's activities. I *will* understand if you are late."

"It's a date," Kane said, then changed gears. "Have you heard from Lani?"

"No," Sora replied, her voice changing from amused astonishment to cold concern. "Was she still at the club when you left with the tall, dark stranger?"

"His name is Gade Williams. He told me it's short for Renegade," Kane said. "And La left before I did. I think she went home with the deejay."

"Sheesh."

"I think that's worthy of some good, old-fashioned profanity, Sora. You can say *shit*."

"You know what I mean, Kane," Sora said, like she always did.

"It's going to be some serious shit when Chase starts calling around looking for her. Her phone is going straight to voicemail."

"Leave Lani to me. You have your hands full—or you better have your hands full."

Kane smiled. "All right. See you at two."

"Or later," Sora said with a wink in her voice before she hung up.

Kane sat there for a minute. Gade was just on the other side of the door. He had had enough whiskey last night to maybe impair his judgment. What if he regretted taking her home with him? What if things got awkward when he awoke? Kane suddenly wished she could somehow sneak through the back door, but there was only one way out of the bathroom. Besides, did she even know him well enough to care if he thought it was a mistake or not? If he were weird about it, she could grab her things and get out.

She opened the door. The bed was empty.

The door to the master bedroom was open. Kane could hear the sounds of Gade making breakfast. Smells slinked in through the open door—frying bacon and toasting bread or bagels. Kane realized she was very hungry and extremely thirsty. She followed her nose out of the door, down the hall, into the open living space that featured the kitchen, dining area and living room.

"Good morning, Princess," Gade greeted, his tone more cordial than a man admitting carnal knowledge. "Breakfast?"

"Yes. I worked up quite an appetite."

A ghost of a smile touched his lips. He guarded his emotions—a soldier through and through. Was there a hint of fond remembrance in that little curl of his lip or an embarrassed acknowledgment?

He wore pajama bottoms that were loose and airy, but nothing to cover his magnificent chest. Kane had appreciated sculptures at the art museum of marbled figures with no less perfect of a figure. But this was real life, and she had the memories of touching and tasting to confirm it. Certainly, Gade wasn't made of stone.

Kane sat at a stool and pulled herself up to the raised bar top. Hadn't this all started at a bar? His Air Force T-shirt was longer than any of hers, but not long enough to conceal most of her mocha legs. Her bare feet dangled, her toes brushing his tile floor. She leaned her elbows on the granite countertop and watched him work.

Gade was masterfully efficient, clearing debris like eggshells and dirty utensils after their use was up, wiping away spilled messes on the polished surface as soon as the ingredients were mixed, the balance between flipping eggs and turning bacon a thing to behold. In his previous occupation as a soldier, competence had likely been necessary for survival.

There was a single bright flower in a vase at the center of the countertop. It seemed out of place in the utilitarian workspace of Gade's kitchen. He noticed her interest.

"I had to go around to the corner market for eggs," Gade said. "I thought you might like a little color this morning."

"When did you have the time?"

"Before you woke," Gade said. "I was up early then crawled back into bed."

To buy me a flower. "A pink rose," Kane marveled. Her favorite.

"I thought it seemed to fit you."

She smiled. What did he know of her? Enough to impress, she decided.

He served her on a plate that looked ready for posting on her social media homepage. This thing they were having was probably not ready for that. Wendy the boyfriend-stealer might have been fine advertising her new status online, and it might be oh-so-much-fun to sting Dillon back with a post of this gorgeous homemade breakfast at a strange man's home, but Kane wasn't sure what the night with Gade had even meant.

They ate across the bar top from each other. Gade had coffee, black. Kane was offered and accepted orange juice. She smiled and tried to catch his gaze, but he seemed to be avoiding eye contact. *Does he regret this? Was it a mistake? Do I have bacon stuck between my teeth?* There was something wrong.

"Are you married?" Kane blurted. She'd been out of the game too long and this guy was too new to monkey around with silly shit.

"No."

"Girlfriend?"

The thought of her being the Wendy to some other Kane made the eggs and bacon bubble in her belly.

"No."

"Then what is it?"

"It's complicated," Gade said.

"Just what every girl wants to hear," Kane quipped.

She stared at him for an explanation, and he suddenly seemed to think something on his tile floors offered more interest than her face. Kane got up and marched back to the bedroom. Gade followed, but she slammed his door.

"Kane, come on," he said through it. "I'm trying to find a way to tell you."

Kane was pissed. Disinterest might have been better than this bullshit. He was hiding something and didn't trust her to explain. That spelled trouble. Gade was *all* trouble.

Kane collected her garments that had been strewn about the room and played a game of hide and seek with her purse before finding it behind the bathroom door. Redressed, Kane reached out to hang his Air

Force T-shirt where she had found it on the hook, but she paused. Instead, she stuffed it in her purse. A souvenir. It was more of an adventure than she'd had in all her three years with Dillon.

Gade still stood outside the door when she unlocked and opened it. He held her rose, so pink. But she only saw red.

"Let me explain," he tried.

"If it took you that long to think up some story, save it for some other gullible girl," Kane said, striding across his apartment to the door. "I've had enough of lies lately."

"It isn't a lie, Kane," he called after her as she exited. "But you might not believe what I tell you."

Kane didn't know what that meant—and she didn't care. Gade was just another guy with another something to say. She had no reason to trust anything that came out of his mouth.

* * * *

Kane went home for a while after she'd stormed out of Gade's apartment. She should have been early for her appointment with Sora, but being back in her apartment proved detrimental to her emotional state. Kane lost herself again in the grief of heartbreak. By the time she found her way out of the fog, it was already two o'clock. In her autopilot of an afternoon, she'd managed to shower, get dressed and put on a splash of makeup. Realizing the time, she rushed out of her place and was only fifteen minutes late by the time she got to O'Malley's.

O'Malley's was the oldest restaurant around. Established by one of the original founders of the town, it has been in continuous operation for nearly two centuries. The sign in the front window was the original wooden shingle that Lewis O'Malley himself might've hung outside over the front door when he'd opened the restaurant to his very first customer. The refurbished oak floors looked exquisite. Reclaimed pieces of original trim hung about the establishment. A preserved letter from Charles Carroll, a delegate from Maryland who'd signed the United States Constitution, to the original owner was framed and featured prominently behind the bar. Now, Sora sat in the back beside a brick wall that has existed since Thomas Jefferson had been still breathing.

As Kane crossed the restaurant to the corner table, Sora wore a smirk. Two in the afternoon, O'Malley's was almost empty, and the girls had the corner of the room all to themselves. Sora sipped an iced tea with lemon, watching the news stream on a TV screen hanging on a wall near their table. She apparently supposed Kane was late for a different reason…a better reason.

"Kane Liberty, you absolute tigress," Sora taunted.

"I wish," Kane said. "It wasn't like that. It wasn't anything like that."

"Details," Sora said, leaning forward. She wore a beige suit jacket perfect for a business meeting, even though it was Saturday afternoon. Sora forever looked ready to close a deal.

"He told me 'it's complicated'."

"Ouch."

"Mm-hmm."

"Wife? Girlfriend?" Sora asked.

"He said no," Kane said. "But he wouldn't be stupid enough to say yes. He said I wouldn't believe him if he told me the truth."

"Maybe because his truth is a big fat lie," Sora said.

Kane shrugged. A waitress came and asked what she wanted to drink.

"Whatever she's having," Kane said.

Kane preferred something strong, but Sora had a sweet tea. The thought of Gade's muscular form crossed her memory. She had had enough of 'strong' these last few hours.

"You get through to La yet?" Kane asked.

Sora's eyes narrowed until they were nearly closed. "Finally."

"And?"

"She spent the night with the deejay."

"Like passed out on his couch? Or they stayed up and binged on Netflix?" Kane asked hopefully.

"Let's just say you weren't the only one who had an active night."

"Shit," Kane hissed. "And Chase?"

"Lani told him that she had too much to drink and spent the night at my place," Sora said. "She told Chase it was *my* fault for not messaging *her* husband about it. So I had to lie when Chase messaged me. And it's just a matter of time before it comes up between Chase and Sevin, so I have to tell Sevin to lie about it, too. She's such a bee."

"Like a bumble bee?"

"You know what I mean, Kane."

"You can say 'bitch', Sora. She's really acting like one."

Is Lani any different from Dilly? Lani cheated on Chase just like Dillon cheated on Kane. Kane felt sick about it.

"She's the one wrecking her marriage, and you're more upset about the ordeal than she is," Sora said.

The waitress returned and took their food order. The grinning young woman must have sensed the tense topic of conversation at the table and seemed determined to overwhelm them with sunshine. Kane applauded the effort but was irritated by the experience.

Kane and Sora both watched the television while they waited, a distraction from the disaster of this day. The tragedies paraded on the news always made real life seem less terrible. Maybe that was why the only news was bad news. What kind of heartless network bastards would rub the viewers' noses in good news all the time and make everyone feel all the more shitty about their regular lives?

Onscreen, the news anchor flashed his perfect white teeth. If a mold existed for the generic personalities that hosted these kinds of talk shows, Dash Dameron was the original template—strong chin, piercing eyes, superlative smile, supernatural hair. The silver fox had been a staple of cable television for three decades. He had interviewed every president since Clinton. He schmoozed with the celebrity gods. Sports figures and business titans both came on Dash Dameron's show when they wanted a fluffy interview with just enough edge to make it credible. Dash styled his hair with oozing charisma.

"Tonight on *DamTime*, Senator Sidney Cambridge will be live in the studio for an exclusive interview. The chairman of the powerful Ways and Means Committee promises us a bombshell revelation that will change American history as we know it. Don't miss it!"

Dash signed off with his signature wink. Kane had never been sure if the gesture was supposed to playful or if he thought the audience was in on some secret joke. When she was younger, Kane had wondered if the wink meant Dash Dameron knew something that she didn't, and when she got older, she started to think it was just a commercial gimmick, trademarked to sell the *DamTime* brand.

"So what are you going to do about this new guy?" Sora asked, tired of news that was never anything new.

"He was just a distraction," Kane dismissed.

"I think it was more than that," Sora said. "Kane Liberty never had a one-night stand in her whole life. You're certainly allowed a night of fun without any strings attached if that's what you're looking for, but it looks like that wasn't quite what you expected."

"I didn't expect it to be so awkward. He took the time to make breakfast but then he seemed like the whole night shouldn't have happened. It was like he wanted me to leave and he didn't want me to go at the same time. He wanted to tell me something, but he wouldn't say it."

"Why don't you hear him out?" Sora suggested. "Maybe he's in the witness protection program or from outer space or something."

Kane glared at Sora as the server brought out their order. "Is that a joke?"

Sora scowled. "Why does everyone always act like I don't have a sense of humor?"

"Well, I haven't heard you try to be funny since that time we had to rush Lani to the emergency room when she was in labor with Callie. Callie is five years old."

Sora huffed and took a bite of her pasta. "I think you should call him."

"I didn't even get his number."

"Kane, you little *vixen*. That is some serious out-of-character behavior. I like the new, bold direction."

But Kane wasn't bold. She didn't want a new direction. She had been content with the old one—the one she'd been traveling in with Dilly. Now this was all new. *Bad* new.

"It doesn't matter," Kane said. "It's too soon. Gade was a diversion—a *great* diversion—but I'm not ready to start up anything with anyone right now. I need to get over Dillon."

"Well, that piece of trash shouldn't take up any more of your life," Sora said. "I understand if you want to take some time to rebuild Kane Liberty, but don't make one more minute about that scumbag Dillon Durfee."

Kane's phone chimed between bites of key lime chicken.

"Is it Gade? Did he track you down like in the movies?"

"You mean stalk me like a creeper?" Kane asked. "No, it's my sister."

Mary was two years older than Kane and twin sister to Mark. Kane's parents had both died when she had been very young, and her Aunt Polly had raised Kane alongside Polly's own two kids. Mark and Mary had always been protective of their younger 'sister', so it wasn't surprising now as Mary texted.

Need to talk. Can you come over tonight?

Kane figured her sister had finally found out about Dillon and his cheating.

Kane texted back affirmatively. She had a busy day—from a stranger's bed to the place she'd shared with Dillon for the last three years to her childhood home. A circle…all the way back to where she had started.

Kane sighed and finished her chicken. On the television, Dash Dameron came on for another promotion for his interview with the Senator. Repeat. Cycles. The same thing again and again.

* * * *

Kane parked outside her sister Mary's flawless little two-story home. She locked the car and zipped her keys in the outside pocket of her crossbody bag then slipped it over her head and started up the cleanly swept walkway. Immaculate flowerbeds aligned the foundation on either side of the front door. The bright blue door featured a homey welcome mat out front. Aunt Polly had lived an idyllic life here as she'd raised three kids, and Mary was trying mightily to follow in her mother's footsteps. Mary strove to replicate the perfect life presented by her parents.

Aunt Polly and Uncle John had retired to Florida years before, and they'd sold the family home to Mary. They had discussed the decision with Mark and Kane before they offered it to Mary, to ensure that there would be no hurt feelings. Mark had wanted something bigger and better than this quaint little home, and Kane had been content with her apartment. Mary had already started a family. She was a stay-at-home mom, like Aunt Polly had been, so it had just made sense.

Kane had lived there until she'd left home at eighteen…a lot of good memories. She never remembered her natural parents as anything more than dreamlike impressions and fleeting images, so their absence was more of magical wonder than a grief-stricken loss. Aunt Polly had done everything she could to make Kane feel like she fit in. This was as much Kane's family home as it was Mary's or Mark's.

Kane had slept in a tent in this very backyard when her friends had stayed over, Sora and Lani always among them. Kane's first date had had to pick her up right there and meet her Uncle John. She'd experienced her first kiss later that night at the end of the cobblestone walkway. How many times had Kane walked around this block with thoughts swimming in her head of whatever boy she had liked at the moment?

A car rolled slowly through the intersection, cautious in a neighborhood full of chasing children. Kane just glimpsed the driver before the car disappeared behind Mr. Clopper's big brown Victorian two-story on the corner. Why did she think she'd seen Gade driving by? Was it her overactive imagination? Was Gade really that much on her mind? Or had he really just cruised by her old family home?

Kane shook the thought away. She was tired of thinking about guys, either former flames or recent ones. At least when it came to her sister, Kane had almost thirty years of experience dealing with that kind of crazy.

Kane noted a brand-new Mercedes in the driveway as she approached the front door. *Certainly not the minivan style of Mary Smythe.* Kane guessed that it meant Mark was also over. Suddenly, she wondered if she'd been summoned for bad news. Had something happened to either Aunt Polly or Uncle John? Kane's stomach turned, not ready for any more twists in her life right now.

Mary answered the door…another ominous sign. When Kane rang the doorbell, it *always* resulted in Artie and Agnes making a mad scramble as to who answered first. When it opened and neither niece nor nephew stood inside the entryway, it was the first time since Artie could toddle that Mary herself had opened the door for Kane.

"Where are the kids?" Kane asked.

"Larry took them out for ice cream."

Mary was just two years older than Kane, but she'd already lived the iconic American life—married, two kids, cute house, SUV. Those two years looked like ten. After a decade of household management, Mary was no-nonsense and displayed no sense of humor. She had forgotten what fun was. Her dark face had become consistently glum, as if she were always somehow disappointed with the disposition of something. Wider than Kane by double and with unruly hair frizzed and frenetic, Mary made taking time for herself seem like the last thing she had room for on any given day. Mary had looked perpetually tired ever since she had given birth to Artie ten years before.

"And Mark is here?" Kane asked.

"He's in the kitchen," Mary said, "having some wine. He brought the good stuff. Want a glass?"

"I think I'm going to need one."

Mary didn't confirm or deny. She just turned and walked down the hallway toward the kitchen, and Kane followed. The walls were adorned by Emerson family history, and Kane figured prominently in the chronology. There was a graduation picture, candid shots of the three of them growing up, a family portrait from when Kane had been an awkward teen and a group photo from last year's family trip to Florida to see Aunt Polly and Uncle John.

Mark sat at the kitchen island, drinking a large goblet of red liquid. The label on the bottle looked old and weathered. *Only the best for brother*. He wore expensive clothes and a watch worth more than Kane spent in a year. With hair styled like a politician's, thinner strands on top striving to cover his growing patch of premature baldness, Mark appeared to be ready for any unexpected interview by a roving local reporter. Like his twin sister, he tended toward extra pounds. His distributed around his waistline and chest, making for manboobs bigger than Sora's bustline. He lately favored a mustache that reminded Kane of Uncle Carl on that show with Urkel they had watched when they had been kids.

Mark was staring at the small television mounted over the coffee pot, *DamTime* just starting with its punchy theme song, Dash Dameron setting up the historic interview with Senator Sidney Cambridge.

"Just in time, Kane," Mark said.

"Is this some sort of intervention? Did you find out about me and Dillon?"

"What happened with you and Dillon?" Mary asked.

Damn, Kane thought. She didn't have to even get into that.

"We broke up," Kane simplified. If this wasn't about that, then what sort of shit was going to hit the fan?

"I'm so sorry, Kane." Mary folded Kane into her arms, and they stood there like that for a long while. It was nice, just like Mary had done when Hollis Wentz had stood Kane up for junior prom or Anthony Reed had talked trash about her to the other girls on the volleyball team. The Black boys would make fun because Kane's skin was too light and the White boys talked smack because her skin was too dark. Mary had hugs that could make a person feel protected from the whole wide world. She always tried to make things better, although the look on her face when she and Kane uncoupled made Kane think that things would soon get worse.

"If this isn't about Dillon, then what's it about?" Kane asked, worried. "Is Aunt Polly okay? Uncle John? The kids? Larry?"

"Yeah," Mark said. "They're fine. No one is hurt. No one's sick or dying."

"Okay," Kane sighed. The possibilities otherwise were endless and she didn't know what to expect. Her stomach rebelled. This felt like last week when Dillon had sat her down on their sofa and told her that they needed to talk about their relationship. The look on his face had been evidence that he wasn't about to propose. She had known before Dillon said a word that he was going to break up with her. Now, she didn't know what was coming.

"It's about your dad, Kane," Mark blurted out.

Kane knew almost nothing about her father. Her mother's family had surrounded her since the day Kane had been born. Aunt Polly and Uncle John had raised her, and she knew her maternal grandparents, her cousins. There were picture albums piled high with photos of her mother as a baby and a teen and a beautiful young woman, but her dad remained a mystery. Kane had no pictures from before he'd married her mother. There was no history lesson there. It was as if Reese Liberty had only come into being when he'd met Kane's mother.

Her parents had died in a car accident when Kane had been just two years old. Aunt Polly had been babysitting Kane at the time. It was supposed to be just for the evening, but it had turned into forever. Aunt Polly had told tons of stories of Kane's mother from when Polly and Desiree were young, but she had so few stories about Kane's father. Polly had known him for such a short time before he was gone, so this revelation by Mark came as a surprise.

"My father?" Kane repeated.

"There's something you need to know," Mark said. He darted his focus to the television screen, where Dash was shaking hands with the Senator. *Is he monitoring the screen as a way to avoid eye contact with me?* Why did it seem like what was happening on *DamTime* somehow connected to what Mark was telling Kane Liberty in Mary's kitchen? Mary stood close to Kane, as if ready for more support if this new information proved too much for Kane to handle. *What the hell is going on?*

"There's something Uncle Reese never told you," Mary said. "Something he never had a chance to tell you."

"There were things in your father's past that he was trying to run away from," Mark added. Kane didn't like the way Mark's black mustache twitched, like this secret was itchy. "When he fell in love with Aunt Desiree, your paternal grandfather disapproved."

"Because she was Black?"

"Maybe not color. Maybe more because of our pedigree," Mark said. "So, your grandfather made Uncle Reese choose between his family and your mother. Obviously, you know how that turned out."

"My parents were like Romeo and Juliet? And they ended up just as dead."

"Not exactly the Montagues and the Capulets, Kane," Mary said. "Mom and Dad, and our Gran and Gramps, they all *loved* Reese. It was just *his* family that disapproved. Your grandfather, to be exact. But the Emersons welcomed Reese with open arms. They didn't care where he'd come from, that he was white or what his family thought of Aunt Desiree."

"It sounds like my grandfather was racist," Kane decided.

"I never met him," Mark said with a shrug. "No one ever said exactly why he didn't want Uncle Reese to marry Aunt Des. You would have to ask him what his reasons are."

"Hard to ask someone I've never met," Kane said in a huff. They had kept this secret from her for thirty years. She was pissed.

"Mom always planned on revealing the truth, but it just..." Mark trailed off. Aunt Polly had dropped the ball. He apparently had no good excuse.

"Just come out with it, Mark," Kane demanded. "I have had a week of shit. What's just one more damn thing making a stink?"

"Your father's real last name isn't Liberty," Mark said. "Uncle Reese had been hiding from his father. He'd changed his last name and disappeared off the face of the planet."

Liberty. A lie. Kane's world, already turned upside-down, was now kicked across the universe. For thirty years, she had believed she was Kane Liberty. And now she found out she was someone else. Dillon was a lie, Gade was an enigma and now her own legacy was just a word picked out of a hat.

"Why now?" Kane asked. Why now, during this week of hell? Why one more messed-up moment on the mountain of muck? "Why wait until I'm thirty-one years old and suddenly spring this shit on me?"

Mark's eyes went to the television again. *What is so goddamn interesting about Dash Dameron and Senator Cambridge?* The Senator was telling Dash that he knew something about United States history that would change the way the country thought about everything—something that would revise every history book in every school in America.

"Senator Sidney Cambridge..." Mark said. "He's your grandfather."

* * * *

The only grandfather Kane had known in all her thirty-one years was Gramps. Roland Emerson was known as Roly around the neighborhood where he had lived since he'd been just a kid himself. Gran told how he had always been a bit round—and was ever jolly. With a large white beard and twinkling eyes full of joy, Gramps was a light if ever there were dark times. Kane always thought that if Santa were black, her maternal grandfather would be suspect number one.

The man on television was white and severe, tall as a signpost and half as wide. He looked the opposite of Roly Emerson. Kane recalled having seen him address the Senate in a scathing rebuke to the President some time ago on some biased news network that fawned over such melodrama. Sidney Cambridge obviously craved the spotlight. The news crawl across the bottom of the screen announced he had represented Maryland since the seventies.

Dash Dameron flashed his famous smile. The playful twinkle in Dameron's eye reminded Kane of Gramps and was in stark contrast to the man Dash interviewed. Kane imagined both of her grandsires facing off, one of the most prominent men in American politics and a humble custodian from Detroit. Seeing the pompous ass basking in the spotlight, Kane could imagine the circumstances where her father had become excommunicated from the family.

"So, you have announced that you possess some earth-shattering news for the people of America, Senator Cambridge," Dash prompted. "What information are you ready to divulge in this exclusive interview with *DamTime*?"

"Thank you, Dash," Kane's grandfather replied. "I wanted to make this announcement on a respectable program such as yours, where I can reach as big of audience as possible. There is information of historical importance that has been kept secret by my family for generations. Two hundred and fifty years ago, it was agreed that the truth should be kept under wraps in the interest of the greater good of a new nation. But I think the time has come for Americans to know the truth of the beginnings of our wonderful country.

"There was documentation drafted in 1787 that served as a companion to the original Constitution of the United States of America. It was a separate amendment that was ratified and accepted by the Continental Congress. It endorsed an ancillary arm of the federal government, largely ceremonial and only advisory. In keeping with history and with an eye toward our European legacy, an American monarchy was established in the new nation."

Dash looked genuinely taken aback. Apparently, Senator Cambridge hadn't revealed the big news to him privately—or else Dash Dameron was just a damn good actor. "An American *monarchy*?"

"Yes," Kane's grandfather confirmed. "Little different than the British monarchy now, it was just a vestigial venue. While the Continental Congress was eager to split from British rule, they couldn't be so sure the citizens of a tenuous new nation could break entirely with their European history. So before ratification, they added an amendment establishing the American monarchy."

"A King of America?" Dash asked.

"Queen, actually. My great, great, great grandmother," Senator Cambridge said. "Eleanor Cambridge, the niece of King George the III, the daughter of Prince Edward, Duke of York and Albany. She was sent to live in the colonies after her father's death in 1767 and took up the Cambridge surname. She was just twenty-five years old at the time of the ratification of the amendment declaring her Queen of America."

"This is crazy," Kane said to Mary and Mark.

"This is nuts," Dash Dameron blurted out onscreen.

Senator Cambridge continued—"Queen Eleanor was short-lived for the American throne. It's where the saying comes from, 'Queen for a day'. Patrick Henry, who was in attendance at the signing of the Constitution and privy to the amendment that created the American monarchy, threatened to move against the Founders. As the former governor of Virginia, Henry promised a new rebellion in his state over the idea of a federally endorsed queen. He argued that the War for Independence demonstrated a definite divorce from any sort of monarchy. Virginia, he promised, would never bend the knee, not even in meaningless ceremony. So when the framers sent William Jackson to carry the Constitution to New York City to present to Congress, he did so without the amendment marking the monarchy. The founders were sworn to secrecy lest Patrick Henry fulfill his promise. They believed the document ratifying the amendment had been destroyed. But instead, William Jackson delivered it to Eleanor Cambridge before he left Philadelphia, as he was smitten with the young and beautiful American Queen. And so it has remained in the possession of the Cambridge family ever since—a secret…yet no less official than the Constitution itself."

"So what you are saying is that you, Senator Sidney Cambridge, are the lawful King of America?" Dash asked.

"Indeed," Cambridge said. "I have the original document and I am ready to submit it to authentication by any number of experts. It is signed by Washington,

Franklin, Hamilton and all the rest of the framers. They never bothered to rescind the amendment, so it remains officially valid. I will submit the document to any test."

"Why now? If this has been a secret for two and a half centuries, why reveal the truth now?"

"Politics has never been nastier," the Senator said. "The country has never been more splintered. Celebrities have taken over media and they are a corrupting influence on the American Way. The royalty of the United States has no governing power, but the Cambridge family could be an inspiration. We could be a better example than the tinsel kings and queens of Hollywood or the diabolical dukes and duchesses of D.C. The people need that shining castle on the hill, like Camelot in the time of the Kennedys. We are here. It is time."

"You are a widower, Senator," Dash reminded Kane's grandfather. "Your only son died in a tragic car accident decades ago. Aren't you the last in the line of American royalty?"

"No. I have a granddaughter," Sidney Cambridge said, looking into the camera. Looking right out of the television…right at Kane. "The American princess."

* * * *

"No," Kane sighed as Dash Dameron signed off on the television. "Impossible."

"It's true," Mary said. "Mom always knew. She just never could figure out how to tell you."

"Your grandfather wanted to reveal the truth of the American royalty a long time ago," Mark added. "He wanted your father to be a prince, but Uncle Reese chose love over lineage. Your dad rejected his heritage because your grandfather wouldn't let Aunt Desiree become a princess. She wasn't…royal. Now, you are his last descendent. You are the heir to the American throne."

"That's crazy," Kane said. "This is some kind of a joke."

"Your real name is Kane Cambridge, sis," Mark taunted, trying to keep it light. "Get used to being Princess of America."

Kane's head was swimming—first Dillon, then the one-night stand with Gade and now this. It was too much. She felt lightheaded. Mary's hands were suddenly at her elbow, steadying her. Otherwise, she might have toppled over.

"Just give her a minute, Mark," Mary snapped. "She needs to let it soak in."

"I thought it would be like a dream come true," Mark said defensively. "You used to parade around like Cinderella when you were a kid. This is like the end to some kind of modern fairy tale."

Kane leaned against the jamb of the large picture window looking out over Magpie Lane and she thought she glimpsed Gade's Camaro again, almost too far down the street for Kane to see. She felt sure it was the same car she had spotted when walking into Mary's house. *Is he following me?*

"I need some fresh air," Kane said. "I just have to be alone for a minute, guys. Just a minute."

Kane went out of the back door into the yard where she had enjoyed many a campout, where she had chased Mary and Mark around and around, where they had planted a garden every year since she could remember. She had snuck out of her bedroom window that faced this backyard when she had been a teenager, and she knew every concealed route to escape undetected from the neighborhood. Kane considered just ditching Gade, but she was pissed. First, he showed up out of nowhere the day before she found out she was a princess and now Gade was stalking her. He must know some damn thing about all of it.

Kane used a concealed pathway through the Beckers' backyard next door and cut across the empty lot on the corner of Magpie and Aspen. She wound around the small copse of elms next to the three-car garage on the Lipkes' double lot and came up behind Gade in his Camaro. It was him, all right. She hadn't seen much of the back of his head during their interactions, but she recognized the hulking biceps sticking out of the open driver's side window.

"So," she said when she came up on him, avoiding detection in his rearview mirrors. He jumped so that his head struck the roof and made him wince. Kane felt a little vindicated. "This is like level-ten creepy. You didn't strike me as a stalker-type. Is my crazy-radar off or do you have an extremely damn good reason for spying on me?"

"Shit, Kane," Gade said, rubbing his head. "Shitshitshit."

"You're lucky I didn't call the cops."

"It's a free world, Kane," he huffed. "I can park my car wherever I want."

"Outside the childhood home of the woman you banged last night?" Kane asked. "Then wanted nothing to do with and you followed me all through town? This is some seriously screwed-up shit, Gade."

"I can explain," he said.

"We tried that already," Kane said. "You didn't want to talk."

"Just get in already," Gade snapped, although it was less a command and more a desperate plea.

Kane leaned against the Camaro. *What am I doing?* She was still reeling from Dillon dumping her. A United States Senator had just revealed himself as her long-lost paternal grandfather, and now she was a friggin' princess! Like some serious Snow White shit. Why did she care what the hell part Gade played in this?

Because they'd had a night together.

And it had been so damn good.

Kane texted Mary that she was leaving with a friend—with bulging benefits—and that she needed to clear her head and think about what had just happened.

I'll see you tomorrow when I get my car. Love you, sis.

There were a lot of 'just happeneds' that Kane needed to process. Then she marched around to the passenger side and got in—not because Gade had told her to but because she wanted to.

As Gade started to drive away, Kane asked, "You called me 'Princess'."

"So?" Gade asked, sounding defensive.

"Last night," Kane said. "At the club."

"Lots of guys call a pretty girl 'Princess'? What of it?"

"The news," Kane said. "There was just something on the news."

"There's always something on the news."

"No. You knew. You knew last night. Before we—You knew about my grandfather. About the truth."

Gade didn't reply. He just drove.

"Damn it," Kane said. "Have you been a part of this the whole time?"

"I'm here to protect you," Gade said. "I am supposed to watch over you."

"You work for him? Senator Cambridge?"

"He's worried about you," Gade said. "When the truth comes out, you'll be in danger."

"The truth is already out."

"No one knows the Senator was talking about you, Kane. Right now, he might have been referring to any young woman in America. Until you come forward, no one will know that you are a princess."

"You know," Kane said.

"I'm not dangerous," Gade said, turning the Camaro in the direction of her apartment.

"I wouldn't exactly say that." Kane sighed, looking into his deep brown eyes as he pulled up to Kane's place. He noticed and looked away.

"We can't," Gade said. "I am supposed to protect you. I work for your grandfather."

"I don't want to hear another thing come out of your mouth," Kane warned.

"I understand," Gade said. "I'll let you be. I can protect you from a distance."

"I didn't say anything about distance," Kane said. "I just said I want you to quit talking." She leaned forward and kissed him—and he didn't say anything else...all night long.

Chapter Three

Kane woke up alone. The Sunday morning light leaked in through the pleated shades over her window. The bedroom door was open a crack and the smell of coffee and waffles wafted in. Soft sounds of shuffling containers and the fridge opening and closing filtered through. Her first thought was *Dillon*, and that was followed by a sinking feeling soon squashed. She sat up, stretched, more fully awake, and remembered the things she'd done with Gade in the night. *Three times*. A smile touched her lips.

She used her bathroom, not so en suite as Gade's, hers down the hall between bedroom and kitchen. She took a shower to wash the cobwebs away from the last few hours. Alcohol had not played a part during their second night of passion. Kane just couldn't seem to get enough of Gade. She was getting action for the purpose of distraction. She let the steam and stream wash away her train of thought every time it turned to anything past the moment they had slipped between the sheets.

The Air Force Fighting Falcons T-shirt she had swiped from Gade's house was hanging in her bathroom now, but she didn't put it on this morning. She didn't know what to expect with Gade and she didn't want a carbon-copy replay of yesterday morning's events, so she finished, pulled on a pair of yoga pants and a sweatshirt that seemed to swallow her top half then went out into the kitchen.

"Good morning," Kane said.

"Good morning, Princess," Gade replied. He didn't meet her eyes.

"We are not going to do this again," Kane sighed.

"We can't," Gade agreed, meaning something different. "And soon, you won't even consider it."

"Don't tell me what I'm going to want, Gade."

"Everything's about to change. You'll have other important responsibilities, Princess. Your grandfather wants the royal line to be a shining beacon for the American public—a noble role model, to be a pillar of grace and poise. It wouldn't be appropriate for you to be sleeping with the help."

He wore a white undershirt that Kane had peeled off him after unbuttoning his collared 'work' attire the previous night, seconds before his pants joined them in a pile in the corner of her bedroom. She couldn't see his bottom half from where he stood behind her kitchen island, but she had seen enough of it for her imagination to fill in the blanks. He was a massive man, a moving mountain that seemed immense compared to her small kitchen. Gade seemed like he wouldn't be afraid of anything, but he constantly tried to get out of the way of any future they had together.

"Waffle?" Gade offered.

"I'm not giving in just because you want to give up," Kane said. "I don't know what all this means, but I'm not going to close doors just because new ones are opening."

"You don't know what will happen next," Gade said. "There's so much more to your story, Princess."

And the rest of the story always seems to hurt, Kane thought.

He slid her a plate with two waffles. Embedded blueberries perfected the perforated pastry. Kane hadn't even known she had blueberries in the apartment. Had Gade gone out to the market? Had there been some forgotten in her freezer? Was there a magic blueberry bush in this weird fairy tale she had lived these last twenty-four hours?

"So, what's next?" Kane asked.

"When you're ready, your grandfather would like to meet you," Gade said. "In person."

"What if I'm never ready?"

"You will be. You're a princess. You have a responsibility to your constituents."

"My father walked away from those responsibilities."

"You are not your father. You're Kane Cambridge. You'll come to your own conclusion."

Gade seemed to think that Kane couldn't have it both ways. If she embraced her role as princess, then she couldn't have a relationship with her bodyguard. Her father was not allowed to choose her mother, so he'd turned his back on his legacy. Could Kane do the same? She barely knew Gade. By all accounts, Kane's parents had enjoyed an epic love that had ended tragically too soon. Now, it was premature to even know what this was between Kane and the mountain of man, yet she had to decide the future off a too-brief present.

"Do you like me, Gade?" Kane asked.

He managed to look at her. His eyes were so brown and intense that they seemed like sights centered on Kane and she was his target.

"Isn't it obvious? I have risked my career over this…two nights in a row. I'm a warrior who has been tested in the fires of battle, Kane. But against your beauty, I am defenseless. The most difficult thing in my life thus far has been resisting you."

She came around the corner of the island. He was only wearing his boxers below the hem of his shirt. "Then quit resisting."

"This can't last any longer," Gade warned.

"Maybe a little longer," she teased, pressing herself against him.

She parted her lips, inviting his mouth. He surrendered, a soldier against an obviously overwhelming opponent. He kissed her, pulling her into his embrace. His arms were like strong, steel pistons, making her feel safe and dangerous at the same time. The taste of syrup and berries were on his soft lips and his hard chest felt like a marbled sculpture against hers.

He lifted her, sitting her bottom on the island countertop after peeling her yoga pants away. They dropped to the floor as her toes dangled a few inches above the kitchen tiles. He moved his mouth south, nuzzling at her neck, nibbling at her breasts. Her breath was faster, deeper, hungry. He kept moving in the same direction until she sighed as he arrived at his destination. Then there was just pleasure and nothing more for a long while.

****

She sat on a blanket in Clinton Park waiting for Sora and Lani. Kane needed their advice, so she had invited them out for a Sunday picnic. Her head swam with thoughts of Gade. There was something there between them, and she wasn't ready to discount it just because he thought it couldn't work. Obviously, Gade couldn't resist the temptation when she'd initiated impropriety. His duty was eroded by the allure of Kane Cambridge.

The name still sounded strange in her head. Kane *Cambridge*. She had been someone else for thirty-one years. Now she was a princess. She was someone else's granddaughter. Her last name wasn't Liberty. Her life teetered at the possible precipice of major change. Kane could become a part of history.

She watched a frumpy guy jog by along the walking path who looked a little like Dillon, and she realized she hadn't thought about him in hours. There was nothing to help get over a breakup like finding out one was American royalty and sleeping with a perfect specimen of human physique. Her life with Dilly now seemed like something out of a dream. Her future as a princess also seemed like some kind of fantasy. Kane was stuck in a moment between two fairy tales.

"Again?" Sora asked as she approached the quiet place in the park where Kane had placed the blanket.

Sora carried a wicker basket. She looked dressed for a photograph on a feature story in some business magazine's idea on leisure. Fashionable and less comfortable, Sora seemed more prepared for a portrait than a picnic.

"Is it obvious?" Kane asked.

"If you glowed any brighter, I would have to put on sunglasses," Sora said.

"The sex is pretty damn amazing," Kane admitted.

"You like him."

Kane nodded.

"And he's obviously into you. Several times now, by my count."

Kane blushed.

"Did he tell you what you wanted to know? Did he confess that thing that he said you wouldn't believe?"

"I found out what he was talking about," Kane said.

"Is it such a big deal?" Sora asked.

Kane shrugged. "Maybe. That's why I wanted to talk to you and Lani."

Lani arrived, strolling across the grass with a wine bottle in one hand and three stemmed glasses in the other. She walked like she was still a little drunk, or… *Is that what I look like? Does Lani have the same glow Sora is talking about?*

Sora had one black eyebrow raised suspiciously. She'd clearly noticed the same thing Kane had. "Does that mean you and Chase made up in spectacular fashion for your excessive partying on Friday night?"

Lani plopped down between Kane and Sora. Her grin was less moonstruck than Kane's—and more diabolical.

"I haven't been home yet," Lani revealed with a sinister smile.

"I am not covering with Chase with any more lies, Lani," Sora snapped.

"You don't have to, Snore-a," Lani said with an eye roll. "I know covering for a friend goes against your goody-two-shoes instincts. I've already told Chase I'm leaving him."

"What?" Kane cried. "Leaving, like, *forever*?"

"I want a divorce," Lani said. "I'm done."

"You're leaving him for that deejay?" Sora asked in disbelief.

"Scatch is *am-a-zing,*" Lani gushed in the tone of a teenager crushing on the drummer in the high school band instead of sounding like a soccer mom with three kids.

"His name is 'Scatch'? It sounds like a venereal disease."

"You're going to throw away all those years with Chase, La?" Kane asked. "Turn your back on your family?"

Lani turned defensive. "What good am I to my family if I'm miserable in my marriage, Kane? What example am I setting for my girls if I stay in a loveless relationship for the next fifty years for the sake of 'family'? We only have one life. And I'm not getting any younger. If I want out, I have to get out *now.*"

"Scatch is worth flushing ten years of work on your relationship with Chase down the toilet? All the time and effort with him and your kids? Everything you've achieved and all the conflicts you've already survived?" Sora challenged. "All just gone in one night?"

"It was a hell of a night," Lani pointed out with a devilish smirk.

"What do you see in him anyway? He seems so…dirty."

"Yeah." Lani smiled. "Maybe it's because I haven't known any different for such a long time. And Scatch *is* different…so damn different." She licked her lips, apparently remembering. "Maybe it's the piercings."

"Sheesh, La," Kane sighed. "Maybe you should try a trial separation—or just tell Chase you're conflicted right now."

"I already told him everything," Lani said. "I confessed every last detail."

"Why?" Sora screeched. "You didn't have to drop a nuclear bomb on the last ten years!"

"I would rather have him mad than hopeful," Lani whispered. "I prefer him to hate me than want me back."

"Y'know, we're supposed to be here because Kane has something to tell us, and you turn it into being all about Lelani Travers," Sora said. "*Again*."

"I'm done," Lani pouted. "I was just informing you. I didn't ask for an opinion or to be judged. Let's talk about Kane."

They both looked at her. With Lani imploding, it seemed like the wrong time to talk about fairy tales. How could she tell them about the last twenty-four hours without it seeming like she was crazy? She couldn't. But life was not normal, anyway. There was always something crazy around the corner.

"Have you seen the news lately? Last night? Today?" Kane asked.

"It's all about that American princess," Sora said.

"It was even on Scatch's morning show on the radio this morning," Lani added. Sora scowled at the mention of the deejay.

"Does that have something to do with your weekend beau's big mystery?" Sora wondered.

"Uh, sort of," Kane said. "Gade works for Senator Cambridge."

"Everyone at the radio station was talking about the mystery woman—an American princess from some secret historical agreement," Lani said. "That's better than being a celebrity. She's going to be bigger than Duchess Kate or the little English lords."

"Does Gade know who the lucky woman is?" Sora asked, the gossip sidelining her from Kane's reason for calling them together. She didn't know that the answer and the reason were one and the same.

"It's me," Kane said. "I'm the princess."

No one said anything as Sora laid out the items from her picnic basket. There were little sandwiches made with tomato and cucumber and cream cheese, so flawless they may have been assembled by a master chef. Each one was perfectly square and could have been a carbon copy of the next. Sora was particular to the point of psychosis, but damn did the girl make a pretty lunch. On the side, Sora served a bouquet of broccoli precut and pre-washed, each floret pruned and arranged like the most expensive presentation of roses. Sora also made a dip as delectable as it was decorative, replete with a swirl of whipped avocado in a green spiral through the white sauce.

Lani, on the other hand, had left the price tag on her bottle of wine showing the discounted price of seven dollars and ninety-nine cents a bottle. Upon closer inspection, the wine glasses were made of cheap plastic.

Still, no one managed either a compliment or a complaint as they ate their sandwiches and drank their cheap booze.

Kane had left them speechless, and it lasted for a full fifteen minutes. It was the longest period of silence the three of them had shared since Lani and Sora had both transferred in to Kane's elementary school when they had all been in third grade.

"A fucking princess," Lani finally managed.

"Despite my activities over the last two days, I would like something a little more formal as we refer to my situation from now on," Kane requested.

"Shit," Lani said instead. She was a more vulgar attendant than the likes of which Princess Rapunzel ever had to deal with.

"How…?" Sora managed, then she looked at a loss for even another syllable.

Kane told them the story of her grandfather, Sidney Cambridge, and how he had driven away his only son. When Kane's father had renounced his name rather than relegate his true love to a dustbin, Senator Cambridge had been left without an heir. "Apparently, he either just discovered he had a long-lost granddaughter and decided to out the whole family to all America or he has always known about me and chose to force me into the spotlight on national television without consulting my wishes. So far, I haven't even met the man."

"And that magnificent hunk from the club the other night is on the Senator's payroll?" Lani asked.

"Apparently, he's like a royal guard or something," Kane explained. "Gade said he was hired to protect me in case anyone discovered my heritage. He said there could be dangerous people out there with reasons to hurt anyone who might overturn the balance of power in the United States."

"Power?" Sora asked. "Even if this is all true and the framers of the Constitution have a valid amendment installing an American royalty, isn't the position entirely ceremonial?"

"Celebrity is the new power in America," Kane said. "Gade told me that my grandfather decided to come out with the truth now because Hollywood has become the new monarchy. Senator Cambridge wants a better role model for American youth than rock icons and reality stars."

"How noble," Lani sneered.

Silence overtook them again as they packed up the ornate glass saucers, little ceramic bowls and expensive silverware that Sora had brought for the picnic. They collected the plastic wine cups and threw them into the proper receptacle for recycling. The three women worked together to fold the blanket that Kane had brought. Lunchtime had turned to mid-afternoon.

"What will you do?" Sora finally asked.

What am *I going to do?* Kane thought. *Am I ready for everything to change completely? Hasn't my life already been upended by Dillon dumping me?* This would make a bad breakup look like a bump in the road. And what about Gade? Could they continue this steamy thing they had going if she was in the spotlight? Would he dare touch her? Could he resist if she tried to seduce him again? Wasn't he just a distraction from Dillon anyway, and Kane would be distracted enough if she waltzed into the world as the American princess?

"That's why I want to talk to you guys," Kane said as they carried their accessories to the car. "Mark and Mary kept the truth from me this entire time, so I don't feel much trust toward those two right now. But you two have been there for me almost my whole life. You know me better than anyone. What do you think I should do?"

"A princess?" Lani exclaimed. "Hells yes, girlfriend. You would rock a damn tiara."

"Make the choice before the choice is made for you, Kane," Sora said. "This is the age of aggressive information gathering. Your grandfather revealed the royal line on a national news program, so expect reporters from all over the country probing every aspect of the story. This is what *everyone* is talking about. Your secret is only safe until it is uncovered."

"So you think I don't have a choice?" Kane asked.

Sora shrugged. "Probably not 'if' or 'when', but you can always control *how*, Kane."

"Princess Kane," Lani corrected, smiling.

They arrived at the parking lot and Kane noticed there were only a few spaces occupied. She felt too out in the open, as if her secret were stamped on her forehead. She moved between Sora and Lani's vehicles. Why was she so worried when surely no one could have figured out her real identity that quickly? It had taken her thirty years to figure it out. *Chill out, Princess,* she told herself.

They put the items from the picnic into Sora's trunk. Lani paused for a moment, her head hung, and Kane wasn't sure if she was having an adverse reaction to Sora's healthy lunch or if she finally felt some effects from upending her ten-year marriage. Then she looked at Sora.

"Can I crash at your place tonight?" she asked. "I don't want to go home and fight with Chase."

"What about Scatch's place?" Sora asked with disgust coloring her tone.

"Not tonight," Lani answered.

Was it something about Kane being a princess? Whatever Lani's reason for asking, Sora nodded.

"Ms. Cambridge?" came a voice from behind the three women.

Lani and Sora looked, but Kane had thankfully had thirty years of practice not responding to that particular name. She didn't turn. Sora had said she couldn't control the *if* or the *when*. She'd said it just a moment ago. How prescient. But Kane could control *how* everyone heard her story.

"Just a few questions, Ms. Cambridge?" the reporter pressed.

Kane turned. "I'm not sure you have the right person."

The guy looked more paparazzi than reporter, disheveled and overweight. His hair must have been victim to a windstorm, although it had been calm all weekend. His jacket was two sizes too small and unnecessary on this warm Sunday. Instead of a notebook like an intrepid investigator from a good novel, this guy pointed a camera phone in Kane's face.

"Her name is Kane Liberty," Lani snapped, taking charge. She moved between the reporter and Kane, so that the camera's lens was filled with Lani's enviable bosom, her breasts smashing against the face of his phone. "And we were having a girls' day out. You're not a girl, are you?"

"I-I, uh…" the reporter stammered. The interview questions had been turned on him instead, and he didn't know how to answer.

A Camaro pulled into the parking lot while Lani interrogated the reporter on his qualifications for manhood. Gade sat behind the wheel. Kane's heart soared and her belly did a dance. *This is it. This is the moment that everything changes*. She could lie to the reporter and maybe delay her debut for a while, but certainly there must be dots that could be connected. Enough people knew the truth. And there would be public evidence once someone looked in the right place. Kane's birth certificate could connect Kane Liberty to Reese Liberty. There had to be documents showing that her father changed his name from Cambridge to Liberty. Maybe this reporter had already found the paper trail.

"Get in," Gade said.

She looked at Sora. Sora nodded, then turned to give Lani backup in distracting the reporter. Kane got in beside Gade and they took off. She didn't know where they were going, but Kane believed it was somewhere she had never been. Everything ahead of her would be something new.

"Where are you taking me?" Kane asked Gade as the Camaro wound through the backstreets away from the park where the reporter had ambushed her.

"That's not my place to decide," Gade said. "I just drive."

He was the hired help…nothing more. He looked at her out of the side of his eye, a twinkle there that was something other than just a bodyguard checking on the object of his protection. *Maybe* something more. But he didn't say it. He *wouldn't* say it.

"Your place?" Kane asked. "They won't think to look for me there."

"How long do you want to run from the truth, Princess? When will you have had enough hiding from all the ways your life has changed, will change?"

Was he talking about her new status as American royalty or was he admonishing her for trying to use their amazing sex to avoid dealing with her breakup with Dillon? Maybe both? For an employee, Gade was pretty damn brash. Of course, they had spent more time together undressed so far rather than fully clothed.

"You're right," Kane sighed. "Sora said I can choose how I want this story to unfold."

"So you're ready?" Gade asked.

"I'm not ready for everything that comes next," Kane said, "but I am ready to take the first step and see what happens. I want to speak with my grandfather."

"I'll contact Senator Cambridge," Gade said. "He wants to meet you in person. In the event that you decided to take the next step, he instructed me to escort you to the Royal Palace Hotel. He has a room on permanent retainer this week. He will join us as soon as he can book a flight out of Washington."

"A hotel?" Kane teased with a twinkle. "One bed or two?"

Gade ignored the insinuation and answered her literally. "The Grand Suite. Heavily guarded. Highest anonymity. Three individual bedrooms."

"What are we going to do with the other two?" Kane quipped, not ready to give up on a third night of Gade. Her life was about to go upside-down, so she wanted just a few more hours of being horizontal before everything turned topsy-turvy.

Gade drove past the hotel's public parking lot and pulled into a private entrance. The guard at a gate nodded as Gade pulled in.

"Some security," Kane observed. "He didn't even check your ID."

"Dirk and I served together in the Air Force. We are brothers. Your grandfather hired on a lot of my former colleagues. We work together as a seamless unit."

"So how did you end up the soldier with babysitting duty?" Kane asked.

"I volunteered," Gade said.

Kane smiled to herself. There was a possibility for more than room service and a pay-per-view movie yet tonight.

They parked in a private garage that could have housed a Hummer or a limousine, more than adequate for the Camaro. The overhead door was reinforced and had four locks. The walkthrough door opposite where they'd entered had a scanner coded to Gade's biometrics with a redundant requirement of a keycard that Gade swiped across a scanner. They took a private elevator to their own floor, where another door required additional security approvals. A live guard stationed right outside greeted Gade and didn't even look at Kane. *A good soldier and probably another of Gade's buddies.*

"The hotel is really called the Royal Palace?" Kane asked as they walked into the opulent alcove inside the suite. "A bit on the nose, isn't it? Is it really the best place to hide a princess?"

"Half the hotels in town have 'castle' or 'crown' or some royal title in the name," Gade said. "This is as good a place to hide away as any. The paparazzi would track us to your apartment, or even mine, before they'd ever find us here."

Kane walked into the main vestibule of the suite and looked around the room. A patio door led to a balcony that overlooked the main avenue, a view that would have been acceptable to millionaires and power players—or even royalty. Exquisite tiling inlaid into bamboo flooring cordoned off a living area. Fixtures worth in excess of Kane's annual income glittered around incandescent lighting. An antique table featured an expensive crystal vase filled with a dozen roses, all as pink as the one Gade had purchased her at the market after their first night together. A bar shaped with exotic wood curved around the east wall. As Gade had described, three doors opened to bedrooms going three different directions. A fourth door led to an opulent bathroom.

Gade checked his phone. He had been texting since they'd gotten out of the Camaro. He looked serious. She tried to remember if she had ever seen him really smile. *Is he ever happy?* At least, had he ever seemed happy *with his clothes on*?

"Have you contacted my grandfather on my decision?" Kane asked.

"I have," he said.

"How soon will he be here?"

"Tomorrow. His flight leaves first thing in the morning."

"Then we have the whole night to ourselves."

"I'm sure you wouldn't mind some rest," Gade suggested. "You haven't gotten much sleep the last couple of nights."

Gade blushed. He seemed to realize what he had said too late, acknowledging their intimacy when trying to put it behind them. He was pretty damn sexy when he was embarrassed. The color in his cheeks made his dark brown skin turn the color of stained cherrywood. He darted his gaze away, unable or unwilling to make eye contact.

"So, you call yourself my guard?" Kane asked coyly.

"Yes. Your royal guard."

"My *body*guard?" she quizzed, slinking in front of the white drapes over the patio door that led the balcony, the light of late afternoon illuminating every part of her.

"I suppose you could put it that way," Gade said, as she walked across the room. She plucked one pink rose from the bouquet and smelled it. *Sweet*. She smiled beneath the pink petals.

"*This* body?" she asked, unbuttoning her blouse and letting it fall to the floor. She still held the flower.

Gade exhaled so loudly that she could hear his hiss from across the room.

"A man has to appreciate the things he protects," Kane said, her pants joining her blouse in a pile on the tile. She carried the rose as she walked away from her bottoms.

"Princess," he managed in a breathless voice.

Kane wore just her underwear—black lace, just in case. She hadn't known when she'd gotten re-dressed after their kitchen escapade, before her trip to the park to meet Lani and Sora, just what the day would bring. She would rather be ready than be caught unprepared with her pants down.

She left her underwear and bra on the polished wooden bar top, between a bottle of Jack Daniels and a crystal jar of mints. She placed the pink rose into an empty champagne flute. Kane leaned back against the brass trim that bordered the top, the cold metal against her spine making her nipples hard. She propped her toes on the foot-rail of the bar, letting Gade look at whatever he wanted to see.

He was her bodyguard. He was supposed to protect her from attack. But Gade ended up being the one who attacked her, his mouth a weapon that could make her mewl. He was supposed to be the one who saved her, and instead she surrendered to his touch.

Chapter Four

Kane woke up in the plushest and most comfortable bed she had ever experienced, mounds of pillows and blankets like a landscape—mountains, foothills, valleys and a mass of naked man. For the first time in three mornings, Gade was still asleep, a slumbering ridge of muscular ebony rock, like Mount Rushmore as sculpted by DaVinci.

She slipped out of bed without waking him and padded across the master bedroom, pausing to reach for a silk robe with 'Royal Palace' written upon the breast, but then on second thought, left it draped over a chair. She walked naked out to the main living room. It was early and Kane was supposed to be at work by nine. *No work today*. She called in sick, leaning naked on the bar and faking a hoarse voice. A touchscreen next to a high-backed barstool offered her a menu of room service. She ordered, left instructions, then went for a shower.

The place was a palace, indeed. Shower heads ran the full length of her body along the marbled wall as another fixture dangled from the ceiling and made a rainfall directly over her. The water washed away all the uncertainties of yesterday, dissolving everything into just the now. Right now. She didn't know if she had spent twenty minutes or an entire hour in the shower, but when she got out and exited the steamy bathroom, someone had already delivered breakfast just inside the hotel room door.

Kane picked up the platter off the cart and carried it into the master bedroom. Gade started stirring, blinking sleep out of his eyes. Surely he had worked up quite the appetite the previous night, but his focus traveled across her naked body before he turned his attention to the platter.

"Not homemade, but my talents do not tend toward the kitchen," Kane confessed.

"What is this, anyway?" Gade asked as Kane lifted the lid and revealed an omelet that looked like it had been concocted by some famous chef.

"I think they make it with eggs," Kane said, pulling off a piece with her fingers and plopping it in her mouth, very un-princesslike. It was not the first thing that she had done in the last twelve hours that was most definitely unlike royalty.

Gade was eating a bite, too, seemingly replenishing calories. "I mean…between us," he said. "What are we doing?"

"I think there are a few different names for it," Kane said, shrugging. "Fornication. Sleeping together. Amazing sex. A lot of folks would break it down to just four little letters."

"This is crazy, Kane. I'm not a part of the plan. You have a big future right around the corner. It starts today. You can't be falling into bed with your royal guard every night."

"Well, in defense, we didn't start in the bed last night," Kane pointed out. "It was against the bar. Then we continued on the sofa and again in the shower. Then it was technically morning before we did it in the bed."

He glowered. It was hypnotic. Kane was fascinated by a man who looked like he could bend a steel bar in his bare hands and yet wasn't strong enough to resist her. She was completely naked yet had never felt less vulnerable. Kane had a power over Gade that made her feel emboldened. Potent. Fearless.

She felt like a goddamn princess.

"Why don't we just see where this goes?" Kane asked. "You quit telling me how this thing we have is not in my best interest, and I promise I won't announce a royal decree that you wear the tightest damn pants we can find."

His frown turned around. He lit up when he smiled, like a ferocious bear revealing a tender side.

"All right. I'll quit pushing you away. I am your royal guard, so I'll just stand at attention. I'll be there whenever you need me."

"That's right," Kane teased. "I'm the princess around here. Just make sure you aren't too far away. Never know when I might…need you—and I like the 'standing at attention' part."

Gade nodded. The way she was looking at him, he probably couldn't manage any other reply. Kane crawled into bed beside him, but instead of another round of sexual gymnastics, they just sat side by side, her arm brushing his, her thigh against Gade's, and they finish the breakfast with a side of fresh blueberries.

Kane watched him walk toward the shower, a machine-made man with pistons pumping and gears turning. He shaved his hair close to the scalp and the rest of him had little fur, the tone of his skin radiant. She liked looking when it was covered by nothing.

What next? she wondered.

Kane's world was at the edge of transition. She felt like Cinderella transformed from a lowly servant girl by her magically fairy grandfather, ready to go to the Royal Ball and see what wonders would greet her in some new world. These might be the last moments of a real life. The life of Kane Liberty would soon be her past, back there with Dilly and her parents and a dead-end job. *Back there with Gade?*

The future wasn't here yet. It was coming this afternoon…but not this morning.

Kane got out of bed and padded across the room, out into the main living area. She felt so alive, naked and with nobody's eyes on her. These were her last moments of anonymity. Soon, she wouldn't be able to walk down the street without fans asking for a selfie or eat peaceably at a restaurant without paparazzi filming her every mouthful. But today, right now, she felt as free as she had ever been.

She leaned into the doorway of the bathroom, watching Gade in the steam of the shower. His silhouette through the fogged glass was all angles and contours of perfection. He was big, her superman, and she felt safe whenever he was around. He was her royal guard.

"So, you'll be there?" Kane asked as he peered out the glass door of the large, tiled shower. "Whenever I need you? Like a good soldier?"

"That is my duty," Gade said.

"Are you standing at attention now?" she quizzed, walking over as he opened the door to let her in.

He didn't have to answer. She could see for herself.

* * * *

Senator Cambridge had arranged everything. Being the King of the United States surely offered all sorts of perks. As princess, Kane wondered about her own available resources. Already she had spent the night in a fancy hotel, had enjoyed extravagant room service and had *really* appreciated a personal bodyguard.

Like a wizard, Senator Cambridge had made it all happen. Where? A restaurant right here in the hotel. When? An elegant dinner for two. He'd even arranged the what. He'd sent up a personal assistant with a selection of eveningwear from a nearby designer boutique. Kane picked a beautiful dress in soft pink that almost exactly matched her bouquet of roses. It was not too formal and not really casual. She didn't exactly look like a princess. *Perfect*. She didn't really feel like one, either.

The restaurant on the main level of the Royal Palace Hotel was as fancy as anywhere Kane had ever eaten. At four o'clock in the afternoon, the place was entirely empty. Her first thought was that maybe people couldn't afford to eat at a place like this, but then she knew better. Plenty of people could afford this. They just weren't people who Kane really knew—maybe Mark on a special occasion or Sora if she needed to court a wealthy client.

The hostess informed them that Senator Cambridge had reserved the entire restaurant for dinner. That kind of power, wealth and influence was beyond Kane's experience. Her grandfather had managed to book the entire posh establishment. Certainly, word of the royal King of America dining at the restaurant was worth millions in publicity.

Kane had arrived early. Gade had escorted her down to the restaurant and posted himself at the entrance by the hostess stand. Other brawny men were stationed at every exit. Kane recognized Dirk from the parking garage. The rest were probably more of Gade's brothers-in-arms. It was a major mass of manly meat. Lani would be like a cougar surround by fresh cuts of beefcake.

Kane sat alone at a table dressed with embroidered linen cloths in immaculate white. Silverware made of actual silver was arranged in two place settings. A waiter poured Kane fine red wine into a crystal goblet while she waited. Every table had its own candelabra with six candles, but only the wicks on Kane's table were lighted. A fresh bouquet of peonies smelled succulent. Somewhere unseen, someone played piano, beautifully and softly.

They entered through a side door, two escorts in front and two behind. Sandwiched between was a man taller than any of his entourage, slender, walking with perfect posture. His hair was a silver mane, a stoic style befitting a statesman…or a king. His eyes were as gray as his hair, steeled, sternly observing every guard at every door. Satisfied with safety, his focus turned toward Kane. She felt like she was in grade school all over again, her teacher was looking at her for an answer and Kane didn't know what to say.

Kane wondered about proper protocol, if she should offer her hand or bow like a loyal subject. He might not have but recently revealed his royal lineage to the world, but he obviously had practiced being majestic his entire life. By comparison, Kane wouldn't know a scepter from a sigil, and everything she had ever learned about kingdoms came from bingeing *Games of Thrones* when she'd had laryngitis last February.

Kane stood, dismissing a bow as being too submissive for a woke woman like herself, and instead offered her hand like she was ready for a hearty handshake. The stern expression on her grandfather's face turned into a warm smile, as stark an effect as a pumpkin transforming into a chariot. He took her hand, turned it sideways and kissed the back.

"Thank you," Senator Cambridge said, dismissing his royal guards. He took the place across the table from Kane. So tall and thin, he looked like he had stepped right out of a history book. Kane almost expected him to be in black and white, like some portrait of a historical figure from colonial times, so the pink rose in his lapel was a shocking splash of color. He no longer featured the bemused expression he had favored Kane at first, but neither had it reset to the serious countenance he had worn as he initially surveyed the room.

"I am sorry we have not met before this day, my dear," he started off. *An apology.* Kane had expected him to make no mention of the thirty years that he'd ignored her.

"So am I," Kane said. "I was going to call, but I…y'know…didn't know you even existed."

"I was respecting your father's wishes," Cambridge replied calmly. "He renounced me and my name. *Our* name. I did not wish to impede upon his decision."

"My father died a long time ago."

"Which makes honoring his ideals all the more sacred."

The servers brought salads full of vegetables that Kane didn't recognize, along with olives imported from Italy, avocado sliced impossibly thin, shredded something mixed with crumbled other, all atop a leafy bed that looked nothing like lettuce. It was delicious.

"So why did you decide to meet me now?" Kane asked. "Why not just let it be? The story of our secret royal stature would've faded away and the world would've been none-the-wiser."

"Exactly, my dear. If I did not introduce you to the world before my passing, there would have been no more Cambridge name. The royal line would have been a victim of American amnesia, relegated to a fairy tale and never believed."

"Nonsense," Kane replied. "You could have revealed the amendment to the Constitution. You would have claimed fame in revealing your ancestor as Eleanor Cambridge, Queen of America. You could have still secured your place in history."

"What is history without a future?" the Senator asked. "I want my legacy to extend beyond the few years I have left, Kane."

"I'm your only descendent?"

"Yes," Senator Cambridge acknowledged. "I tried to have other children, but it just wasn't meant to be."

"I'm sorry," Kane offered.

Cambridge shrugged it off, as if the weight of fate had clearly been accepted long ago.

"But lately, I have become preoccupied with hopelessness—nasty politics, numbing social media, mindless entertainment, addictive gaming platforms. The world needs some positivity to balance all that damn gloom," her grandfather said. "I want to ignite a beacon of light in a world growing progressively darker. Maybe something to look up to when someone gets down. The very notion of a royal family could be uplifting and inspirational. But I cannot do it alone. You are the fresh face that can bring brightness to these gloomy times."

"You seem to think this royal announcement is going to change the world."

"It already has," Senator Cambridge said. "Now it is up to you to decide whether the change ends with me or if our legacy goes on. What do you say? Are you ready to be Princess Kane?"

* * * *

When Kane had been sixteen, Armie Evans had invited her to the Disco Ball. Uncle John had said absolutely not when she'd asked permission to go, but after a hysterical breakdown worthy of Scarlett O'Hara herself, an intervention by Aunt Polly about 'girls being girls and that this was no longer 1965', Uncle John had relented. He hadn't stood a chance once Aunt Polly had declared for Kane's side.

Mark and Mary were two years Kane's elders, seniors in high school at the time of the event. Uncle John had never had a problem when they'd gone to their first dance the past year, probably because they'd gone with each other for their first ball. But only Kane knew that Mark had snuck off with a busty sophomore named Bethany Barman under the bleachers and that Mary had made out with Annabeth Langford all night long in the backseat of Annabeth's G6.

Yet Uncle John had won in the end as Kane had gotten stood up by that asshole Armie Evans after busty Bethany Barman, now a junior, had asked Armie to escort her and her fulsome twin accessories to the Ball. Her uncle seemed to feel sorrier for Kane *not* going than he had been angry when she'd first said she *was.* It had broken his heart.

"Mark will take you," Uncle John had suggested, although Mark was already taking Harriet Loudeen, a sure thing out at Tawdry Point after they'd put in a brief appearance at the dance.

Mark had his eyes wide open and his mouth wound up to protest when Kane had let him off the hook. *"I'm fine going by myself,"* she'd said. *"I don't need a man to turn heads at any Ball."*

And she didn't. Her dress had been half chiffon, half silk and all sass. As pink as bubblegum and twice as poppin', Kane strode into the ballroom like the fiercest Oprah in the world and disco'd like Travolta mainlining energy drinks. Her hair was as wide as little Mikey Jackson's and the platforms on her shoes made her almost six feet tall. She looked like Diana Ross, supreme as H-E-L-L.

Armie Evans had even reconsidered and asked her to dance. Kane had told him to go fornicate with the big papier-mâché disco globe hanging in the center of the decorated high school gymnasium.

"You want to have a Ball?" Kane asked her grandfather now, as it needed repeating.

"Just the thing to announce the coming out of a young American princess," the Senator said. "Media. High society. Celebrities. Politicians. We will give out random free tickets via a lottery system so even regular folks can attend. It will be the biggest event New York City has seen in decades."

"When?" Kane asked. Her life was about to change. How long did she have before societal impact? What number of days could she sneak around with Gade before everyone in America was watching?

"The weekend."

It was only Monday. "I don't think I can avoid reporters that long," Kane said. "One of them spotted me today. I barely got away without being cornered."

She looked at Gade, who had saved her in his Camaro. He stood sentry in one corner, so still he seemed like a stoic totem just for ceremonial purposes…a very deadly statue.

"We will have you tape an exclusive interview with Dash Dameron beforehand that will be aired the night of the Ball," the Senator detailed, as if he had thought of everything. "Once the rest of those paparazzi realize that *DamTime* has the exclusive, they won't have any reason to hound you."

Kane looked at her plate. It was empty. She hardly remembered eating the three courses served by the most professional waitstaff she had ever seen…or had barely seen. They were like wraiths that came and brought and retrieved dishes, like they had mastered some magical ability of to be invisible. Now she was left with just an empty dish that had once contained a delicious cheesecake, the flavor still phantom on her tongue. So distracted by being a princess, she had missed fully appreciating the fine dining experience.

There will be more, she told herself.

"So, what is your decision, Kane?" her grandfather prompted, his hands steepled and staring at her as if he had asked her to choose between going to medical school and being a barista at the local Starbucks.

"Senator Cambridge," Kane replied, "I have to consider how this will affect the rest of my family."

"Please, call me Sidney," he said. *Not Granddad. Or Papa Sid.* It was still less formal than 'Senator' or 'Sir'. He reached across and put his hand over hers—a grandfatherly gesture, at least. "I understand the ramifications of your decision. I am sure your family has considered the fallout from the truth coming out over the course of these last decades. If they are as dear as you suggest, then I'm sure they will support your decision."

He had reminded Kane that Mary and Mark had known all this time about her royal heritage. Aunt Polly had told them the secret. They had all known and had never told Kane. What did she really owe them in regards to her decision, after being lied to all her life?

She looked at Gade one last time. Sidney noticed.

"I trust your royal guard has performed admirably," the Senator stated. He was a perceptive man. Did he realize more than he was letting on?

Several times, Kane almost said.

"He makes me feel safe," she answered instead.

"Good," Sidney replied. "If anyone lays a hand on you, I want swift and ferocious punishment. That goes for everyone in your family, too, Kane. They will all be protected."

She looked away from Gade. Her next words would doom their relationship. Sidney would never let her *be* with a bodyguard. He had plans for their royal premiere. For now, Kane would have to cool it with Gade. But once she was Princess, she would do whatever she damn well pleased.

"All right," she said. "So what's the next step?"

"You have twenty-four hours to wrap things up here," Sidney said. "Then you will meet me in New York."

Chapter Five

Kane woke up with the rising sun. For the first time in three days, she didn't have Gade next to her. She'd spent the night again at the Royal Palace Hotel in the same room. Gade was in another. He had probably been up all night, standing sentry. Kane couldn't go to him. Next door, her grandfather stayed in another suite with his own entourage. It was too close to risk being caught.

Besides, Kane needed to think. She had met Gade while a greater whirlwind whisked around her, unknown. Now, she was about to become a royal celebrity. The Kardashians would soon be usurped as the premier American monarchy. There was a new princess in town.

She called up work. Her boss, Pauline, didn't seemed too pleased with Kane calling in for a second day in a row. Kane listened to Pauline complaining then faked a coughing fit that lasted until her boss said she hoped Kane felt better by the next day. It was more a threat than well-wishes. Soon, Kane would be calling in sick from New York City.

Her grandfather had given her one last day to get her affairs put in order. She had to pack the things she needed before she left. Mary had texted late the previous night, and Kane had promised to stop in and see her. Lani and Sora wanted to meet her later for dinner and maybe Mark would join them. Then tomorrow morning Kane would be on a flight to New York.

Kane pulled on a heavy sweatshirt and sweatpants that concealed enough of her so that she felt she wouldn't be inviting Gade into anything untoward. She steeled herself at the door to the bedroom for the encounter, then opened it. She had expected her royal guard to be standing at his post outside her door, but Gade had become a girl.

"Who are you?" Kane asked, feeling less like a princess than she ever had in her whole life.

The woman wore a suit as professional as any CEO, tailored perfectly to her long legs and trim form. She sported glasses that maybe were meant to distract from her beauty and accentuate her intelligence. They succeeded in the latter but failed in the former. She was gorgeous. Her blonde mane cut off at her shoulders and her smile should have been on a magazine cover.

"My name is Abigail Morgan," the woman introduced in a lilting proper British accent, looking Kane up and down with a small frown. "I am your personal attendant."

"Am I getting married?" Kane quipped.

Abigail glowered as if Kane might be the unfunniest person that had ever been born. "That is not why I'm here today. My purpose is to prepare the princess to go public."

Kane frowned. "You're here for a makeover?"

"That's part of it," Abigail said. "I've been a part of Senator Cambridge's staff for years. I studied history at Oxford with an emphasis on the British monarchy. He brought me on as an expert on historical context. In my tenure, I've studied your family and its secret. I formulated a hypothesis on the impact of the advent of American royalty on modern society."

"You make it sound like we're about to tell the world witches are real or that aliens live among us," Kane said.

"We just want you to be prepared."

"Where's Gade?" Kane asked as the conversation dwindled.

"Mr. Williams?" Abigail clarified. Kane made an awkward gesture that was a mix of shrug and nod. She didn't want Abigail to realize she and Gade were way past last names. "The royal guard is gathered with your grandfather to plan the security details for New York."

"So are we left unprotected?" Kane asked.

"I assure you, we're quite safe at the moment, Princess. Mr. Williams will escort us as we endeavor to enhance your wardrobe," Abigail assured, looking Kane's rumpled sweatshirt and baggy sweatpants up and down. "We need to find you some clothes befitting someone of your stature."

"You mean this won't do for the Ball?" Kane asked sarcastically.

"Oh, no," Abigail replied seriously, as if sarcasm were a concept as foreign as American royalty. "We are going on a proper shopping spree, your highness."

Kane grinned. She had seen *Pretty Woman* a hundred times and she knew the scene where Julia Roberts gets a makeover by heart. Despite her carnal activities the last three nights, she wasn't promiscuous like the character Ms. Roberts played, but she did have the outfit from the cover of the film, complete with thigh-high black hooker boots, bought for a kinky night with Dillon on their first anniversary.

She turned her thoughts away from Dilly.

"I need to see my sister first," Kane said. "I promised I would stop by."

"I'm at your service, your Highness," Abigail said. "Why don't we invite her along? I'm sure she will want something new to wear to the Ball."

"Great," Kane agreed. "Let's go."

"Not before you change," Abigail said. "At least put on a blouse and some regular pants."

Kane sighed and turned back to her room. She pictured the look on Mary's face when the housewife and harried mother tried on something new and beautiful to wear to the event. That decided it for Kane. If there was going to be a marathon montage of beautiful, expensive gowns, she wouldn't experience it alone. It was the perfect sister thing.

* * * *

When Kane texted her sister that she was coming to pick her up, maybe Kane should have warned Mary about the elegant transportation, but the look on Mary's face when she opened her front door and saw Kane standing beside the limo was priceless. Mary scurried down her front walkway like a schoolkid late for the bus and ducked into the back as if sneaking out to the prom with a boy—or a *girl*—who her dad didn't like.

"Do you think the neighbors saw?" Mary whispered in the back of the limo.

"Hell, yeah," Kane said with a grin.

"You should've told me," Mary said, fidgeting. "I'm not dressed for this."

Mary wore a simple blue blouse and jeans that had seen better days. Those days were at least a couple of years and judging from how tight the jeans were, a size or two ago. She wore her old, scuffed white tennis shoes, the same ones she'd had since high school. Her feet were about the only things that hadn't gotten bigger in the last ten years. As soon as the kids had come, Mary had forgotten to buy anything new for herself. That was why Kane was so excited about today.

"This is something else, Kane."

"My life is something else now, Mary."

As they exited the neighborhood, Mary relaxed…a little. It was relaxed for Mary anyway. She was the worrier in Kane's circle of acquaintances. She always stressed out over something that could maybe go wrong. Even if a story headed toward a happy ending, Mary always imagined a dozen ways it could be derailed. Mary thought of *Romeo and Juliet* less as a tragedy and more of a lesson on the way things always seemed to go.

"You're sure we'll be done by three o'clock?" Mary checked. "I have to pick up Artie and Agnes after school. Artie has clarinet practice and Agnes needs to study for her spelling test tomorrow. I can't be late."

"We'll be done by then, Mary. And even if we aren't, it might be good for those kids to experience waiting for someone instead of you waiting hand and foot on them all the time."

"Are they royalty? They sound like a little prince and princess," Abigail said.

"Yes, I have seen for years what it takes to be a personal attendant," Kane said. "I just didn't know it was a profession. I thought it was just called being a wife and mother."

"That reminds me," Mary interjected. "I need to text Larry and let him know I left some lunch warming in the oven."

Just the three women rode in the back of the large limo. Gade sat in the front beside the driver. Abigail faced backward toward the two sisters, while Kane and Mary faced forward in the vehicle.

"Did you make arrangements for the kids so you can make it to the Ball in New York?" Kane asked.

"I'm still looking for a sitter," Mary said.

"Aunt Lydia can watch them," Kane suggested. Aunt Lydia was the spinster sister of Polly Emerson and Kane's mother. She had acted as the default sitter when Kane, Mary and Mark were growing up. Now in her sixties, she still had more bustling energy on any given day than Kane. Her thirteen cats kept Lydia young.

"Maybe so," Mary said.

"You *have* to be there," Kane said. "It's a friggin' Princess Ball."

Mary smiled and her eyes lit up. As younger girls, the two sisters would dress up in Aunt Polly's old clothes, fancy gowns she had worn to great school dances from the '70s. Kane and Mary would use half a can of hairspray to make their black curls puff up like the head of a dandelion gone to seed. Balancing precariously on high-heeled shoes five sizes too big, they would parade up and down the hall in a grade-school promenade. Now to attend a real-life Royal Ball…

"All right, shopping," Mary said. "I'm kind of an order-it-online kind of shopper. Where do we go for a ballgown if it isn't ordered from Amazon?"

Abigail smiled. Mary lit up. Kane was sure this would be one magical afternoon.

Mary tried on twenty different outfits. Abigail sat with a discerning look on her face as Kane's sister paraded back and forth like a model on a catwalk. After ten years of being a homemaker, this obviously felt like one of those makeover episodes on a cable TV style show. Mary tried short skirts and lavender pantsuits and flowing gowns and spectacular evening dresses. She considered plunging necklines that accentuated the effects of nursing two kids, even if it had ended half a decade ago. She didn't shy away from tight fits that highlighted her wide hips and broad backside. Kane noticed Abigail looking interested. Her personal attendant attended to Mary more than to her, Abigail roaming her gaze over Kane's sister with every switch of attire, and Abigail's opinion seemed to sway Mary every time. Kane couldn't help but think of the rumor of Mary and Annabeth Langford making out in Annabeth's backseat at their high school prom.

In the end, Mary dazzled in a dress hemmed at the knee, revealing just enough of her shapely calves. The top exposed her ample bosom, her proud cleavage revealed to all the world. Elegant silk gloves accentuated the outfit, balancing what she showed off with what she covered up. The smile on her face looked as fresh and fierce as any expression Kane had seen on her sister since Mary's own wedding day.

This dress was even more amazing than the one she had worn then.

"What about Kane?" Mary asked, after her final selection. She seemed suddenly flustered, as if she'd just realized that she had taken up the whole day while the princess was waiting.

"I already have the perfect dress picked out for Kane," Abigail said. "She just needs to be fitted."

The curator of the establishment led the women back past the dressing room where Mary had tried on her endless attire. Gade kept watch from the main part of the shop while the women followed the seamstress into the private section. There, in the back, with a room of its very own, was a dress on a rack that looked as unique and magical as if it had been darned by small animals á la Cinderella. It took Kane's breath away. It was *perfect*.

* * * *

"I'm going to be late picking up Artie and Agnes," Mary realized, checking her phone.

Kane had just finished lacing up the high heel Christian Louboutin gladiator sandals featuring real diamond studs worth more than the limo parked outside. It had taken her half an hour to get strapped in, and it would take just as long to get out. Not even the promise of her future firstborn to this establishment would allow Kane to walk out without a deposit of something in the seven-figure range.

"We're done here," Abigail said. "I can take Mary in the limo. We can pick up the kids."

"My Camaro is just a few blocks from here. I can escort the princess to her dinner arrangements," Gade suggested. He'd moved from farther away to nearer.

Mary looked from Gade to Kane with a little smirk on her face. She had known Kane long enough to sense when something was going on with her sister. Mary seemed to think Kane's romantic notions were amusing. Kane looked from Abigail to Mary with a sterner expression of concern. There was something percolating between the two of them. Mary was married and not allowed to be smitten.

"That works for me," Mary said, giving Kane a hug. "I'll see you in New York."

"Just be careful," Kane warned.

Kane didn't know if Mary knew what she really meant, but Mary nodded. "Of course."

It did take a half-hour to unlace her shoes. This was certainly not the footwear she would choose for the Ball, but she couldn't pass up a chance at trying them on. Abigail already had the exact right shoes being designed in Manhattan especially for Kane.

"They are going to look like glass slippers," Abigail had told her.

"Just like Cinderella?" Kane had asked.

"We have to play into the myths created by Hans Christian Anderson and Walt Disney," Abigail had replied. *"You are the American fairy tale, Princess."*

Instead of a white stallion or a rainbow unicorn, Kane rode shotgun in a cherry red Camaro. Her strong, valiant warrior fell straight out of a storybook, fantasy biceps and all. At least this fairy tale was progressive enough to include people of color. Gade stared straight ahead, seemingly as if he were afraid of falling under her spell if he looked at the princess in the passenger seat.

"We're going to be early," Kane said.

"I'm not too often late in this," Gade said, revving an engine that growled like some animal sidekick.

"We have some time," Kane suggested, unbuttoning the top few of buttons on her blouse and revealing a good deal of cleavage. "If you want to stop for a while."

Kane had watched him all day. Gade was powerful, disciplined, beautiful. He'd avoided her every leer. Each time Kane had tried to give him a playful look, Gade had stared at something else. His avoidance made her more aggressive. She wanted his eyes on her, his hands, his lips.

"Princess," he protested with much effort, "maybe we—"

She didn't want any 'maybes'. Kane ripped open the last two buttons on her blouse. She had purposely left her bra behind in the dressing room after her last fitting. She'd tried on a red lace set of underwear, perfect for the night after the big ceremony, when she planned on making Gade her consort, whether he thought it was a good idea or not. She wouldn't sleep alone on the evening of her own Royal Ball.

Now, she was topless. The tinted windows in the Camaro prevented the drivers at the stoplight on her right from seeing a thing, but Gade could see everything. She reached back and grabbed the headrest, thrusting her breasts out toward the windshield. She looked at him with a wry smile. "Maybe we *what*?"

He roamed his gaze over her, so intense she almost felt it, like light fingers touching her, tracing her long neck, lingering at the hollow between her collar bones, making a trail between her firm breasts. Her breath heaved at the thought of his hand leaving the steering wheel and traveling over the surface of each one.

"Princess, I—" he started, but Gade seemed incapable of forming complete sentences.

"You have a green light," Kane said. "You can go."

She gave him permission. The car behind them honked and Gade seemingly realized the streetlight had turned. He took his foot from the brake and started forward. Gade took his right hand off the wheel and reached across the console between the front seats. His large hand covered her entire left breast and Kane melted under his touch.

Gade took an exit, which would be the long way to O'Malley's. As soon as Kane realized he'd chose to be a participant rather than a party pooper, she leaned back and let his hand massage her. Around her, cars slid away like butter warmed on a skillet, the Camaro fast and quiet and moving like the wind.

She wore a skirt with a zipper down the side. She'd left her panties behind at the same place as her bra. She hated to break up a set. At the next stoplight, Kane unzipped the skirt and wriggled it down to the floorboards. She was bare, out, free. In a few days, she would be the most famous person in the country, but now, she was naked, out in the daylight, commuters on her left and right, in front of her and behind—dozens of people all around separated by just smoked glass. It might be the last time she ever felt so exposed while going unnoticed.

The feeling of being so scandalous made her dizzy. Gade traveled his hand down from her breasts as the Camaro moved across the miles. He made a pit stop at her belly button, tracing the rim of the divot. Then he continued on, making turns, taking the long way around, moving toward his apparent destination then going completely in another direction. He would get there in time. Kane closed her eyes and opened herself to him. He was doing the driving in every regard.

Pleasure. Waves. The rhythm of the car. The sounds of traffic. She would open her eyes briefly while he was taking her curves and weaving in and out of openings. Sometimes, someone would be looking her way, appreciating the car. Or maybe…? The glass was tinted, but she wondered once or twice if they could see her anyway. If they were watching *her*.

Gade maneuvered his hand like he moved through gears on the manual transmission, shifting her into ever higher states of arousal. Her engine revved to compete with the Camaro vibrating under her bare bottom. She arrived at her own destination around Third Avenue but didn't stop coming until somewhere around Twenty-Sixth Avenue.

* * * *

The bottom buttons on Kane's blouse were not going to get repaired, and she didn't have a change of clothes. If Sora or Lani noticed, they would understand. Gade was an irresistible specimen of mandom. If Mark joined them, he would be oblivious to such fashion details. He'd be half drunk before he could count enough buttons to wonder if some were missing.

Sora and Lani already had a table as Kane walked in. She still felt a little lightheaded from her climax in the car, but she managed to walk a straight line. It reminded her of when she had been a junior in high school and had sampled shots at Cindy Salazar's seventeenth birthday party, then she had to walk by Aunt Polly and Uncle John when she got home without a wobble in her step. Gade took up a position at the bar, close enough to intercept any aggressors, yet far enough away not to hear the vulgar first sentence to come out of Lani's mouth.

"You are glowing like a neon sign, Princess. You look like a woman who just stepped off the Orgasm Express."

"Lelani Travers," Sora scolded, "what would your mother say about such filth coming out of your mouth?"

"My mother wouldn't have anything good to say about any of my choices lately, Sor," Lani said. "But then, she never did."

"Try to remember when you're talking to royalty," Sora whispered. "At least make an attempt at being proper."

"Being *proper*?" Lani asked with a knowing smile. "The flushed cheeks on this princess suggest a little *im*proper behavior of her own."

"Speaking of improper behavior, are you still messing around with that deejay?" Sora snapped. "Or have you come to your senses and begged Chase for forgiveness?"

"Has Sevin come crawling to you on hands and knees and apologized for his online porn addiction?" Lani clapped back.

Sora flinched like Lani had slapped her across the face.

"Shit, La," Kane swore, "that's harsh. Sora just cares about your marriage."

"Maybe I just care about Sora's happiness? What's the difference between cheating with a young, talented musician that's hot as hell and masturbating to pay-by-the-pull porn pussy?" Lani looked at Kane with a sarcastic sneer. "No offense."

"Everything about you is offensive," Sora said tersely.

Mark arrived just in time to defuse a bomb on the verge of explosion. "Sounds like things are getting a little heated," he said, taking the seat between Sora and Lani, right across from Kane. "Sora, if you're surprised by anything that comes out of Lani's mouth, then apparently you haven't been listening to a word she has said over the last twenty years."

"It gets tiring," Sora sighed.

"Then allow me to speak for a while," Mark said, smile flashing. He already had a drink in hand, picked up at the bar as he passed, but Kane saw it wasn't his first drink of the day. It was only five o'clock. "It seems being royal suits you, sis."

"I'm not sure the tiara quite fits just yet," Kane wondered aloud.

"Mary texted me about the limo," Mark said, "and the shopping spree. You guys were so into it that she didn't even have time to pick up Artie and Agnes. When I dropped them off at home, they made me promise that Auntie Princess Kane would stop by as soon as possible."

"You picked up the kids?" Kane asked, confused. Mary had left in the limo to get them from school...with Abigail.

"That must have been one hell of a shopping spree," Mark said.

What was Mary doing? With Abigail? Everyone in Kane's circle of friends and family seemed to be spinning out of control. It made the rollercoaster week

Kane had seem almost par for the course among her group of acquaintances.

The waitress stopped at the table. Mark had already emptied his glass. Kane hadn't ordered yet. Sora and Lani still sipped at their cocktails.

"What can I get you?" she asked Kane first.

"Vodka Sunrise for me," Mark interjected. "And she'll have a Screwdriver. Right, Kane?"

Kane shrugged. Mark had been ordering her Screwdrivers at bars since she was twenty-one. Ever since her first drink, when she told a server, "I'll have what he's having."

"So," Lani said, apparently sensing a way to turn the conversation away from her infidelity, "I see you brought the sex machine."

"He's my royal guard," Kane corrected sheepishly.

Mark looked at the man Sora and Lani stared at. Gade seemed to know he was the topic of conversation and looked anywhere else but in Kane's direction. His gaze swept the restaurant crowd, constantly on the search for threats to the princess. She knew that if their eyes met, his gaze would be trapped like a fly in her web.

Mark frowned. "You're screwing the help?"

Kane gave him that glare that always preceded a punch to the arm if Mark continued to taunt her. "What is it, your business?"

"It's the 'I care about my little sister' kind of business. You're on the rebound. Suddenly some dude with a perfect body comes along for some action? Might be fine under other circumstances, but you're going to be the most famous woman in America in a few days. An empty romance is too much of a distraction."

"Empty?" Kane cried, offended. "What do you know of it?"

"I know that you have a broken heart and it isn't ready to be filled up with someone else," Mark said. "I know he's supposed to be guarding you, protecting you, your loyal subject. Instead, he's the most dangerous thing around. He needs to protect you from himself. Maybe he's in awe of the American Princess…or obeying you because it's his royal duty. But how do you know what's love and what's just ogling? Or obligation?"

"Shut up, Mark."

"How can you know what's real at a time like this, Kane?"

"Nothing about any of what has happened to me lately is *real*," she snapped.

"Exactly," Mark agreed. "Your life is a damn fairy tale."

Kane looked at her girlfriends for rescue. Neither one of them disagreed with her brother.

"Which of you is going with Kane to New York tomorrow?" Mark asked, changing the subject before he got knuckles to the biceps.

"I can't get out of my commitments to my clients until the end of the week," Sora said.

"I'm not leaving Scatch right now," Lani said. "Things are red *hot*."

Sora glared, but apparently held her insults. This was clearly not the time.

"Mary won't leave the kids that long," Mark pointed out. "That doesn't mean you're going alone, does it, Kane?"

"Gade will be there," she said.

"The bodyguard?" Mark scoffed. "I'm talking about one of us – someone who you know will have your best interests at heart. I'm talking about *family*."

"My grandfather is accompanying me," Kane answered.

"Family isn't determined by pedigree, Kane, no matter how royal the bloodline," Mark said, taking a gulp of his drink. "I'm coming with. You need someone you can trust."

Kane stared at him and Mark stared back. No piece of paper said he was her brother, but he was. Kane sighed and nodded. Then she looked at her royal guard. Did that mean she didn't trust Gade? Mark's words had cut deep. Gade *was* dedicated to her…a loyal subject. And she was just a broken-hearted girl on the rebound. *Is that all it is? Empty? A foundation built on duty and desperation instead of romance?*

If she discovered that was all it was, she would want someone like her brother nearby in New York. She would need her family.

Chapter Six

Kane woke up in her own apartment for the first time in days. Her grandfather wanted her to stay another night at the Royal Palace Hotel, but Kane had worried that the awkward familiarity between her and Gade would be obvious to anyone as sharp as Senator Cambridge. So, she had insisted she stay at her own place one last night, making the excuse that she would be able to pack all night instead of rushing through it in the morning. "I'm too wound up to sleep, anyway."

Kane hadn't invited Gade in. He hadn't insinuated that he'd expected anything different. Gade had remained posted outside her apartment all night. She wondered when the man ever slept. Even when she'd had occasion to see him in bed, it had rarely been with his eyes closed. They were usually doing the opposite of resting.

Kane called work. She had planned on making up something about walking pneumonia and being contagious, then her boss cut in while she was crafting the most heartbreaking story of sniffles and coughs—"I know you're faking it, Liberty," Pauline interrupted. Pauline was always a total bitch. "Get your ass in today or find something else to do with your life." Kane was sure Pauline thought that would set things straight, but Kane was now a damn princess.

"If I had more time, I would bring my ass down to the office one last time so you could kiss it, Pauline," Kane snapped. "I quit." Before Pauline could comment or retract, Kane disconnected.

She showered. Afterward, Kane stood in front of her half-empty closet. It hadn't been that full even before she'd started packing. She selected a T-shirt that she'd gotten as a souvenir from the Kanye concert she'd attended with Dillon the past October. She paired it with some black jeans that were worn and comfortable. Kane considered whether or not she wanted to put on underwear first. The ride to the airport would be long and the flight to New York even longer. It would be a lot of time with Gade, so lot of opportunities to make a mistake. She put on the least sexy underthings she could find before pulling on the shirt and jeans.

Gade stood sentry right outside her apartment door. She dragged two suitcases out of her entrance and had four more waiting in the hall. He offered to carry the heaviest two. Kane took the lightest pair and started toward the first floor, down steep steps. They left the middle-sized ones beside her apartment door for another run.

"I'll run up and grab the last ones," Kane said while Gade packed the first load into the Camaro's trunk.

"I'll get them," he said. Then he looked at her like he expected her to follow him up the stairs and not carry anything back down.

"I'll be fine for five minutes, Gade," Kane promised. "I won't ever be directly in your line of sight every second of every day."

Gade didn't move. He obviously had protocols and was evaluating them. How long was the leash? Then she remembered that *she* wasn't the one on the end with the collar.

"I mean it," Kane said, commanding. "I will not be treated like some helpless child."

Gade nodded. He clearly knew as well as anyone alive that she was a woman in full. He disappeared up the steps, moving double-time.

"Who the hell is that?" came a voice from around the corner where Gade had parked his Camaro in Kane's parking spot. The owner of the voice used to share the spot with Kane.

"Who the hell do you think *you* are?" Kane attacked. "What are you doing here, Dillon?"

"I wasn't expecting some British brute amped on 'roids making all googly eyes at you," Dillon said. "Are you sleeping with him?"

"That's none of your damn business anymore," Kane snapped, her insides a sudden turmoil of emotion. Dillon made her so angry, yet her heart cried out at seeing him again. She wasn't ready to deal with Dilly. She wasn't over him enough to handle his shit. "You're living with that trollop."

"She's actually Puerto Rican," Dillon corrected. He was never known for his vast vocabulary. "And it didn't work out. I made a mistake, Kane."

"Don't you dare say it, Dillon Durfee," she warned. "You don't get to take it back."

"Look... I think I was scared of commitment, Kane," Dillon said. "I was running away. The thing we have is so powerful and real that I just didn't know what to do with it."

"Please, Dilly, don't do this."

"I want you back, Kane."

No. Nonononononono. She couldn't hear this right now. Kane was moving on...moving up. This was everything she had wanted to hear a week ago, but this weekend seemed like a lifetime and now she was living someone else's life.

Gade slammed Dillon like an armored car sideswiping a Hyundai. He threw Dillon up against the brick sidewall of Kane's apartment building. His arm was as big around as Kane's thigh and pressed against Dillon's throat. Gade glared at him like he would snap him in two if another sound came out of Dilly's mouth.

"Gade, wait," Kane cried. "He was just talking. He wasn't trying to hurt me."

"He doesn't need to use his hands to hurt you," Gade said. So Gade knew who he was.

"It's all right," Kane said. "I have to deal with this sometime."

Gade let him go. Dillon coughed for a long minute then glared at Gade like he thought daggers in his eyes made up for being tossed around like a light salad. Gade stayed standing between Dillon and Kane.

"Is this 'roid monster going to let us finish our conversation?" Dillon asked.

"If I wasn't going to let you speak, I would have done more damage to your trachea, Mr. Durfee," Gade said.

"Can we have some privacy?" Dillon inquired.

"You have forfeited your right to privacy," Gade said.

"Just because you're banging a princess doesn't give you the right to rule over my life," Dillon said.

Kane stepped forward. She passed Gade, standing right in front of Dillon. "You know about that?" she asked.

"Yeah, I heard you were hanging out with some fucking English bastard on steroids," Dillon said. "We still have friends that move in the same circles, Kane."

"I'm talking about the other thing," Kane said. "You know who I really am. That's why you're here."

"I still love you, baby," he tried.

Kane shook her head. Tears were falling from both hurt and anger. *He only came here because he wants to be a prince.* He smashed her heart all over again. Kane turned and walked away. Dillon took a step forward, reaching for her.

"Take another step," she warned as she kept walking, "and I will have Gade break you in two."

Awkward.

The whole rest of her day after Kane encountered Dillon was *awkward.*

Mark met her at the airport. Mary had offered to drive him and drop him off. She came into the airport lobby to say farewell to Kane—or so she said. Mary would see Kane in a couple of days anyway. They had gone weeks in their adult life without crossing paths. And since when did Mary offer anyone a ride to the airport during the day, when she was responsible for housework and shopping and laundry and chores?

Abigail waited for Kane and Mark with first-class tickets. The look that Mary and Abigail exchanged confirmed *something* had happened between the two of them. The sexual tension felt as thick as the stink of jet exhaust and the stench of unwashed travelers. The women worked hard at avoiding each other's gaze as Mark told Abby and Gade the story of Mary's atrocious driving on the way to the airport. They failed to convince Kane that nothing happened.

"I need to use the restroom before we go through security," Kane said. "Mary, come with me."

"You haven't needed my help in the bathroom since you were three," Mary replied.

"I just want to spend as much time with you as possible before I leave, sis," Kane schmoozed.

As soon as they were out of earshot—"What the hell, Mary? What's going on between you and Abigail?"

A look of horror crossed Mary's face. She apparently thought no one had noticed. Did she think she could get away with it? Things like that never stayed secret. Kane didn't know what story Mary had told her husband, but it damn sure wasn't the truth.

"It just happened, Kane," Mary cried. "One minute, we were in the limo, going to get the kids. Then I kissed her. Abby told the driver that she needed an Evian. She told him to pull over in the first available space and that he needed to take an hour to get the bottle of water. He didn't ask any questions. As soon as we were alone in the limo, with the dark tinted windows and the soft music... I don't even remember what I was thinking, what I was feeling. It was just..."

"You slipped down the slope," Kane said.

"It won't ever happen again," Mary promised.

Mary had tears running down her face. *Shame? Fear that Larry will find out? Maybe heartbreak over the feelings that she has to tamp down?*

"But you're here," Kane said, "to see Abigail."

"I'm here to see *you,*" Mary argued. "I'm dropping off Mark."

"Bullshit, sis," Kane said. "This is about Abigail. What did you think would happen? A repeat performance of your tryst in the limo?"

"No," Mary said.

She means yes.

"You can't," Kane warned. "Look at Lani. She blew up her whole life. What about Artie and Agnes?"

"It's always about my kids," Mary suddenly snapped, seething for a moment. Then fresh tears accompanied fresh guilt. "It's *always* about them. This was just about me. This was just for *me*."

"Then keep it to yourself," Kane clapped back, "and never speak of it to anyone else. Now go home. Nothing good can come of this."

Kane walked away and she didn't turn back. She wasn't sure if Mary followed or left until she rejoined Abigail, Mark and Gade. Her brother asked, "What happened to Mary?"

"She had to go," Kane said, looking at Abigail. "Her family is more important than anything at the airport."

Mark shrugged. Mary the family woman, Mary the housewife, Mary the mother… He seemingly figured it made sense—and Abigail got the message.

Awkward.

Then Mark made things even more weird the whole flight to New York. Abigail, Mark and Kane had seats in first class and Gade rode in coach. Mark couldn't help his fascination with Kane's ill-advised relationship with the hired help.

"Is it weird," Mark asked when Abigail went to use the bathroom, "that your boyfriend is sitting all the way back there while you sip champagne up here?"

She saw where Gade was sitting, in a space half the size of her while he was twice her width and girth.

Gade sat between a woman who was very, very pregnant and a man who looked like he had been expecting for the last twenty years. That was one very full aisle.

"He's not my boyfriend," Kane hissed.

"Well, I'm glad you're not getting ahead of yourself and updating your social media status," Mark quipped, a jibe at her ex-boyfriend. *Did he hear about how I ran into Dillon earlier?*

"I have enough going on without your juvenile remarks, bro," Kane said.

Mark was on his second complimentary flute of champagne. "You're the one who started it, Kane. I'm just here as the voice of reason."

"Your 'reasons' are starting to slur," she said.

Abigail returned and thankfully Mark wasn't drunk enough to keep flapping his liquored lips.

Then there was Gade.

Kane had scolded Mary on the illicit encounter between her and Abigail, but there was just as much on the line in the affair between Kane and Gade. When they were close, she could feel the heat coming off his rock-solid body in waves. The scent of his cologne made her swoon, transporting her in time to when they had worn much less clothing and space separating them. Kane looked back every so often during the long flight to New York City—whenever Mark was distracted—and when her eyes met Gade's across the aisles, she felt warm all the way down to her toes.

Deplaning, a flight attendant flirted unabashedly with Gade, lightly touching his big biceps. The attendant laughed like she wanted to have his babies, right then and there. When Kane was close enough, she could hear the attendant offering to write her phone number on one of his deltoids. Kane wanted to corner the hussy and tell her to keep her goddamn hands off the princess's man and stick that ink pen up the wrong way of her runway. But Gade wasn't her boyfriend, and he wasn't her 'man', so Kane just shot the flight attendant a glare of pure contempt and moved on.

Awkward.

And things were only going to get worse.

* * * *

The morning seemed so long ago—like it belonged in some other year—that Kane Liberty had woken up in the apartment she had shared with Dillon the last three years, a puddle of drool drying on her pillow, wearing a pair of footie pajamas she'd had since junior high. Now, twelve hours later, Princess Kane Cambridge sat across from Dash Dameron at the restaurant in the lobby of a posh Manhattan hotel.

There was a damn waterfall in the room. A black granite ledge twenty feet up spilled a sheet of water as thin as crêpe paper, a crystalline curtain backdrop against the semicircle of immaculately adorned tables. Chandeliers with teardrop gemstones twinkled overhead. The tables on either side of Kane and Dash were unoccupied, no one within earshot. The drone of cascading water drowned out the sound of their conversation beyond a few feet.

"Is this an official interview?" Kane asked, as the famous television host flashed his fabulous toothsome smile.

"This is the pre-interview," he said, his grin never faltering. "It's just an informal chat to get your vibe. I like to call it 'confab foreplay'—just a little small talk.

We aren't going to discuss anything about the *big* story."

His every word was a flirtation. His bright blue gaze played with her, teasing at the edges of her lips, her long neck, the neckline of the blouse she wore, piercing her own whenever their eyes met. Dash reminded her of George Clooney with his elegant gray hair so perfectly styled and his playful demeanor.

Dash was older than Kane by twenty years. He had been at the top of the industry since Kane had been little. *DamTime* was an iconic infotainment program that regularly ranked as the highest rated show on cable news. Certainly, the audience tilted heavily female, attracted to Dash's suave allure. Kane was in awe of the magnetic charisma of the man. Was it pheromones? Magical charm? Some genetic super-mutation that made him sexy as hell? Within just a few seconds, Kane was smitten.

"They will put your beautiful face on every magazine in the world, Kane," Dash said. "You have the look of a cover girl."

Kane blushed. She had hardly ever thought of herself as 'beautiful'. Her hair was forever a tangle of curls, unruly and a wreck. She never really knew what to do with her makeup. Aunt Polly and Mary had a lot darker skin than she did, so they had an entirely different scope of color scheme than Kane. Her skin was shades lighter since she had a white father, and her mixed-race skin had never taken the same kinds of product that they'd used. Kane had never really found a palette that matched her complexion. And her wardrobe was usually more 'boyish' than 'babe'.

But Abigail had helped with all that. As soon as they'd arrived in Manhattan, a small army of her grandfather's interns had intercepted them. Four college kids who worked out of Senator Cambridge's office in an apprenticeship program from Georgetown University had been directed to escort and assist her in transportation around town. Kane had parted ways with Mark, sending her brother to a hotel with one of the interns. The other three apprentices had accompanied Kane and Abigail to a beauty shop where no expense was spared. Gade had escorted them, standing sentry outside the front door of the shop as Kane was painted and remolded. They had done her hair and makeup and she had changed into a dress Abigail had brought along. Kane had walked into the beauty shop looking like a boho beatnik from Greenwich Village and had exited as an uptown socialite ready for Park Avenue. Her transformation had even made Gade stare. He had seen her completely stripped down, but he had never seen her looking so made up.

Now Gade and Abigail sat across the room at another table, out of earshot of everything Kane and Dash conversed about. The three interns lined up at the bar, ready to be summoned for any menial task. Kane had her back to Gade and was grateful. She would hardly be able to handle being distracted by Gade's beautiful buffness and Dash's dazzling dentals at the same time.

"Oh, yes," Dash continued. "The twenty-four-seven cable news cycle is going to just love your smile…and that *hair*."

"My brother always called me a tomboy growing up," Kane said.

"Well, you are prettier than any boy I've ever met," Dash replied. "And considering the Hollywood crowd I hang out with, that's really saying something."

"You are pretty smooth. I'll give you that," Kane said.

His grin never wavered. It was like a self-sustained power source that dazzled nonstop—like the sun in a cloudless sky, eternal energy beaming out in a steady stream of warmth. Kane basked in it, soaking it up. Dash made it so easy to just be, just say, just let all those worries and wonders wash away for a while.

A server came over, an exotic Asian woman as beautiful as any person Kane had ever seen, but Dash hardly spared her a glance. His attention was focused on Kane, as if a spotlight shone down directly upon just her.

"What'll you have?" Dash asked Kane.

"I'll have whatever you're having," Kane said.

"So you want a Negroni?"

Kane shrugged. She had no idea what a Negroni was. "I'll try it."

"I don't think you want a Negroni. What do *you* want?"

"Well, I don't know what they serve here," Kane stammered. She didn't feel comfortable ordering a drink in a place as fancy as this.

"They will make you whatever you want, Kane. Anything at all."

She thought for a few seconds. "Well, when I was a kid, we went out for Christmas dinner at this fancy steakhouse every year. Uncle John let us order anything we wanted off the menu. There was a funny drink on the list. I ordered it one year then they didn't have it after that. It was called a 'Freddie Bartholomew'."

"Of course," the server said. She disappeared to retrieve their drinks.

"A virgin drink, huh?" Dash asked.

"Not what one of those famous people you always interview usually order?"

"All those famous folks? We call them 'stars'," Dash said, his teeth actually twinkling in the dim light of the dining room. "It's such an appropriate word. There are a million stars in the sky, and we may pay attention to some for a while, watch them twinkle, then we move on to another star. Some shine for a while and fade out, while others are bright for an entire lifetime. There are clusters we name in collective formations—like the Kardashian constellation. Yet there's always some different star, the next thing to twinkle, because we can look around and there's always another.

"But every once in a while, a new star is born—something brighter than the others, a light that outshines the rest of the heavens. A star that dominates the field and lights up the darkness. Oprah. Elvis. Madonna."

"You're talking about me?" Kane asked. "You think I'm something so special?"

Dash shrugged. His gaze played across her face, like he absorbed every detail of her. He was intense and interested. She felt like the only woman in the room.

"I have interviewed everyone from presidents to porn stars," Dash said. "I know special."

"You're good," Kane complimented, smiling. He knew how to engage his interviewee. He made her feel like she was standing in the spotlight, the star of the show, even in a two-way conversation. "You know that?"

"I've seen the ratings," he replied with a wink.

The server brought their drinks. One sip of her Freddie Bartholomew and Kane was transported back twenty years. She smiled. Dash watched her, smiling himself. He never stopped grinning.

If he were a little younger...or if she were a little older... And if Gade weren't sitting right behind her...

They talked some more. Dash was flirty but not forward. He made her feel free but not without tether. She would have told him anything, but he didn't ask about most things. They just talked, two hours slipping away as quickly as two minutes. It was empty conversation, but after it was over and he was gone, Kane still felt full of him, Dash's smile lingering in her head like the evening star shining in the twilit sky.

The interns dropped Kane, Gade and Abigail off at the hotel and were dismissed for the night. Abigail escorted Kane down the hall, Gade following the women at their heels. They each had their own room tonight, the best suite available reserved for Kane. Gade, Abigail and Mark were sheltered nearby. A private elevator took them up to the top floor where no public lift had access. Gade nodded approval at the effective security.

"Dash is pretty impressive, isn't he?" Abigail asked as they walked down the hall from the elevator.

"He's a charismatic interviewer," Kane said, trying not to sound like she was gushing.

"Just don't let him charm the pants off you, Princess," Abigail warned. "That man has a notorious reputation in some circles."

Kane noticed Gade glowering at the prospect of Kane being seduced by a celebrity lothario. *So he can be jealous.* It was cute seeing him puffed up with envy. Kane *tsked* and shook her head, her perfect curls staying right in place. "You don't need to worry about me," she said. "I do not intend to sleep with Dash Dameron."

Kane didn't need any more complications in her already-confusing life.

"Intentions are often exclusive of incident," Abigail said, her eyes looking away and down. "Sometimes things happen, whether we want them to or not."

Is she talking about Mary? Or is it something else? Kane saw a gravitas cross Abigail's face when she spoke, a hint of terrible regret. Was it because she'd had sex with a married woman? Or did Abigail have some other sinister secret?

"Good night, Princess," Abigail said, and was inside her room before Kane could reply. Abigail's comments would remain cloudy, at least for the night.

Gade escorted Kane to her room. He was so large, towering over her in the corridor between the doors to their respective rooms. He seemed out of proportion with the rest of her world, looming large every time she turned around. Kane couldn't help but assign the man his own gravitational pull, tugging her nearer every time she got too close. She looked up and he looked down.

"He was pretty smooth," Gade said. "It looked like you were having a really good time."

"Dash Dameron was preparing for the interview that will reveal Princess Cambridge to an American audience," Kane dismissed. "That's it…end of story."

"There is *always* more to the story," Gade said. "And it's the rest of the story that often tends to sting."

Then there was silence between them. They had been intimate over and over, but something separated them now, where there had been nothing between them before. Kane was a princess, and Gade was her royal guard. That had meant nothing when she had only been Kane Liberty back home nursing a broken heart. Now she was Kane Cambridge in New York City. There was that...and Dash. She couldn't stop thinking about Dash's dazzling smile. Gade waited, like he wanted her to ask him inside, but she couldn't.

"Goodnight, Gade," she said, instead of kissing him.

"Goodnight, Princess," he replied, knowing better than to overstep her boundaries.

She watched him walk away to the next door down. He waited to close his door until she went inside, always making sure she was safe.

What a room! Modern to the point of futuristic, it featured exclusively black and white decor. White marble floors extended everywhere with plush black carpets so soft that she wondered what poor animal had had to die for the comfort of her soles. Photographs of old Manhattan decorated the walls, faded black-and-white prints with white matting in black frames on white walls. She felt like Lelia in *Shadows*, an old movie set in New York in the fifties that was one of Aunt Polly's favorite films to watch on throwback Thursday movie night.

Kane shed her dress as soon as she was inside. Her undergarments might be more expensive than her entire previous wardrobe, so she carefully hung her bra and panties on hangers in the walk-in closet in her room. She pulled on a gossamer-thin robe that covered her in translucent material, outlining the shape and shade of everything underneath.

Still wound up from Gade's presence and Dash's energy, Kane couldn't just go to bed. A balcony overlooked the city, with square black aluminum balusters and a round black handrail with more white marble tile on the floor. Skyscrapers surrounded Kane, rising into the sky and blotting out the stars. A million points of light glowed all around her, from countless windows and neon signs and streetlights up and down the avenues. Kane was just one shimmery soul among millions.

Dash had said she was a star. He'd compared her to Elvis and Oprah. *Maybe soon…but not tonight.* Tonight Kane was still anonymous. She was still free. She was a princess-to-be, fame still existing only in some nebulous future. Kane was no more noticed tonight than anyone else in the sea of souls. Her star hadn't yet started to shine.

She could be anyone…no one. For tonight, she was nobody.

Kane had a thought…a devilish one, a wonderful, exhilarating thought. She was still no one for tonight but soon that would change…forever.

It was the last night to try something bold before everything changed ever after.

She let her robe slip off and the breeze wafted over her naked body. Standing under the starshine of the city's lights, she felt both exposed and unseen. If anyone happened to gaze at the balcony on the upper floor of the hotel, they would see just a naked woman too far away for them to ever recall a face. If someone watched out of a nearby window, the shadows of her balcony and the backlight from her room would conceal her features enough to ensure anonymity. It felt too good to be free and uncovered to worry about being noticed.

She stood there for a long time, nothing at all between her midnight skin and the night all around her. There might be endless eyes that could turn her way. Kane remained outside, under the sky and among the millions, thinking about Gade, and Dash—and being famous. Despite the cool breeze, she was warm and getting warmer. She closed her eyes and touched herself. Maybe someone was watching…maybe not.

She wanted Gade, dammit. She moved her hand against the places that were warm and wet. She pictured Gade then she wasn't picturing anything, because stars in her mind were blossoming and blowing up, brighter than anything in the sky or out among her in the world.

Finally, when she was flushed and feeling fine, Kane went inside.

Chapter Seven

Kane had a dream. She'd come in from the balcony the previous night and crawled into her princess-sized bed, still naked. Sometime in the night, Gade entered the room. He gently stirred her from sleep. He was wearing as little as she. Soon enough, they became entangled, entwined, one. And for a while, nothing else mattered. They made love until dawn broke and the thin light of sunrise lulled them asleep.

Kane woke up alone. For a moment, she wondered if maybe it had been real instead of a dream, but then she recalled pulling on a comfy pair of gym shorts that said 'Booty' on the butt and the Air Force Fighting Falcons T-shirt she had swiped from Gade's place on the first night of their one-night stands. She was still wearing the same thing. The far side of her bed was cold and undisturbed. She had slept all night alone.

The Ball was set for the weekend. Her interview with Dash Dameron would air right before the event. Her casual introduction to Dash yesterday had been prelude to the official meeting today and the formal sit-down tomorrow to tape the segment. The thought of being the subject of nationwide interest made Kane's head buzz.

She took a shower and put on one of the outfits that Abigail had picked for her when they had been out shopping with Mary. She chose a button-up blouse in lavender that recalled the spring lilacs back home and designer jeans that hugged her curves better than any pair of denim ever purchased at the discount stores that had been her familiar stomping grounds these last thirty years. When she exited the bathroom, Gade was waiting in her room. He placed her room service breakfast on a small table that looked out the grand balcony doors. There was bacon with an omelet, garnished and plated to perfection, a meal that looked too picturesque to eat. But Kane was famished. The omelet didn't get a reprieve for being beautiful.

Gade stood sentry like one of those British blokes who guarded the royal palace over in London, yet his focus could not remain disciplined. It wandered over to her again and again, watching her eat. He was also plated to perfection, armored like a knight with muscle and mass. A bulge under one arm was the garnish of a gun, his version of a valiant sword. The bulge under his waistband was the sword Kane was more interested in, her Lancelot too alluring to the young Princess Kane.

"What is this, Gade?" Kane asked, finishing her breakfast. "What are we doing about this thing between us?"

"You are the princess, m'lady," he answered. "I'm your guard."

"I thought we were going to see what happens?"

"Nothing can happen. Not again."

"What if that's not what I want?"

"I'm supposed to protect you, Princess," Gade said, like a parent telling a child that it's for their own good, "not co-conspire to put everything at risk."

"Since when is exploring something physical between two consenting adults a bad thing?"

"Often," Gade simply replied.

"So it's just over?" Kane asked, irritated that he thought he could unilaterally decide for the both of them. "You think you can just turn off your feelings? Just like that?"

"No," Gade admitted. "But my first responsibility is to protect you, Princess. So if that means guarding my feelings against putting you in danger, then I will perform my duty. I'll stop myself from bringing you harm."

"Maybe I want to be in a little danger?"

"Then I'll protect you from yourself."

Kane was miffed. She stood up from the table, spilling the rest of her orange juice and knocking a fork onto the floor with a clatter, glaring at Gade. A dozen curses sizzled on the tip of her tongue, but she stopped the worst of them from tumbling out. She puffed out a hot exhale and turned away, walking out onto the balcony where she had stood last night, naked for all Manhattan to see. She had felt so empowered then—now, she felt like she was at the mercy of her whirling emotions.

Kane sighed. "If it's going to be such torture to be around me without being *with* me, then why don't you just resign? I'm sure there are plenty of bodyguard jobs in the world, especially with a body like yours."

"I'm the only person I trust to protect you, Kane. My only desire is to keep you safe, both professionally and personally."

She turned around and faced him again, calmer. "That's your *only* desire, huh, Gade?"

"That's what I'm going to focus on, m'lady," Gade said.

"Very well, Mr. Williams," Kane sniffed. "You can escort me across the hall. I'm supposed to collect my brother before we meet with Dash Dameron for the pre-interview luncheon."

A quick expression passed over Gade's face, like he had caught a waft of something that smelled rancid. Kane realized it was the whiff of jealousy. So he didn't like Dash. Gade apparently wanted to turn off his feelings for Kane, but that wasn't how it worked. He could only turn his back on them. But they were likely still there, like a shadow that could be ignored but not extinguished. Kane was seemingly his sunlight, and her effect could not just be eliminated.

When she was ready, Gade escorted her down the hall. Kane knocked on Mark's door. He was supposed to be ready by ten to accompany her to the pre-interview. But it wasn't Mark who opened the door. Instead, it was one of her grandfather's interns, the blonde who had escorted Mark to the hotel the previous day. She was easily half his age and wearing half his clothes, his blazer hanging mid-thigh with obviously nothing underneath. Her face turned red when she opened the door and saw it was the princess knocking. *Who did she expect? Room service?*

"Where's my brother?" Kane asked, already expert with a tone that brooked no bullshit.

"Uh, he's in the shower, your grace," the girl stammered, trying to tug the hem of Mark's blazer down to cover her nether bits, but only succeeding in exposing more of her ample cleavage in the process. "I'm sorry, your highness."

"He was supposed to accompany me for lunch," Kane said, turning away before she saw more of Mark's concubine than she cared to. "Just tell him to meet me there."

Kane stalked toward the private elevator, Gade easily keeping up with her. She would have to sprint to ever outpace him. Abigail texted that she was already at the restaurant for lunch, coordinating with the *DamTime* people for Kane's luncheon. At least Mary's illicit lover was professional and dependable. Mark needed higher standards.

"My brother needs to keep it in his damn pants," Kane swore under her breath as the elevator descended.

"Since when is exploring something physical between two consenting adults a bad thing?" Gade asked, quoting her own words back to her. He smirked, a little curl of his beautiful lips that almost made her late to her own lunch. She had no more self-control than her boondoggled brother and nearly undressed right then and there. And if she did, she knew that no matter what Renegade Williams represented in mind and voice, his body would have no option but to do what it was built to do, right there in the damn elevator.

Kane shook her head. She warned, "Y'know, just because you can't bring yourself to quit this job doesn't mean that you can't get fired, Mr. Williams."

And Gade remained silent for the rest of the descent, for the rest the drive. In fact, Kane wouldn't hear him utter one more word for the rest of the day.

* * * *

Dash Dameron sat across from Kane, that smile shining as brightly as the sunniest of afternoons. After her morning catching Mark with his pants down and Gade pushing her away because of some stupid sense of nobility, she was having a shitty day. Kane gulped another mouthful of the lime-green drink in front of her. A Midori sour. No virgin Freddie Bartholomew today. It was only one o'clock, but Kane needed something to take the edge off.

The bistro was obnoxious with a Mediterranean theme. Teardrop bulbs dangled from stringed wires like someone had mistook the restaurant for a Christmas tree. Round windows were opaqued to give patrons privacy from New York City tourists teeming along the city sidewalks. Scenes of coastal cafes from across the Atlantic seemed almost cruel examples of authenticity in a relic of replica. Three walls featured arched doorways, none left unguarded. Kane felt like a valuable treasure who everyone wanted a piece of.

Abigail consulted with *DamTime* producers and made final arrangements for the official interview the next day, and Gade stood by one entrance. Mark sat outside the private room, at the edge of Kane's line of sight, saddled up to the bar in the main restaurant, sipping wine and texting like a teenager. Probably asking that blonde to send him nude selfies.

Kane sat across from Dash. They were the only two people sitting inside the secluded section.

"Fame," she sighed.

"Already seeing the effects?" Dash asked, charm oozing from every syllable. He had an accent that Kane couldn't place, like he had invented his own inflection. *Alluring*.

"I shouldn't talk about it," Kane said. "It doesn't have anything to do with what my grandfather wants me to talk about. He gave me some specific talking points, like he thought he needed to slip me the answers to the exam."

Dash smirked. "Just a part of the game. The only rule is that you have to break the rules."

"It feels like I'm cheating."

"So, let's just talk off the record then," Dash said. "This isn't a meeting to get all the talking points out, Kane. Every famous person always says the same thing, anyway. I already know what your grandfather wants you to tell me—*Blah blah blah*. I can fill in those blanks. Instead, let me have a chance to get to know the *real* you before I have to ask questions from the fake you. I can make the mundane a little more exciting if I know what you *really* want to say."

"So, all your big interviews with celebrities and politicians? They just tell you what they want people to hear?"

"Of course," Dash said. "This is America. You read from the American script. Everyone says one thing and does another. The person on the camera isn't any more real than a character in a book of fiction. Fame is a fairy tale, sweetheart and you're an honest-to-goodness princess, so it certainly won't be any different this time."

"I *want* to be different," Kane said.

Dash shrugged. "That's just not how it works. You might be a nice-enough person, but you have things that you think or do or want that have to be kept in the shadows. The world doesn't want the real you. They just want the fairy tale."

"Maybe I will give them the real me and see what happens?"

"Then they'll push you to the side and ignore you," Dash warned. "Or they'll find some secret part of you to expose and destroy you. You play the part—or they tear you apart."

"The public?"

"The public absolutely adores elevating the anonymous, giving power to someone who is no one. Even more, the public *loves* taking it away," Dash said. "The two greatest American stories are the tale of rags-to-riches and the spectacular fall-from-grace. Give them the former and play the part or challenge the public and they will see you in ruins."

"Vicious."

"They're the ones who give you power, so you have to follow their rules."

"What if I don't want the power?"

"Can you use it for good, Princess Kane? Can you inspire the masses? Can you make the world a better place?"

"I think so," Kane said. "I want to."

"Then that's the tradeoff. The truth loses. But what matters is what you do with the lies. Can you wield the power of fame for the purpose of good?"

Kane considered. Maybe she could be a force in the world for positivity. Civility. Poise. She wanted to be an alternative to mud-slinging politicians, self-important celebrities, kooky musicians and misogynistic sports figures. There was a purpose for her in the world, but she needed her tiara to be a star.

"What about everyone around you?" Dash asked. This might be off the record, but he remained an adept interviewer. "Are they ready to lose the power they have already tasted, just by virtue of being in your royal entourage? It seems your brother is reaping the benefits of your new fame. How about your other friends?"

"Everyone," Kane said. "Lately, all the people in my life seem to be making these major mistakes."

"But would they have made them anyway?"

Lani had cheated on her husband with the deejay before Kane had even found out she was a princess. Mark and Mary had both taken thorny paths after she'd learned of her royal status, but maybe both had just been waiting for an opportunity to act out. Could Kane blame her own situation for their indiscretions—or was it merely that moment that had precipitated what would have been otherwise inevitable?

"You know a lot about these things."

"I've seen almost everything you can imagine over the years," Dash said. "But I do have to say I've never met an American princess. You are something new and refreshing, Kane Cambridge."

"I want to be," Kane said.

"Well, be what you want to be," Dash suggested, "not what your grandfather wants you to be, not what fickle public opinion wants you to be. Be one thing for the cameras, but be yourself otherwise. Some people lose themselves in the fiction of fame. They *become* the part, but the part is only meant to be played—like a mask that should go on and come off. I usually like people when we talk like this, off the record, no matter how insipid their celebrity role...the *real* people. But there are those that become who the world wants them to be. Don't let that happen, Kane."

"I feel like it's already happening," Kane said.

"There aren't any microphones here, Kane. No paparazzi yet. No reporters snooping for a story. Just you and me…and we have today," Dash told her. "So what do you want, Princess Kane? How do you want to spend your last few hours of relative anonymity?"

"Not like this," Kane said, looking at Gade guarding her, Abigail arranging everything, Mark making terrible choices. "Not right here."

And Dash grinned. "Let me see if I can do something about that."

The producers wanted to shoot some candid video of Kane talking to Dash, to act as background footage to run during promos leading up to the big show and over the show's theme when the interview aired. The substance of their conversation wasn't being recorded, just the camera rolling while they had lunch. After Dash finished interrogating her off the record about fame and her future, the *DamTime* team started breaking down the recording equipment.

"Big guy," Dash called to Gade, "do you suppose you could lend your ridiculous muscles to something other than blocking a fire-exit?"

Two *DamTime* tech guys struggled with a tripod system featuring an LED light as big around as a serving platter. Gade just stared.

"Is menial labor beneath you?" Dash taunted.

"I don't see you assisting them," Gade said, "and it's your own team."

"I'm hosting the lady, and you're just standing there protecting her from some undetermined threat," Dash said. "Does your sense of duty extend to such a nonsensical degree?"

Gade grunted.

"Will you give them a hand, Gade?" Kane suggested. "They look like they're really struggling."

Gade reluctantly trudged over to the techs and their tripod. He started sliding the apparatus down, compacting it into a smaller state. Meanwhile, Dash snagged Kane's hand and lived up to his name. They dashed out of the side exit at the exact time Gade was distracted.

"He might shoot you," Kane worried as she willingly followed.

"He won't get the chance," Dash said, flashing her his dazzling smile.

Dash paused in the hall that led back toward the street, right in front of a full-height portrait of Fiorello La Guardia. According to a small brass plaque, he had been a famous New York City figure during prohibition. Dash swung the seven-foot-tall frame open on a hidden hinge and led Kane into a secret passage hidden behind the portrait. The door closed on their heels before Gade would even know they were gone. Kane and Dash stood in a long corridor lit with faint incandescent bulbs mounted in wall sconces that looked at least a century old.

"Are you abducting me?" Kane teased.

"Do you want to be abducted?" Dash questioned. His grin flashed, even in the gloom. Kane felt like she as part of an interview mixed with a seduction. He started along the shadowy passageway.

"I just want a minute to breathe," Kane sighed as she followed.

"Well," Dash said, coming to the end of the dimly lit hallway and opening another secret passage, "breathe this in."

Jazz slipped through the open door like a snake slinking around her ears. The murmur of conversation acted as an accompaniment to the musicians on stage. There were maybe three dozen patrons partaking in the prohibition-era pub. Some smoked cigars, others cigarettes, one or two something stronger and a millennial in the corner with a vape. All this smoking was of course entirely illegal in New York City bars, where tobacco was the new enemy of teetotalers.

The glow of cell phones may have been proof of modern conveniences, but the dress appeared all vintage attire, common a hundred years ago. The men wore tweed pants, newsboy caps, stylish vests. The women looked so much fun in flapper dresses and wild skirts trimmed with tassels and fringe. The women's hairstyles and the men's hat styles were straight out of *The Great Gatsby*.

Kane had seen such places before in movies. She stood in a speakeasy, one of the secret places where society had gathered to ignore Prohibition in the Roaring Twenties. Now these trendy little hovels in metro areas were where the coolest of the cool were allowed entry. Dash was so cool that he gave Kane chills.

The bouncer at the door made Gade look like an average-sized human being. The man's head seemed the size of a cement block. His folded arms looked like constricting pythons wrapped around his whiskey-barrel chest. The bouncer nodded at Dash and gave him a courteous, "Good afternoon, Mr. Dameron." Dash gave him a smile and said, "Very good, Hector." If anyone could stop Gade if he managed to track Kane through the secret corridor, it might be this mountain of a man.

"My bodyguard is probably going crazy," Kane said as Dash pulled out a chair and offered her a seat.

"He's more than just a bodyguard, isn't he?" Dash asked, his smile genuine and his eyes knowing.

"He was," Kane confirmed. Why did she trust Dash with the whole truth? He was a celebrity interviewer. He could be probing her for answers so that he could excoriate her in an exposé. Yet she trusted him. "We can't be anything anymore."

Dash seemed amused. "You are the Princess of America. Who can tell you what you can or can't?"

"There are expectations. Rules."

"Maybe in London," Dash shrugged. "This isn't the British monarchy, Kane. Americans don't really follow rules."

"My royal guard tends to disagree," Kane said, looking toward the door where the bouncer stood. Gade didn't come through.

"You'd best text him that you're okay," Dash suggested. "I wouldn't want anyone to get hurt in his frantic search for the missing princess. Anyone like *me*, for instance."

Kane texted.

I'm fine. Just need some time alone.

Gade replied instantly.

Where are you?

Safe.

This city is too dangerous for you to run off alone.

I'm not alone.

Then she turned off her phone. Done.

"What would you like, Princess?" Dash Dameron asked, beckoning to the waitstaff.

"No rules?" she asked.

"No rules," Dash agreed, his smile shining in the shadows of the club.

"Show me a good time."

There were drinks. Good food. Dash made Kane laugh and laugh. His smile was infectious. They talked all afternoon, through the evening and into the night. And there was jazz—lots and lots of jazz.

When it came time to leave, Dash led Kane through another secret passage. This corridor was as dimly lit as the first one, but much longer. They exited the hallway several blocks from where they had originated. If Gade was still looking for her after all this time, surely he had no idea she would end up there.

The streets still teemed with people, despite the midnight hour. Throngs of tourists that slept by a different clock murmured in many languages up and down the avenues. City sanitation didn't work bankers' hours like back home, cleaning streets in this city of six million a twenty-four seven job. Fewer cars clogged the intersections at this time of day, but the number of red taillights and bright headlamps still seemed a never-ending parade. The sounds were muted by the dark, yet sounded alive and insistent, like the volume was simply turned down by half. Sirens somewhere, an occasional honk, bad mufflers, banging music… All were the constant somnolent sounds of the city.

"It's late," Dash said, his smile glowing under the bright lights. "Let me take you back."

"I'm not ready to go back yet," Kane said, dreading the ramifications for her actions. Surely her grandfather had been notified, and Senator Cambridge wouldn't be pleased. "Just a little longer. Just tonight. Can't I have just tonight?"

"Who am I to say no? You're the princess," Dash shrugged. "What do you want to do?"

"I just want to see the city," Kane said. New York at night. She had dreamed of such a place when she had been a kid. Manhattan was bright and bustling, even at this late hour. "I'm sure you know your way around Manhattan. I want see the most beautiful view of the skyline you've ever seen, Dash Dameron."

Dash looked down the street. He smiled. Nodded.

"First, you text that gorilla of an ex-boyfriend and tell him you're still okay," Dash said. "I don't want the NYPD filling me with holes because he reported you as being kidnapped by a famous television talking head."

Kane sighed. She turned on her phone. A message from Abigail warned her against impropriety. Five messages from Mark begged her not to blow up the good thing they had going. No messages from him after eight. He was probably banging the blonde again. And no less than twenty texts from Gade, each with an increasing amount of questions marks and exclamation points. Thankfully, he had never resorted to emojis. Gade was not an emoji kind of guy.

She texted them all to assure them she was fine and that she would see them in the morning. After she sent the last text, she turned her phone off again. Kane looked at Dash. "Done." His smile widened and lit the way as they started walking toward a stretch of skyscrapers.

Dash approached one of the taller structures in Manhattan, but instead of going through front doors that looked like they belonged on the entrance to some grand castle, he went around the back.

Kane expected a service entrance or a back door for deliveries, but instead they approached a secondary entrance through an unassuming vestibule all the way at the back corner of the skyscraper. A guard who looked like he might have been a brother to the bouncer at the speakeasy stood sentry at the secret entrance. "Good evening, Mr. Dameron," the big man greeted, nodding almost imperceptibly. Dash flashed him a smile and said, "*Very* good, Ramon."

They took an elevator to the top floor. Kane expected an opulent penthouse with a balcony featuring some amazing view, but Dash took her all the way to the rooftop. There were no rooms, just chairs, a cabana and a small bar along one edge. Most of the rooftop was taken up by an infinity pool that stretched along the entire eastern edge.

Even from the perimeter of the pool, the view was breathtaking. The rooftop overlooked the skyline of Manhattan, skyscrapers arranged in an enchanting order that looked straight out of a painting. She could see the Empire State Building and the Chrysler Tower in the distance. Kane couldn't breathe.

"You think that's beautiful?" Dash asked. "You need to see it from the edge."

Kane looked around. "Did you request swimsuits when you arranged the private use of the pool?"

"No suits," Dash declared, starting to unbutton his shirt. "And I didn't ask for privacy. Anyone could come along at any moment."

Kane watched him undress. He was an older man with hair gone silver, but still fit enough in the way of all rich guys with a gym membership, a nutritionist, a personal trainer and lots of leisure time. His body was tanned from tip to toes, not a square inch of skin unbaked. Dash was completely unabashed as he walked naked toward the poolside. Anyone could come along at any moment, but Dash didn't demure.

Dash paused before he stepped into the pool. A silver bowl on a stand nearest the water's edge contained a selection of shining foil wrappers. He selected one, his smile still in place. Confident as ever.

"You didn't request swimsuits, but you remembered to order a bowl of condoms?"

"Better to be over-prepared than fucked over," Dash said, stepping into the pool.

"You think you're getting laid?"

"I think you're getting whatever you want. I just want to be ready for whatever that is."

"I don't know what I want."

"I don't know, either. All I know is that the water's nice and warm," he said with a smile as he slipped under the surface. He swam to the edge, and he looked like a man perched at the precipice of a waterfall slipping over the edge of the skyscraper. There was nothing between Dash and the city.

There were rules to being a princess—how to act, what to say, proper etiquette, certain expectations, banned relationships. Certainly skinning dipping would be considered an uncouth activity of the royal court.

Kane unbuttoned her blouse, folding it carefully and placing it beside the pile of Dash's clothes. Then she peeled off her designer jeans. The night air was crisp, but warmth radiated from the rooftop and emanated from the poolside. She stood for a moment in her underwear, mostly black and fringed with scarlet. It could be a fancy swimsuit. She didn't have to strip down like Dash. Because what if someone walked in on them?

What if…?

I'm not ready to go back yet.

Kane reached back for the clasp on her bra and Dash watched. His smile never faltered. It wasn't creepy or calculated but comforting, like it was all good. So Kane unfastened her bra and took it off, placing it on the neatly folded blouse and jeans. Then her underwear dropped. Dash wasn't the first guy to see her naked and he damn sure wasn't the sort who would end up being the last. He was just the latest.

Kane waded into the pool and the water was fine, indeed. It was like silk, maybe some special water that seemed softer and wetter than most. There was no sharp smell of chlorine. The perfect temperature. It seemed to caress her naked body like a perfect set of sheets. Kane swam out and joined Dash at the edge. He could've reached out and caressed a breast or touched her intimately but he didn't. He just floated right at her elbow, both of them looking out at the skyline.

"This is amazing," she sighed, looking over the edge, seeing a city seemingly open before her without any walls, any borders. The pool was designed to appear endless, extending over the rooftop, although it was just the impression. It was her first infinity pool, and the effect was breathtaking.

"Yes, it is," Dash agreed, now looking at Kane instead of the city.

"I'm not out here because I want to have sex with you, Dash."

"This isn't about sex," Dash said, his gaze seeming to know more than his mouth was willing to say. "This is about getting what you want."

"I don't know what I want," Kane said.

That wasn't entirely true. She wanted Gade—but he didn't want the same thing.

"This isn't about me at all. It's not about any man at all," Dash said, like some hunky Yoda. "It's about being confident enough to do whatever the hell you want to do."

"I want to be able to decide for myself."

"Take change of your own fate?"

"I need to prove that I can take care of my damn self."

Dash smirked, a smile that surely would've had most women smashed instantly against his fit body. "Then take care of your damn self."

She turned back and looked at the city. There could be a dozen eyes looking back. She reached down between her legs and touched herself. She was so warm. Ready. She started moving her fingers and the lights of the city started to pulsate. Dash gave her some room, treading water a few feet away. She knew he was watching. Ripples of pool water ran between her fingers, swirled over her breasts, made currents across her feet as she moved her thighs farther and farther apart. Skyscrapers rose into infinity before her, countless floors of warm auburn lights. There might be a hundred more eyes on her, watching the young woman in the pool get closer and closer and closer to—

Kane gasped, biting her bottom lip. Then there were just lights, blurry and bright and everywhere, for quite some time.

Chapter Eight

Kane sat in the bathroom of Dash Dameron's apartment in upper Manhattan. It was morning and she stared at the phone in her hands. It was still off. She dreaded the stream of messages once she turned it on. She didn't want to know what Gade had to say. It would hurt and piss her off. He had given up the right to say anything about what she did and with whom she did it.

She pressed the power button. Abigail had texted one last time.

Whatever you wish, your grace.

Mark had texted this morning, maybe after the blonde was done with him.

Just don't get caught and a winky emoji.

Kane remembered masturbating in a public infinity pool in front of an entire city, but no one had walked in on her. She didn't 'get caught'. Then there were the texts from Gade, every half hour, all night long.

Just tell me you're okay. Over and over.

I'm fine, she texted now.

Okay, he replied instantly.

And that was it. Did he understand? Could he imagine what she had done last night? Certainly he didn't picture her getting herself off in an infinity pool while soaking up the Manhattan skyline. Did Gade finally accept that if he didn't want to see what they had, then she could have whatever else she wanted? Do whatever she pleased? He was a bodyguard, not a babysitter. She was still mostly anonymous, enough so that Dash could keep her safe.

Mostly anonymous. Until tomorrow. Until the interview aired and she attended the Royal Ball. Then Princess Kane Cambridge would be the most famous face in America.

Kane took a shower. Dash's place was exquisite. Nozzles along the wall washed her from head to toe while a showerhead the size of a serving platter rained down on her from above. Last night, she had felt like she was swimming in some exotic lake in the Amazon overlooking a concrete jungle, and this morning she stood under a tropical rainfall surrounded by swirled soapstone.

Kane pulled on the same clothes she had worn the day before, retrieved from the poolside table after they had stayed in the infinity pool for another hour after she'd finished. Her blouse still smelled of the speakeasy from yesterday, with a hint of Dash's cologne. Dash had been a perfect gentleman the entire time. He had even escorted her to his guest room and made sure she was comfortable before he left her for the night. Kane had fallen asleep…exhausted.

Kane exited the bathroom, wondering if Dash had slipped out in the meantime. Would he avoid her until their interview this evening? Was it going to be awkward?

Dash sat at a small table off his grand kitchen. His dazzling smile was still in place. He wasn't any different now than he had been before. Wearing just a black robe and matching slippers, he looked like he wasn't going to 'dash' anywhere. He had even waited to start breakfast until Kane joined him.

"Good morning." That smile. *How do women resist it? Most probably don't.*

"You made this?" Kane asked, looking over the succulent salad before her. The kitchen looked immaculate, so she wondered how he had had the time in the short minutes she had taken to shower.

Dash's grin changed, his smile taking on various individual expressions even as it was always on. "Oh, no. I have someone come in very early and prep breakfast. It was ready, in the fridge. I'm not known for my culinary skills."

Kane started eating and Dash took a bite. They talked about his apartment and his job and her agenda for the day. They didn't talk about the night before. Kane left after breakfast and Dash bade her a smiling goodbye.

Her phone made noise and she dreaded a text message from Gade. But it wasn't Gade. It was Sora. *We're in Manhattan. Meet us for lunch?*

The girls had arrived. *Perfect.* Kane really needed to talk to someone about everything. Her mind whirled around like a windstorm.

Kane took a cab to her own hotel. She managed to get to her room without Gade noticing her return. She changed clothes—a nice blazer and stylish pinstripe pants—put on fresh makeup, did her hair in little pigtails poking out left and right then someone knocked on the door.

She wasn't ready for Gade but she answered anyway, as she couldn't avoid him forever. It was Mark and he wasn't alone. He had a blonde, but it wasn't the same blonde as before.

"This is my sister," Mark introduced to his latest conquest.

Kane had to remember her royal manners. She shook hands with the most current blonde and greeted her warmly. Certainly, Mark had told the woman—more like the *girl*—that Kane was a princess, so Kane acted like royalty.

The girl bounced away. She had a *lot* of bounce. Mark called after her, "See you tonight!"

"What happened to the last girl?" Kane asked.

"Kelli blew five grand at the champagne bar and I realized she was using me just because I'm the royal brother. I was pretty bummed and on my way to a pretty serious bender," Mark said. "Then I met Brooke."

"And she's different," Kane deadpanned.

"Oh, yes," Mark said. "We really connect. Not like Kelli."

"I mean, two nights, two different girls."

"Hmm-m," Mark snorted. "Back home, you were mooning over your bodyguard. Last night, I know you weren't sleeping in your own bed—or in this hotel room or with Gade."

"All right," Kane said. Not the same thing, but Mark would only push her on her extracurricular activities if she pressed the subject. Kane worried Brooke would also use Mark for his connection to fame, but he was a grown man and could sleep with as many bimbos as he wanted…or could afford.

"I'm going to meet Sora and Lani for lunch," Kane said. "Do me a favor?"

"Anything for you, Princess Sis."

"Can you distract Gade for a minute while I sneak out?" she asked.

"Not ready for that conversation yet, huh?"

"We're not talking about it," Kane warned her brother, holding up her finger to show she meant business, "any more than we're discussing Brooke and Kelli and whoever is next."

"Next?" Mark checked, like he was both doubtful and intrigued. Maybe 'next' was more exciting than 'existing'. Then he smiled, more sinister than Dash's perpetual expression. "Yeah, I'll help you sneak out."

* * * *

Sora and Lani wanted to meet at a posh new coffee shop facing Central Park. Kane took a cab and found that the ladies were already waiting in front of the café. Customers sat outside at small tables, iron chairs gently warming under the morning sun. The shadows of skyscrapers smashed across the street and sidewalk, blocking the glare of the bright day. Coffees in three different sizes populated the tabletops, all steaming softly, hazy contrails drawing fingers in the air.

The coffee shop was called Jester's and Lani seemed to think that was the funniest shit she ever heard. "Get it?" she snorted. "Like a court jester! Because you're royal!"

"Sheesh, La," Kane muttered. "Can you keep it down till tomorrow?"

"This is New York City," Lani said. "No one's going to notice one more celebrity getting coffee."

The line extended out of the door and halfway around the block. A barista tried to keep order, despite antsy Manhattanites tapping feet and complaining loudly. Even little old ladies dropped four-letter words as if they were breadcrumbs for pigeons. Kane loved a good cup of coffee as much as anyone, especially considering her hangover from the speakeasy the night before, but she wasn't in the mood to stand around waiting to spend fifteen bucks on something she'd flush down the toilet in the very near future.

"Excuse me," Sora said to the barista who was acting as traffic coordinator of the long line, making a scene of her own even as Kane continued trying to silence Lani. "My friend here is scheduled to have an exclusive interview on *DamTime* and we're kind of in a hurry to get to the studio. Is there anything you can do?"

The barista probably got that line a dozen times a day. He rolled his eyes and opened his mouth to start to give Sora some serious attitude, but his eyes traveled to Kane and his tongue stopped. He looked her over. The guy had surely seen his share of celebrities in NYC. Kane must look the part.

"You know Mr. Dameron?" the barista asked Kane.

Know him? She had gone skinny-dipping with him just a few hours before.

"He showed me around town," Kane said. "I met Hector and Ramon last night."

The barista raised an eyebrow. He knew enough to know that Kane had legitimate inside information. He nodded. "This way, ma'am."

Kane got a long line of dirty looks. The little old ladies called her some vile names. A kid who couldn't have been older than eight years old flipped her off. A man in an expensive suit tried to trip her. There was someone Kane recognized as a news-hour pundit on some morning show who called her a 'budging bitch'.

"So worth it," Lani said as they moved to the front of the line.

The three women got their drinks and walked down the street with their coffees, then crossed over into Central Park, walking far enough until they were sure they had left behind any angry customers still in the Jester's line. No one would risk losing their place in line to kick Kane's ass, but they might be eager for retribution once they had a hot beverage in hand. The trio lined up on a park bench facing a public pond and Kane had a brief flashback to swimming in the pool with Dash, skinny-dipping while anyone, *anyone,* could have walked in on them.

She felt warm and wound up again...already.

"So you were with Dash Dameron last night?" Lani asked, insinuating exactly what Kane was thinking about.

"Yes," Kane said, elaborating on nothing.

"Romantically?" Sora quizzed, surprised.

"Not exactly romantic," Kane confessed, remembering her intense orgasm as Dash had watched from a distance.

"And what happened to Gade?" Sora asked.

"He's protecting me," Kane said. "He thinks that keeping me safe means keeping me at arm's length. We can't be together if I'm going to be a proper princess."

"Sounds like you weren't very proper last night," Lani said.

"It wasn't like that, La."

"So you say," Lani teased. "That's what I said about Scatch."

"That's even still a thing?" Kane asked. "I thought you would've gotten it out of your system by now."

"I'm more worried about what Scatch infected her system with," Sora said drily.

"Well, it sounds like *something* happened with Dash Dameron last night," Lani said with a wink.

"He showed me something new. Now it isn't new anymore. End of story."

"That's what everyone always says," Lani sighed, like some wise harlot looking back on a storied career, "until some douchebag husband posts you masturbating on the Internet."

Kane thought about the previous night and how many cameras might have recorded her as she climaxed in an infinity pool. But it had been dark and distant and it could've have been anyone out there. Still, the idea of a grainy video of Kane getting off circulating online made her squirm on the park bench.

"So Chase published revenge porn?" Kane asked.

"No," Lani shrieked. "I'm not stupid enough to let Chase have a video of me diddling myself!"

Kane stared at her cheating best friend, confused. Then it dawned on her, no matter how illogical it might be. What did Lani always do when she was getting attacked for being immoral or irresponsible? She turned the tables and made it about Kane…or Sora.

Kane looked at Sora. Sora had her head hung. She was hiding her shame. What the hell had happened after she'd left town? The whole world and everyone she knew in it had turned topsy-turvy.

"Sevin posted something? With you?"

Sora nodded, her straight black hair hiding her face. Kane reached out and took her hand. Sora grabbed it like a lifeline. She managed to look up at Kane. Her eyes were filled with tears.

"It was supposed to help," Sora sniffed. "He wasn't looking at me anymore, hasn't touched me for months. He just watches girls online all the time. So I asked if he wanted to watch me instead of them—record it and watch whenever he wanted. Better that than *them*. So we did. We made a video."

"Bastard posted it on a website and now it's ev-ree-where," Lani added.

"Shit, Sora," Kane said. "That absolute son of a bitch."

"I don't know why I was so stupid," Sora said. "I graduated summa cum laude. I run my own business. I was featured on the cover of *Entrepreneur Monthly*."

"Now you're featured on the home webpage of 'Autoerotic Asians'," Lani interjected. "I don't know why you're so upset about it anyway. You look damn good, Sora."

"You *watched* it?" Sora cried, her shame turned to rage.

"Jesus, La," Kane said.

"What?" Lani yelped. "I had to see what everyone was talking about!"

"I'm just going to be a distraction here, Kane. Maybe I should go back."

"It'll be fine, Sora. No one in New York City will recognize you from an online porn site."

But hadn't a half-dozen passersby already looked twice at Sora as they'd walked past? What the hell did Kane know about online porn? Maybe half of Manhattan had seen Sora's sex-tape.

"I'm sorry, Kane. I just thought… You were so brave and unselfconscious about Gade. You didn't give a damn what people thought about it. You would risk becoming princess for a chance at love. So I took my own chance. I just wanted to save my relationship with Sevin."

What the hell had happened to her friends and family since this Princess thing had all started to happen? Gade had distracted her and Lani had ended up with Scatch, ruining her marriage. Mary had slept with Abigail. Mark had screwed a string of college coed interns. Now Sora had become a porn star and Kane was getting off under the stars.

"We were willing to go the distance for love. But we trusted a man to be a partner on that adventure. But those men were just along for the ride," Kane said. "That's where we went wrong."

* * * *

Kane texted Gade her location after the girls were done with their coffees. Ten minutes later, a black Humvee with tinted windows pulled up. No Camaro. It was apparently going to be regulation equipment and standard procedure from here on out. Gade wasn't even driving. Kane had seemingly been upgraded to a two-man security team with her own personal driver. Gade exited the passenger side wearing a gray suit and tie that looked more tactical than practical. His eyes were covered with aviator sunglasses that surely had been left over from his Air Force days. He was all about the business.

"Your grandfather wants to speak with you before the interview," Gade informed.

"Fine, but I need to stop at the hotel and change first."

"Do your companions require transport, your grace?" Gade asked, all professionalism and propriety.

Sora seemed to find everything fascinating except for the mountain of manliness in front of her. *Is she really worried that Gade has seen her porn performance?* Kane couldn't imagine the massive man masturbating in front of a computer screen, logged on to 'Autoerotic Asians'. Lani wasn't shy at all. She roamed her gaze over Gade head to toe. Kane gave her an elbow under her big boob.

"My friends have their own plans for the afternoon," Kane said. "They'll meet up with us later."

"Very well," Gade announced, like he was Alfred the Butler instead of the man she'd slept with all the last weekend.

Lani and Sora gave Kane hugs and went off to explore Times Square. Kane started getting in the back right side of the Humvee while Gade walked to the front door to climb into the passenger seat beside the driver. She glared at her bodyguard.

"Really?" Kane snapped. "Is that how it's going to be now?"

"I'm following standard operating procedure, your grace," Gade stated in a drone, like Kane had just asked Siri a question.

"Bullshit," she said. "You're avoiding me. Are you scared to ride in the back, Gade?"

He slid his shaded eyeglasses down and his brown gaze met hers. There was a mix of emotions in his eyes. Gade always had his guard up, his body tensed for action—either violent or vivacious—but there were vulnerable feelings clearly swirling in his stare—hurt, jealousy, regret, tenderness. "Fear has nothing to do with it, Princess."

"I'm not getting into this vehicle unless you get in the back with me," Kane said. "I'm not freight that needs to be taxied around Manhattan like a FedEx package."

"You called me to come and get you," Gade reminded.

"Don't you think you're safer than an Uber?" she asked.

Gade just stared, exhaled then got in the back. Inside, the Humvee was an extended model and featured two bench seats facing each other. Kane had her back to the front seat while Gade faced forward…faced Kane.

Kane made sure the partition between the front and back was closed and locked. Vehicles like this were designed to keep conversations between passengers private. She didn't need a driver overhearing anything she might accidentally say to Gade. Not every driver was as discrete as the one who had given Abigail Morgan the privacy to seduce Kane's sister.

"You're making it exceedingly difficult to perform the objectives of my job," Gade informed Kane, making no attempt to avoid scolding his employer.

"You wanted me to stay away," Kane said. "I stayed away."

"All night long," Gade replied, his mouth set like cured concrete, seemingly resolute against frown or fracture.

"You made it very clear that you wanted nothing to do with my nights, Mr. Williams," Kane said.

"'Wants' have nothing to do with duty, your grace," Gade said. "Never mistake following your heart with doing the right thing."

"Those two things are not the same?" Kane asked.

"Rarely," Gade answered.

They drove the rest of the way in silence. Gade got out first and held the door for her, offering a hand for her to step down from the high Humvee. This could have been a date to prom, but Gade was just being paid to protect her, so this wasn't one. The princess couldn't fall for the lowly soldier. Gade Williams wouldn't allow it.

The Humvee parked in front of the hotel and waited. Gade escorted her up to the room and stood outside while she changed, did her hair and put on just the right jewelry. Everything had to be perfect. She exited a long time later.

Gade stared.

"What?" she asked. She wore a red lace dress with long sleeves featuring scallop detailing about the waist, accented with white sensible heels, diamonds accenting her ears and a simple silver chain across her breast. It was simple, elegant and inoffensive.

"You look like a princess," he complimented.

Kane smiled. It was much better than more insults.

Kane's grandfather waited for her inside the television studio in a posh reception room that featured a full bar, a crackling fireplace, a buffet of fresh fruits and a beautiful bouquet of pink roses. The Senator spoke with one of his aides, a beautiful woman of Indian descent who took notes as Senator Cambridge had a hand placed on the middle of her back, leaning in, whispering near her ear. It seemed inappropriately intimate.

As Kane approached, the aide looked up, her gaze meeting Kane's before darting away. It reminded Kane of subservient wives in certain cultures across the world, where the husbands worked and the women stayed home with the babies. There were still societies where equality was only official and behind closed doors was another story. There was something furtive about the aide.

"Thank you, Aadhya," her grandfather dismissed. "That will be all…for now."

The aide skittered away like a nervous cat.

Sidney Cambridge held out his hands and Kane took them. He kissed her on both cheeks. "My lovely granddaughter," he said. "How is New York City treating you?"

"It's certainly different from back home," Kane admitted. "The city seems alive all the time."

"Yes," her grandfather said, his eyes taking on a twist of knowingness. "One could remain occupied twenty-four hours a day in this city."

Had he been informed that she'd spent all night at Dash's place? Did he somehow know the lurid details? Was it any of his damn business?

"I think I could spend a lifetime here and encounter only half of everything there is to experience," Kane said.

"Some things are better off left to the imagination, I think," the Senator said. "There are unseemly situations that would be best avoided by a young princess in Manhattan."

He did know something. Had Gade reported that she'd gone missing all night? Or had Dash dished on where she'd been? Maybe Mark hadn't been able to resist the gossip? Had Abigail been spying on her? Kane suddenly didn't trust anyone outside Sora and Lani with her secrets.

"Your father loved this city," her grandfather said, reminiscing, a fraught expression on his face that seemed put on rather than genuine. "He said he never felt more alive than when he was in New York. This is where he met your mother. Did you know that?"

Kane shook her head. She had heard so few stories of her dad.

"Maybe some of Manhattan's endless energy translated into the impetuous love affair that made him renounce his heritage," the Senator suggested, as if deflecting the real reason. Hadn't her grandfather been adamant Kane's mother, a woman named Desiree Onwuatuegwu, would never become an American Princess or a US Queen? "The fire between them burned brightly. Shone like the sun. Then snuffed out in one terrible puff, like the universe couldn't abide something so intense."

"It sounds beautiful," Kane said softly.

"Beauty is unsustainable," the Senator replied, pulling one rose out of the bouquet. He walked to the fireplace and held the petals near the flames. The silky surface withered and turned black…curled and died. "It shrivels up if it's exposed too long to the heat."

The Senator looked back at the bunch of roses. There were still dozens more, all fresh and pretty. Plenty more to choose from. That was his point—as sharp as the thorns that pricked his fingers.

"Does that make sense, my Princess?" Senator Cambridge asked his granddaughter.

Kane nodded. She understood. She just didn't like the lesson.

* * * *

Kane sat across from Dash Dameron. He wore a bright blue blazer with matching slacks, a red tie that was the color of cherry Kool-Aid, polished shoes shined to a tee and yet none of it as flashy as his megawatt smile. That grin always said something different than the words coming out of his mouth, as expressive and dynamic as most people's entire face.

His eyes were serious, and his words innocent, but his smile was lascivious. Dash looked like he was shining his white teeth right at her, a bright spotlight that illuminated all her secrets. Dash knew intimate things about her. So did Gade, who was standing just outside the range of the camera in the same room as Kane and Dash.

Gade didn't know exactly what had happened between Kane and Dash, and he didn't need to know. Her 'bodyguard' had made it clear that he wanted their relationship to remain professional, and Kane was not about to command an employee to be her boyfriend. She wasn't ready anyway. Her brother had been right about that. She didn't need to rebound so quickly from Dillon to Gade.

Mark had maybe been right about her readiness, but that was all he was right about. Her brother stood on the other side of a plate-glass partition, not really watching the interview. He chatted up one of Senator Cambridge's busty interns, one that was neither Brooke nor Kelli. *Someone new*. Mark hadn't had a date that Kane knew about in *years*, and now he was preying on his third blonde in less than a week. It was a blonde bonanza, a bimbo buffet and none of Kane's business. If she avoided giving advice about her brother's string of gold diggers, then she could tell Mark to keep his nose out of her own affairs.

Dash didn't hint even once during the hour-long interview about Kane's little exhibition—not using the English language, anyway. His smile insinuated secrets, but the words coming out between his teeth didn't match his expression.

For example, Dash asked, "What kind of actions have you engaged in thus far that illustrate how you want to be seen as the American Princess?" Yet his smile suggested that she had been having an orgasm in an infinity pool just eighteen hours earlier. Kane answered with some inspirational aspirations as perspiration prickled the valley between her breasts.

The studio was cool, but she started feeling very hot.

"There will be those who frown upon the idea of an American monarchy," Dash suggested aloud. "How will you overcome resistance to the idea of your historical legitimacy?" His metamorphic grin wondered if rooftop autoerotica would be the exception to Kane's rule or the new standard associated with her emerging stature.

"I did not run for election. I didn't ask for this position. Instead of being political, my role in this is historical. I decided that I won't run from my legacy. The truth about my ancestry was made known to me at the same time that the secret amendment to the Constitution was revealed to the general public. Like everyone else, I'm processing the new news and trying to adapt accordingly." Dash slid his teeth across each other in a way that seemed to send reverberations across the space between them, a tenor that made her skin buzz. She felt a tingle from the top of her spine to the tips of her toes and particular places in between.

"What do you say to those people who suggest this is just a political ploy by your grandfather, Senator Cambridge, to launch a Presidential bid in next year's election?" Dash interrogated. His smile seemingly wondered silently whether he might ever see her naked again.

"I'm assuming a public role that is purely ceremonial in nature," Kane answered. She felt natural and confident in front of the camera. That was a relief, because this kind of exposure would be her normal going forward. "It's a nonpartisan position that adheres to no political party. I want to be a figure that other young women can look up to." Her answer meant that what had happened last night should remain *just* last night. She wanted to be a role model. Maybe eventually she would see herself as an anonymous footnote in a Dash Dameron memoir, an anecdote about spending a night skinny-dipping with a nameless beautiful woman in an infinity pool overlooking Manhattan.

"Are you prepared for newfound fame, Princess?" Dash asked. "You're about to dethrone the likes of Swift and Winfrey and Kardashians as the new

American royalty." He had some ventriloquist talent to make the sounds mean one thing while he murmured something else. He likely wanted to know if she'd had liked being so exposed last night, if she had enjoyed the danger that anyone could have walked in on her while she was naked, while she was in the throes of pleasure, while she climaxed as she stared out at the busy city all around her.

Kane felt flushed. She worried briefly that her face had turned a shade of mocha-pink, that her eyes had a hungry shine, that the cameras could pick up on her repressed urges. The crew had spent a lot of effort making sure her hair and skin and wardrobe all looked perfect, and Kane was concerned that the thrumming energy running through her body might unravel it all. Her skin was on fire and her hair follicles tingled like Dash was sending electricity across the air between them.

"I'm going to be myself," Kane replied. "Take it or leave it."

Mostly, she amended in her mind. Like a secret addition to the Constitution two hundred years ago, the public didn't need to know about pasts best kept unpublished. She thought about walking the edge of being free and being caught, that tightrope that Dash had shown her last night, or the way she had stood nude on her balcony. She was going to be famous—and have eyes on her everywhere. The balance between free and fame was about to tilt. Maybe she could never do those things again because the danger would be so much greater with so many more people able to recognize the American Princess. Or maybe that would just make those moments all the more irresistible to explore . . .

"Last question," Dash announced, interrupting her decadent thoughts. "I'm sure there will be countless viewers wondering about it, so I have to ask. Tell me, Princess Kane, is there a special someone?"

She didn't look at Gade. Her mouth just moved, making words, answering the question. "No," Kane laughed off. "There seems to be a short supply of princes around here." But she took a page from Dash Dameron. Her smile said one thing, but didn't her heart answer otherwise?

Chapter Nine

Someone gently roused her from sleep. At first, groggy and half-dreaming, Kane thought it was Dillon. Then her mind caught up with her moments and she wondered if it was Gade. But wishes were wonderwisps in fairy tales, and she knew it wasn't Gade.

"Princess," came a woman's voice with a beautiful British lilt, and for the briefest moment Kane wondered if she had tried something new the previous night.

But the voice whispered from her bedside, not beside her in bed—just a visitor and not an overnight guest. Abigail Morgan stood at her bedside. She looked as good in the morning as she did any other time of the day. The woman looked like a Barbie doll who appeared perfect all the time. Maybe she was made out of plastic. Wasn't there someone Kane could ask about that? Surely Mary knew which parts were real.

Abigail wore a skirt that showcased legs that might have been able to stretch all the way across the Atlantic.

Her top was professional and flattering, neither highlighting nor deemphasizing her décolletage. The colors were muted, designed to avoid detracting from whatever the Princess would be wearing. Unnecessary heels made her as tall as Gade. Amazonian. Abigail's makeup was natural, light and perfectly applied. How early did the Brit have to get up to primp so properly? Kane turned and squinted out of the balcony doors, stars still twinkling in the sky.

"Just how early is it?" Kane croaked. No wonder she had been dead asleep.

"It's five a.m., m'lady," Abigail said. "Remember… I told you we would need to get up early to prepare for the day."

"Shit," Kane said, entirely unladylike. "Early's like eight, Abby. This is like the evil hour. I didn't know people who weren't old and golden ever got up this early."

"I assure you that Manhattan is already bustling, your highness."

"This 'highness' wants some more lowness—like bed-level low," Kane mumbled. "Can you give me another hour or three?"

"Your sister is already at breakfast," Abigail said. "She's waiting on you."

Kane sat up, her hair a wild tumbleweed sticking out every which way. There was the shape of the seam of the pillow imprinted in her skin, running from her temple all the way down her jawline, like the scar on some pretty bride of Frankenstein. She felt drool drying on her cheek as she vaguely recalled the ghost of the dream she had been having when Abigail had woken her.

Gade had taken Kane on a lakeside picnic. He spread out a perfect black-and-white-checkered blanket in the shadows made by a grove of drooping willows. Gade carefully arranged her lunch, placing plates in alternating squares like pawns in a chewy chess game. He had made little sandwiches and served fresh fruit. Gade wore a tank top that showed off his bulging biceps and she looked amazing in a white summer dress with nothing on underneath. Things escalated, mouths enjoying other activities than eating. Gade slowly undressed her right there on the checkered blanket, lakeside along a pathway where curious pedestrians became an interested audience. He traveled kisses from her mouth, down her long neck, across her bared breasts, down over her stomach, soaking up the summer sunshine – then all the way down…

"Mary's here?" Kane asked, blinking away the recollection of the dream before she squeaked a little right in front of Abigail.

"Yes, her flight arrived last night. I went to pick her up after your interview with Dash Dameron," Abigail said. "I just left her at breakfast to come make sure you were up."

"*Just* left her?" Kane queried.

Abigail was a professional. She had surely attended some scandalous situations in the political circles of Washington, D.C. before being assigned to Kane Cambridge. She knew how to keep a poker face and she was damn good. But Abby was used to lying for others rather than covering for herself. The slightest hint of a blush colored the hollow of Abby's neck above her collarbone.

"She's married," Kane warned, "with kids."

"We just talked," Abigail said, looking away.

Just talked. Like Kane and Dash had *just talked* for the interview that would air tonight. There was always more to it than *just* anything.

Kane felt awake now, irritation at her attendant's unprofessionalism and her sister's infidelity evaporating the last effects of her dream about Gade. Sex wasn't some idyllic fantasy on a lakeside, making love in the open air under an afternoon sun. More often, it was a tawdry affair that threatened to upend futures and affect the lives of more than just the two lovers. Kane got out of bed and marched across the room toward her en suite bathroom.

Kane paused before she closed the door, looking back at Abigail. The woman still couldn't look Kane in the eye. "Just stay away from Mary."

"Is that a request or a command?"

"Does it matter?"

Abigail knew it didn't. "As you wish, your grace," she agreed, and the words looked like they hurt as much as any other ramification of the affair.

Kane stood in the shower for a long time. Abigail was surely waiting while Mary was sitting alone at breakfast. Those two deserved to be inconvenienced. *What the hell is Mary thinking?* She had been married for more than ten years. And Lani, leaving Chase for some sketchy deejay? Mark chasing one bimbo after another, throwing money and using his status as the brother to the princess to enjoy a buffet of blondes? Sora starring in her own scandalous Internet porn? What was going on with all the people she knew? Had her newfound fortune come at the expense of everyone she loved?

Then Kane looked at herself in the fog-free mirror mounted on one wall of the tiled shower. She had made some decisions these last few days that someone else might judge as foolish. Kane had slept with her bodyguard, which was a breach of her professional relationship. Then she had let him go the first moment he'd resisted exploring their future. She had masturbated in a pool out under the stars while a nearly total stranger watched, a television star who probably went through celebrities faster than tanning sessions. Then there was the exhibitionist exhilaration of standing on her balcony in the nude. Maybe Kane ought not judge so quickly.

Besides, Mary and Abigail were adults. Lani and Mark and Sora were all grownups. They were all long past getting scolded for taking wrong turns in life. So Kane decided she just had to let friends and family find their own way.

But that didn't mean she had to like it.

* * * *

It was a girls' day. Gade was retired until he needed to be rolled out for the evening, fresh and focused on Kane's safety for her debut to the public. Her grandfather had pressing political business to attend to in D.C. before he returned to New York for the Ball. Mark wasn't invited on the afternoon outing. He didn't seem offended, shuffling off with yet another new woman on his arm, this one a redhead, at least.

An armed woman named Regina took Gade's place. She was lean and mean and looked like she thought everything in Manhattan smelled foul, a permanent wrinkle in her nose. What would her recent nights have been like if Regina had been her initial royal guard instead of Gade? Would Kane have still resisted Dillon when he had come sniffing around the new princess at their old apartment or would she have made a worse mistake than anything else she had managed this last week? Would she have snuck away with Dash for a diabolical one-night stand? Certainly, she wouldn't have had as much fun. Gade had shown her entire states of pleasure that she hadn't explored ever before.

But no boys for a few hours… Kane didn't want to think about men. The whole lot of them had been troublesome these last few days.

Abigail joined them, and Kane caught several stolen glances between her sister and the assistant. It wasn't just the guys who wreaked havoc. Sex was an epidemic, and it didn't discriminate by gender.

Lani and Sora joined Abigail, Mary, Regina and Kane in the Upper East Side at an expensive stretch of shops along Madison Avenue. It was only seven a.m., and the stores wouldn't normally open for a while, yet Abigail walked right up to the front entrance of an establishment decorated in crystal and trimmed with laser lights. A man in a suit that cost more than Kane's last car opened the door for them.

"Thank you, Mr. Lear," Abigail said.

The sign softly glowing over the entrance door read 'Lear Luxuries', so they were graced by the presence of the proprietor himself. He had even opened early, just for Kane. Just to serve the official Princess of America.

"This is a great honor, your grace," Mr. Lear said. "I feel very fortunate that you have selected my establishment to adorn your impeccable beauty at the very first American Royal Ball."

"The pleasure is mine," Kane whispered, as if afraid of waking all the sparkling jewels so early in the morning, setting them all a'chiming. Hundreds of gemstones surrounded her, hanging off mannequins and displayed in cases and dangling in dioramas. The place sparkled no less than a midnight summer sky, free of clouds. Mostly they were diamonds, winking, blinking and twinkling. Others cast colors of the rainbow across the room, the sun coming in the front window making the whole shop *shimmer*. "I think this is the most enchanting place I have ever seen."

Hours melted away. Opening time came and went and Mr. Lear's employees turned other customers away for a 'reserved event'. A group started to gather outside on the boulevard, the curious crowd wondering who might be important enough to monopolize Lear Luxuries. Mr. Lear assured Kane and her guests that the special glass let anyone inside see out but no one could see in. Kane tried on item after item, selecting rings, a bracelet and a thin silver chain for her ankle and a priceless cameo that set right against the top of her bustline. The final piece was the tiara, just like a princess in some Disney cartoon she had watched over and over when she was little. *Just like that. Like magic.*

"It's perfect," Mary said and gave her a hug. She was crying. Mary's sister was starring in a damn fairy tale.

When it was time to go, Mr. Lear's employees cleared a path through the crowd out front. Kane's entourage surrounded her, although the gawkers wouldn't know Kane from Mary from Abigail at the moment. Kane wasn't coming out until that night. Then the whole world would recognize her face.

Manhattan paparazzi could smell a payday half the island away. The closed shop and the gathered crowd were red flags, and a couple of overweight and impolite photogs tried to snap an illicit picture of each member of Kane's group. Her new bodyguard appeared eager for anyone to try something, anything. Regina was ready with loaded fists. One paparazzo ended up with a black eye and a broken lens, hollering about suing the whole lot of them, even though he didn't know a single one of his subjects from Adam Levine. Regina actually snarled at the other pushy paparazzo like she was a rabid dog, and he scurried away.

"Food?" Abigail asked.

Kane caught her eye, and she wasn't looking at Kane. Kane stepped between Abby and Mary. "Certainly," Kane said. She stayed right beside Mary the rest of the way. Her sister needed a bodyguard as badly as Kane did.

"What's after lunch?" Lani asked, having the time of her life. Her best friend had just tried on no less than ten million dollars' worth of jewelry.

"We have the dress. The shoes. The jewels," Mary said, asking Abby more than anyone else. "What else is left?"

"My favorite thing," Abigail replied with a smile. "The spa."

Over the afternoon, Kane would be exfoliated, manicured, pedicured, loofahed, hair-styled, powdered and painted, prepped and polished—ready for presentation. She had woken up this morning in Gade's old Air Force tee that she'd stolen the first night they had been together, her hair disheveled and mostly confused as to where she was. Just a girl. Just Kane Liberty. She would walk into that ballroom tonight like she was made of magic. Princess Kane Cambridge of America.

* * * *

The Royal Ball was located at the Gotham Historical Society Hall, as close to a castle as one could find on the entire island of Manhattan. It looked like a palace merged from the stories of both Esmeralda and Merida, Notre Dame mashed with fairy-tale spires and an honest-to-God turret. Kane wondered as she entered with her entourage… If she were sequestered away in the high tower, would Gade come to rescue her? But this wasn't a world where rescues were required from locked rooms. Mostly, people needed to be saved from themselves.

Inside, the hall was as opulent as the exterior, a grand entryway ornamented with gold lamé trim and marble accoutrements. Crystal sconces accented along each wall and a massive chandelier glittered in the main atrium. Dark mahogany wood ran in wainscoting along every wall, shaped baseboards and detailed casings defining the edges of the floors and doorways. Coved cornice wrapped the ceiling made of embossed tin.

Gade stood guard between the main atrium and the next room. She hadn't seen him since the day prior and the sight of him made her heart soar. He stared straight ahead and didn't make eye contact. Kane had her hair styled and her skin was accented by the best makeup artists in the city, but still Gade refused to look. He likely had an iron will.

"You'll go through there, m'lady," Abigail said as she led the rest of the group in another direction. "We'll meet you in the dressing rooms when you're done."

Lani, Sora and Mary looked back as they disappeared through another door. Kane paused beside Gade, waiting for a compliment. He didn't say a word. It hurt her heart a little. Gade was one stoic son of a bitch. Kane exhaled loudly then walked forward. She stepped solo through double doors ten feet tall, featuring beefy brass hinges. Statues of historical figures lined a grand hall on one side, like a greeting line of bronze well-wishers. There were nine metal figures leading down the corridor and a real-life human at the end.

Senator Sidney Cambridge waited for her. "These are our ancestors. Since its inception in the eighteenth century, The Gotham Historical Society was funded in great part by the Cambridge family. The Society honored our generosity by commissioning a statue to commemorate the head of the family in each generation of Cambridges. The Society did not realize its role in chronicling the secret royal line of America. Every member of the line of succession is represented, all the way through to my own mother, Margaret."

The Senator stood next to a life-sized sculpture of a thin and severe woman that featured a familiar face, something in the shape of it reminiscent of the photographs of Kane's father. Maybe she saw hints of that profile every morning in her mirror. Senator Cambridge stood with perfect posture and preternatural stillness, as if practicing posing for his own statue.

"And my dad?" Kane asked.

Kane's grandfather stepped aside and one space down from Kane's great grandmother was a statue of Reese Cambridge. He had renounced his last name and changed it to Liberty, but he couldn't escape his lineage. The Gotham Historical Society used his *real* name. And he was honored for his true heritage.

"Are you ready to take your place among your family?" the Senator asked.

Kane thought about the past week. She wasn't the same woman who could work a nine-to-five job and go home to Dillon Durfee at the end of the day. She couldn't stay anonymous anymore, not just another generic shopper at the local Walmart or a faceless pedestrian padding along among the crowd at the local riverwalk. There was more to life than Sunday mornings in her jammies or the naughty thrill of walking out from her apartment in a thin T-shirt and no bra to get her mail. She was a *Princess*.

"I'm ready," Kane said.

"Are you ready to represent the royal line as the next Cambridge heir?" her grandfather asked, as if it were a heavy burden to bear. "There may be true personal sacrifices in the future, Kane."

Kane wondered if he was talking about Gade. What did Sidney Cambridge know about her illicit interactions with her royal guard? She worried he had learned about her indecorous indiscretions. The last time they had talked, Kane had suspected Sidney knew more than he ought to about her nocturnal naughtiness. Certainly, the Senator talked around something very specific.

"What kind of sacrifices?"

"There will be royal representatives from monarchies around the world in attendance tonight," Senator Cambridge informed Kane. "Some will be in town to court the new American Princess. I just ask you to keep an open mind to any potential paramours. A union between our royal house and an international suitor of royal lineage would further cement our legitimacy on the world stage."

"You want me to marry a *prince*?" Kane gasped.

"I want you to marry whomever you want to marry," the Senator said. "And if you want to elevate the stature of the royal American family, you could do worse than if you *choose* to marry into another royal line. There will be several men in attendance looking to woo the newest addition to the world's monarchy. The young Prince from Saudi Arabia. King Mohato from Lesotho. Prince Richard of England. The son of the Sultan of Brunei."

"I'm some kind of a prize?"

"Of course. You are the first Princess of America, Kane," her grandfather said.

"I didn't know this night had turned into some kind of audition." Kane sighed, the responsibilities of royalty already weighing heavily.

"It was always an audition, my dear. You're being revealed to the world. It's your introduction to your subjects. Tonight, we unveil our history and shine a spotlight on the future of the nation."

It was time to step into the light. No more Kane Liberty. Snack cakes from the supermarket and late-night Mickey Dee shakes had to stop. Midnight skinny dips were a thing of the past. No more feelings for her royal guard. She had to slip her foot into the glass slipper. She needed to get onboard the royal carriage. It was her moment to truly become Princess Kane.

"So I will ask you one last time, Kane," her grandfather said. "Are you ready for this?"

"Yes," Kane answered without a second thought, "I am."

* * * *

When Kane was little, she and Mary would play dress-up. They would put on Aunt Polly's dresses that she had worn in high school and had not fit the woman in many years, running around the house with the hems dragging behind them like long bridal trains. Aunt Polly had made them tiaras of tinfoil wrapped around cardboard. They'd constructed bracelets of colored rubber bands and had saved their candy necklaces for these royal occasions.

Now Kane stared at herself in the mirror. The dress fit perfectly, tailored to a tee. It was cut low and amplified her modest bosom. Her mocha cleavage might be bolder than British royalty's, but it was conservative for American fashion. The color was a soft blue that recalled an autumn sky, diamonds sewn into the woven lace like stars caught in a white web. Crystals like sparkling frost were adhered directly to her bared shoulders and up her slender neck. The jewelry she had acquired from Lear Luxuries accented her earlobes and wrists. A petite necklace with a silver star dangled against her breasts. The tiara wasn't made from tin or foil, but rather accented with exotic gemstones imported from a country she had never heard of.

"Princess," came a voice from behind her.

Kane turned and faced Gade. He held a corsage with a pink rose on the band, looking like a prom date waiting for the homecoming queen. "I think you need one more thing." Kane let him put it on her wrist and stood back. The thought of him thinking of her and yet keeping her at bay made her dizzy. Sad. She didn't want to play this game.

"Breathtaking," Gade said, standing back and looking at her from her head to toe.

"You don't get to comment on my appearance anymore."

"I might be your loyal subject and your faithful royal guard, but I'm not blind, Princess."

"I don't care if your eyes work or not," Kane snapped. "It's your tongue that seems to be malfunctioning."

"I'll keep further comments to myself, m'lady," Gade huffed.

"Is it time?" she asked, back to business.

"Five minutes," Gade said.

"Let me use the restroom one more time before I greet the public," she said, dismissing Gade. He nodded and let her be.

She used the facilities—with great difficulty in the confined space with the copious gown. Kane washed her hands and dried them, then stood looking at herself in the mirror. She had to admit that Gade was right. They had made her up to perfection.

"You're beautiful, Kane."

See, even Dillion agreed.

"Dillon!" Kane yelped, spinning around to where he stood in the corner next to the last stall in the row. "How in the hell did you get in here?"

Dilly hooked a thumb over his shoulder at a supply closet behind him. The door stood ajar and revealed a small cubby stuffed with toilet paper and chemical cleaners. Gade had swept the hotel more than once and he certainly would have apprehended someone sneaking into the ladies' restroom. Dilly must have been folded into the confined space for *hours*.

"You were hiding in the closet?" Dillon nodded. "All this time?" He nodded again.

"I needed to see you, Kane. I need to talk to you. That fucking gorilla that you call a bodyguard wouldn't let me within a mile of you. What an asshole."

A week ago she would have swooned if Dillon had gone to such lengths for a little more time with her. But since then, the world had turned. She had found out Dilly had cheated on her and in fact had already moved in with another woman. It had turned out she was a princess. She had met Gade, and Dash, and soon would be paraded in front of eligible princes from around the globe. Kane was about to become the biggest celebrity in the whole world. *A lot can happen in just a week.*

"*You're* the asshole, Dillon," Kane said. "If I tell Gade you're in here, he'll tear your damn arms off."

"You won't tell him, Candy Kane," Dillon said in that smooth tone that used to make her melt. Dilly-bar and Candy Kane. Three years. All in the past.

"Don't be so sure."

Dillon moved between Kane and the exit. "Just wait a minute, baby. Hear what I have to say."

"Listen… I won't tell him if you get out of my way. I'm late for the Ball."

Dillon stayed in place. He crossed his arms across his skinny chest. He smelled vaguely of floor cleaner and scented toilet paper, body odor and cheap booze.

"If I scream, Gade might come in here shooting first and asking questions to your stupid corpse," Kane warned.

"Sheesh, Kane, just let me talk to you for a goddamn second," Dillon said.

"Words can't walk back what you did to me, Dillon."

"I know, Kane. I know. I treated you like shit. Maybe I don't deserve a second chance. But I love you, baby.

You know I do. I showed it every day for almost three years. It was good. It was so good for so long."

"It's too late, Dillon," Kane said. "Look at me. My world is so different. We can't go back to where we were."

"I'm not here to ask you to go back to the past. I just want to be a part of your future," Dillon begged. "Maybe just give me as much of a chance as any other guy."

Did he really want her back? And was it Kane Liberty he wanted? The girl with an office job and a closet full of sweatshirts? Or was it Princess Kane he wanted, with her jewels and her radiant royalty? Did he love her—or did he love the thought of being Prince Dilly? Did he just dream of becoming the rich and famous Prince of America?

"These aren't just any other guys, Dilly," Kane said softly, as kindly as she could manage. He had broken her heart and acted like a dog, but Kane was not the cruel type. She didn't want revenge on her ex. She wanted to let him down easy. "I'm being courted by kings and sultans, celebrities and movie stars, rich men and sports figures. You're a manager at Wallyworld. Your mom still does your laundry. I'm not even sure how that piece of shit car of yours made it all the way to New York. You don't have an equal chance. You don't have any chance at all."

And with that, Kane sidestepped Dillon—and he let her. He clearly knew that she would scream and Gade might come in, bullets flying, so he had to let her go. And as the pneumatic door closed behind her, she was sure she heard Dillon Durfee softly sniffling.

Thoughts of Dillon disappeared as soon as Kane walked through the ballroom doors. An orchestra was waiting to play on a large stage, a full ensemble fit for a Broadway show. Abigail had told Kane that she booked the same musicians from the Tony-award winning show called the *Queen of Queer*. *Royal-ish,* Kane supposed.

The ornamentation made her high school prom look like it had been decorated by an indiscriminate twister. Silver swirls descended from the ceiling, slowly turning and making the whole room spin. An ice sculpture in the center of the large auditorium was carved into a life-sized replica of Kane, so realistic that she wondered if they had taken her mold while she had slept. Lights floated inside translucent helium spheres that hovered around the ballroom a few feet above everyone's heads. Each table was decorated with beautiful hand-carved renditions of unicorns, strong stallions in myriad positions, each with a striking horn in the center of the forehead.

Abigail appeared instantly from nowhere, like a superpower. "Unicorns?"

"The Cambridge family crest," Abigail explained.

"Really? Unicorns don't even exist."

"Are you sure? There's also supposed to be no such thing as an American Princess."

Kane smirked. "Indeed."

The room was packed with people. Kane recognized politicians she had seen on cable news, celebrities who had come to fame on Insta, YouTube and reality TV, movie stars in the prime of their careers, stuffy billionaire men in suits that cost more than the average family's house who were escorting wives only half their age. All eyes watched the giant screen suspended from the south wall, playing the end of Kane's interview with Dash Dameron on live TV. The producers of *DamTime* had edited it so that her last words were, *"I'm going to be myself. Take it or leave it."*

General applause filled the room as the credits rolled. Dash himself bounded up on stage and took a bow. Then he turned his megawatt smile on Kane and all eyes followed. Everyone in the room looked where Dash was looking. He waved his hand in a theatrical flourish. "May I present Kane Cambridge, Princess of America."

Kane stood with Abigail at her side as everyone clapped all over again. Her grandfather swooped in and took her arm, leading her forward. She passed Mary, Lani and Sora all standing in a group. Mark was still with the same redhead, holding her hand more eagerly than she appeared to want him to. Even Aunt Polly and Uncle John were in attendance. They looked positively regal standing at the edge of the stage.

Gade remained not more than ten feet from her any time she looked, although she never saw him moving the entire night. It was like he just disappeared and reappeared at will, popping from place to place like a stealthy wraith. He had superpowers of his own, like he and Abigail were the wonder twins. Kane never escaped his sight except when she used the bathroom again, though not the same one where she had left Dillon. Still, she checked the supply closet before she used the stall, just in case.

Her grandfather started taking her around to greet dignitaries and famous faces, and introductions didn't stop for more than an hour. Kane must have met three hundred people and she could name maybe three. One of them was a United States Senator from her home state. Another was the actor from the rom-com she'd watched with Sora just several days ago, right after

Dillon had dumped her. The third was Hashim, the son of the Sultan of Brunei, who was one of her potential suitors. He was the only maybe-someday-husband she managed to remember because he was yummyyummyyummy.

Her grandfather had really talked up the Prince of England. He had an uber-white name like Bailey or Richard or Egbert or something and he was pallid and pretentious. Kane stood there for five minutes while the bland British bastard blundered through a boring history of his time in Buckingham Palace. Kane equated the castle with the man—expensively ornamented, overly regarded and mostly empty.

"You must come to England to visit the origins of your ancestry, your grace," the British Prince invited.

"And that's our *common* ancestry, correct?" Kane quizzed. "We trace from the same original line? Your ancestors trace to my ancestors. Sounds very... *an*cestuous."

"That was two hundred and fifty years ago," the prince puffed, like she didn't know either rudimentary math or history or even genetics. *Incest puns? What am I thinking?* Kane just felt nervous, and Dilly had thrown her for a loop.

"Well, nice to meet you, cousin," Kane quickly concluded while the prince was on his heels. "Maybe I will see you at the family reunion."

She skedaddled, ignoring her grandfather's frown, focusing on forward motion. Why couldn't all her potential suitors be as sexy as Hashim, the Sultan's son? He was delicious. His accent had made her swoon. He smelled like sand and sun. Kane could have some fun with that for a while. *Maybe even longer than a while?*

After unending introductions, Kane had made her way through almost the entire room. Her grandfather finally let her go, making her promise to remain available for any new dignitaries or anyone they might have missed. Kane didn't want to meet one single more person who looked her up and down as if weighing her worth in arranged matrimony. Some of them were even older than her grandfather. *Eww.*

She finally escaped to her family. Aunt Polly smothered her with a hug, and Uncle John clapped her on the back like she was his youngest boy. Mary gushed on and on about the ballroom, although her eyes slipped away to Abigail over and over. Her husband stood right beside Mary, oblivious. Mark paraded his redheaded trophy girl around like a prize pony.

"I need a drink," Mary announced as Abigail happened to be at the open bar.

"I'll join you," her husband offered. *Maybe Larry noticed something amiss after all?*

"Wait for me," Uncle John called, following.

"Thanks for coming," Kane said to Aunt Polly when they were alone. "It means the world to me that you and Uncle John are here."

"We wouldn't miss it, Kane," Polly said with a sad smile, "even if it still isn't easy being in the same room."

Kane blinked. "With me? Did I do something to make you mad?"

"What?" Aunt Polly asked. "Oh, no, dear. I'm not talking about you. I meant John and me. We're still getting used to being separated."

"Sepa-*wha*?" Kane blurted.

"We haven't been together since we moved to Florida," Aunt Polly said. "We didn't know how to tell you kids."

"For three years?" Kane cried. The patrons nearest her, including the perplexed British Prince, looked at Kane and Polly. "I guess keeping secrets is what you do best, Aunt Polly—like hiding the fact that I'm a goddamn princess."

Kane stalked away. She wanted to just be alone, but she was surrounded by her public. She was careening out of control, and there was no safe haven in which to retreat. Stamping like a spurned child, she was caught by Dash, his smile shining. He took her hand in his. Kane glanced at Gade, who glared.

"Dance with me?" he asked.

Kane nodded.

Kane glided across the herringbone tiled floor in Dash's arms, and for the first time since her debutante debut, she felt like the belle of the ball. All the bitter thoughts and latent anger that had boiled up in Aunt Polly's face instantly dispersed. Dash smashed her frown to smithereens and made her heart turn from a frown upside-down. Kane was soaring.

Dash wore tailored Armani, likely put together by professional preeners. His smile shined brighter than any disco ball, so that he twinkled like a silver star. A silver *fox*. He moved like he had once won *Dancing with the Stars*. In actuality, Dash had finished runner-up to William Shatner.

Dash Dameron was not like Dillon Durfee. He neither begged for one more dance nor gave mopey declarations of his preening adoration. Dash lived in the moment without consideration of a sordid past or some possible someday. Dash wasn't like Gade

Williams, either. Mr. Dameron moved with a free fluidity that wasn't conscious of propriety or duty. Dash did what he wanted, when he wanted.

He'd wanted to dance—so they danced.

All eyes were on them…interviewer and interviewee. Perceptive audience members of the televised sit-down might suspect something sexual simmered between them, but the majority of the crowd just watched two people at the pinnacle of pop culture sharing a shining moment in the public eye…a ceremonial shuffle.

"How are you handling the spotlight?" he asked in her ear.

"It's bright," Kane confessed.

"Relax," Dash suggested. "You're really charming this crowd."

Kane looked around at everyone. She saw Sora and Lani watching from the sidelines. Mary stood beside Larry, her husband between Kane's sister and Abigail Morgan. Mark wandered through the crowd, probably looking for his redhead. Aunt Polly sat at a table at one end of the auditorium while Uncle John remained at the other.

"I feel like I'm walking a tightrope and one wrong step will make me totter and fall," Kane whispered. "The space between me and everyone below just keeps getting greater. It seems like the distance to the ground is a lot farther than the space between me and the stars."

"Just don't look down, Kane," Dash said. "Look at me."

She did. Dash was dazzling—and not just his superstar smile. His eyes were bright and bold, confident and unclouded by any doubt. Anxiety melted away under the green gaze of his easy eyes. She felt the pressure of her princessdom evaporate. He saw through the glitter and gold, beyond diamonds and tiaras. He had seen her as she really was, without a fairy-tale dress, any Egyptian silk underwear and all this princess properness—when she had just been Kane.

"Better?" he asked.

"Much," she said.

"You're the only one in this room, Kane—the only one who matters. All the rest of us are here for you. This is a brand-new thing. The bright and shiny bauble that has everyone interested. But you're not an object. Don't let anyone treat you like a pretty prize—not the public, not your people, not your bodyguard, not even your grandfather. They might call you the first Princess of America, but you're still just Kane Cambridge. Remember that."

Kane nodded.

"You got it?" Dash asked.

"I got it," Kane said.

"Prove it," he whispered softly, his lips against her ear, his breath sending tingles all the way downtown. "Show me that you're still the woman I saw blossom the other night—bold, brash, on the edge. Under all this fancy fringe, convince me that you're still that same cool and kinky Kane."

"I will," she promised, looking him in the eye.

"What do you have in mind?" Dash asked with danger a'twinkle in his dazzling grin.

"I'll bring you a token of my promise—a small souvenir made of silk in a size six."

The music ended and they went their separate ways. Kane glided off the dance floor. Lani and Sora both waited, the girls looking like lovely Barbies stepped right out of a Malibu Mansion.

Lani wore severe scarlet that was tight and tiny, her boobs overspilling her neckline. Beside her, someone who ripped his wardrobe off from 1990's Eminem and somehow thought that a T-shirt that read 'Fuck the Power' was appropriate to a Royal Ball. Scatch's shoes had more holes than his pierced face.

Sora came to the Ball covered all the way to her chin, a full-length gown that managed to conceal everything everyone might have already seen online. She attended with Sevin, and Kane could hardly hold her tongue from scolding Sora's husband for posting her masturbation video on some skanky website. Sora stood with her arms folded, like everyone in the room was probably picturing her topless. Not everyone in the room watched Internet porn, of course, and many wouldn't have recognized the upstanding Asian in front of them for the online vixen diddling herself to a rather loud and jerky orgasm.

"You're like a rock star, Kane," Lani gushed. "Goddamn Madonna."

"Totally bangin', bee," Scatch added.

Who the hell invited Scatch to the Ball, anyway?

"I don't know about bees or banging," Kane said, "but I do know I have to pee."

She took Sora and Lani each by the hand and dragged them across the ballroom behind her. Gade was ever on her perimeter, somehow blending with the crowd her entire way from one end of the room to the other. He surveyed the ladies' room before Kane entered—Kane almost told him to check the supply closet for ex-boyfriends—then gave her the all-clear. He was all business and nothing funny about it. Kane tried not to care.

Kane wedged her wide dress into a stall. Once inside, she had little room to maneuver, but she managed to complete the mission she had pledged to Dash. Kane flushed to keep up appearances. She stuffed her silk underwear into the chiffon sash around her cinched waist. Sora and Lani stood by the sink when she emerged, smirking like they were back in high school and Kane had just spent the lunch hour making out with Bryan Burnside behind the bleachers.

"This is like some fairy tale, Kane," Sora said, uncharacteristically close to gushing.

"It's like something straight out of a movie," Lani sang. "I thought the rock star life was glamorous, but this is like…like…"

"Enchanted," Sora sighed.

"Yeah," Lani said. "*Magic.*"

"It's just my life, guys," Kane said. "This will be what it's like some days."

Lani looked at herself in the mirror. The spell faded, and her eyes reverted to reality, that look she'd had when she'd told Kane she was pregnant with her first child, that look that said things would never be the same ever again.

"Is there a place for us in all this, Kane?" Lani asked.

Sora looked away and down, thinking of sordid things. Shades of shame.

"You're American royalty," Sora said. "And we're just royal screwups."

"I told Dash out there that I felt like I was walking a tightrope, and everyone was watching and waiting for me to fall. I felt like it would be the end of everything if I managed to lose my balance," Kane said. "But it wouldn't be, guys. I still have you. And you will always have me. We aren't what they want us to be. We are what *we* want to be."

Lani smiled. Sora nodded. They exited. Kane smirked. Dash got his token. He stuffed the Egyptian silk size six panties into his Armani pocket—and Kane spent the rest of the evening bare-bottomed under the bell of her beautiful dress.

Chapter Ten

Kane woke up after noon, alone, undressed.

The Ball had lasted all night. Elderly attendees who ought to have been in bed before the end of Kane's *DamTime* interview had instead watched the sunrise from the balcony of the Belmont Hotel. Celebrities whose time was worth so much money had chosen to spend it with the new American Princess. A small group consisting of professional baseball players had finally left after dawn, complaining about a doubleheader that started just a few hours later. Politicians who maybe should have been focused on legislation had instead barely focused two feet in front of them, stumbling toward limos that had waited for them all night.

Dash had left around three in the morning, grinning like a sly wolf who'd stolen something from the henhouse. Kane had caught sight of him as he exited, pausing to put his hand against his heart, where a hint of red silk undergarment peeked out of the breast of his

Armani suit like a pocket square. He had winked, then he was gone.

Sora had stormed out of the Ball around four following a fight with Sevin, after a heated argument in the corner of the vast ballroom. She had spent the evening conscious of every stare and suspicious of any man watching a video on his phone, sure they were aware of her indiscretion. Finally, after a few gin-and-tonics, she had let Sevin have it in the harsh whisper that was always Sora's version of shouting. Lani had chased after her, leaving Scatch standing alone at the chocolate fountain.

Mark had left around four-thirty, about an hour after his redhead had disappeared for the last time. She had been avoiding him all evening, more interested in high rollers and powerful politicians than roly-poly Mark Emerson. He had given Kane a hug before he went.

"Maybe she went back to our room," he'd said, checking his phone for a message from his current consort.

"I think she just went, Mark," Kane had suggested gently.

Mark had shrugged. *"There are other fish in the sea."*

Mary told Kane after their brother had left that the redhead had used Mark to go shopping for a long list of expensive clothes the day before the Ball. She was certainly gone for good.

Mary had stayed as long as Abigail had. Larry had started yawning in the corner by two a.m. and Kane wondered if Mary had secretly prayed that he'd fall asleep sitting up so she could sneak away for some Abby satisfaction. Instead, Larry had fought off exhaustion and kept his eyes open enough to trace his wife's every movement—and perhaps saved his endangered marriage in the process. Mary and Larry had finally left together for their hotel after five in the morning, holding hands like newlyweds, although Kane suspected it was less romance and more to keep Mary from running off to play in sapphic traffic.

Aunt Polly and Uncle John had stayed the longest out of her friends and family, finally waving a white flag just before sunrise. In the end, Kane wondered if it had been a contest between them as to who demonstrated greater loyalty to their adopted daughter. Polly had exited through one door and John had gone the opposite direction. Sometimes, when love soured, the stink was too much for the other person to endure.

Maybe more than sometimes… Gade had remained, standing sentry among the aristocracy of NYC. He had watched Kane like a hawk. Had he noticed when she passed her underwear off to Dash? Had he realized she wasn't wearing any underpants under the long princess dress? Had any memories of their nights together flashed across his mind while he was doing his job? Or had he excised those experiences with military precision, their moments together reduced to a mission filed and forgotten?

Gade had paid particular attention to Kane's interactions with the Prince of England and whenever she spoke with Hashim, the Sultan's son. These two had emerged after the long night as the two suitors most eligible to court the American Princess. The others had eventually lost interest in the daunting task of wooing American royalty—or, as in the case of the King of Bhutan and the Prince of Andorr, the men became more interested in each other than any female in the room. Others were simply too old for consideration.

The Ngwenyama of Swaziland attended with his mother. He was at least eighty and his mother was more than a hundred years old. Kane disqualified some candidates for reasons of legality—the Prince of Moravia already had three wives. Only two believed they had the stamina to survive the American press and the brutal court of public opinion under the spotlight of social media.

Prince Richard of Britain had impeccable manners and an astute knowledge of all things royal. By sunrise, he had graduated from forgettable to inoffensive, perfect politeness giving him the air of some old-fashioned suitor. He was like a Prince Charming, stepped right out of a Disney cartoon, if Charming looked less like a Hollywood Chris and more like a crispy baguette. Rounder than skinny Dilly, ripped Gade or personal-trainer-sculpted Dash, he became a puffy alternative to her recent paramours. The Prince and Kane's brother both looked like they might eat at the same buffet table.

The Sultan's son was a sultry alternative. Hashim wore confidence as well as Kane wore a tiara, shining and precious, a swagger that was infectious. He was presumptuous without being pretentious. He had brought her a flute of champagne and dominated the conversation for a half hour near the end of the Ball, but no one in attendance had taken offense. Hashim was interesting and invigorating, his sexy accent enough to engage her attention for long periods of listening.

By dawn, both the Prince of England and Hashim had expressed interest and arranged further interaction with Princess Kane. Their people had spoken with Abigail Morgan and she had scheduled them time with Kane over the course of her weekend—with Kane's approval, of course. And while it had never been confirmed, Kane suspected that Abby had consulted the Senator for his approval of her choices. Kane didn't like the unsaid issuance of his permission.

By the time she had staggered to her room, alone, Kane was absolutely exhausted. Gade had hovered just close enough to intercept any threat and yet had remained far enough away to eliminate the possibility that the threat was himself. She hadn't even bid him good night as she closed the door behind her. She had been ready for sleep, but she was really tired of Gade's games. She had stripped out of her expensive dress and left it laying on the floor in the vestibule of the suite. Her corset had been removed next, tossed beside her bed. She had been thankful she hadn't had to make the effort to shed one last piece of undergarment before she collapsed into bed. Kane had fallen asleep before she'd pulled the cover over herself.

And she was lying in the exact same position when she woke up six hours later.

* * * *

Kane took breakfast—*lunch?*—on her balcony overlooking Manhattan. The sounds of the city were a comfort, the ambient noise of bustling life enough to offset the chattering thoughts that careened and collided in her head. She didn't want to think about royal suitors. She didn't want to daydream about Dash Dameron. Gade stood with his arms crossed and his eyes concealed by sunglasses not ten feet from her, his shadow stretching and touching her toes. The honks and hollers and sirens slinking up to her penthouse suite on the top floor distracted her from interaction.

For a while.

"You know, you can sit and eat with me if you're going to be out here anyway," Kane said.

"I had a protein bar an hour ago," Gade informed, his mouth barely moving and the rest of him as still as stone.

"Can we at least talk to each other like we aren't complete strangers? Conversations with my Starbucks' barista are more personal than this."

"We have a professional relationship, not a personal one."

"Don't say that like it's somehow my fault, Gade. I'm not the one who decided that we have to be one or the other."

"It wasn't a decision, Princess. It's just the only way it can be. Anything else is impossible."

"I'm a claims processor from suburbia who woke up a few days ago and found out I'm a princess. I've gone from a dumpy apartment with a leaky roof and stained carpet to a penthouse suite in Manhattan with a view that's to *die* for. A week ago, I had to dig in my sofa for enough coins to tip the pizza delivery guy and now I'm having champagne for breakfast. I guess I don't believe in impossible anymore, Gade."

She finished her brunch without another word. Kane paused a long moment after she was done, looking out at the city of millions—beyond, a nation of citizens who were now her subjects. Could she ever find true love with any one of them? Or was she limited to just a very short list of suitors who had the proper pedigree? Gade certainly thought so.

She left him on the balcony and joined the crowd inside her suite. Her grandfather watched cable news on a large screen that had descended directly from the ceiling. A woman who appeared as if she might have moonlighted as the star of Broadway's *Moana* brought the Senator some tea. Abigail was in attendance with a small entourage of young women who all looked like likely candidates to be Mark's next conquest. She was communicating relentlessly, her fingers racing across the screen of her phone.

It looked like the cable news anchors had been on air all night, as if the event had been a national tragedy or they were waiting for the Presidential elections results. Reporters covered every angle of the Royal Ball—who wore what, who arrived with whom, interviews with everyone from Clooney to Madonna, live reports from after-parties across the city that were still going on. There was a shot of the street right below the balcony where Kane had just enjoyed her brunch, the street clogged with paparazzi and news vans staked out at her hotel. One photograph flashed by showing her eating breakfast, Gade standing guard, the image taken from some elevated perspective within just the last fifteen minutes. Cameras were *everywhere*.

"You're famous," Senator Cambridge announced.

She starred in video clips that played over and over again. A montage featured a dozen shots of her throughout the night at the Ball, shown in rotation as some pundit drawled in the background, on and on about the importance of an American monarchy. Kane couldn't help but notice that all but three were clips that had been recorded *after* she'd given Dash her underwear. The world stared at the new princess airing out her undercarriage.

They showed videos of her arriving, dancing with Hashim and a few other dignitaries, schmoozing with celebrities and finally leaving at the end of the Ball, still beautiful after an entire night of activity. It helped to stave off the effects of exhaustion when one had a team of doting attendants. The producers had interspersed footage from the Ball with clips from her interview with Dash Dameron, her own voice lending itself to narrate the replay of her night.

Then the anchor introduced a pair of guests—a tenured professor from Harvard and a retired scholar of global monarchies who'd written a book called *A Consideration of Kingdoms*—two old men who were esteemed experts in their field. They spent the next five minutes dishing on who might be best suited to be paired with the American Princess, like busybody hens discussing the latest episode of *The Bachelor*. Both Hashim and the Prince of England were mentioned in the shortlist of approved possible pairings.

"Are they really trying to pick my future husband?" Kane asked.

"There will be endless speculation on your romantic interludes, my dear," the Senator said. "You will be the subject of every tabloid-trash story for the foreseeable future."

"If you think this seems too invasive of your personal life, your highness, then I'd advise you to stay away from the Internet," Abigail suggested.

Kane's life had been turned upside-down. There would be no more sneaking down to the 7-Eleven in her pajamas for a late-night donut run. Her days of shopping at the supermarket without makeup or a bra were over. Maybe her days of even going to supermarkets at all were over. She could never again stand outside on her balcony in the buff like she had the other night.

"You have several appointments today, Kane," her grandfather said. "Your first meeting is with Prince Richard…in one hour."

"Are *you* going to pick my future husband?" Kane asked.

There was no way she would ever enter into an arranged marriage. She would renounce the crown before that happened, just as her dad had.

"Of course not," Senator Cambridge said. "This is the twenty-first century. Princesses have tattoos and ex-husbands nowadays. We don't do arranged relationships."

"But you want me to meet with Prince Richard? And the Sultan's son?"

"The choice is yours, Kane, whether you're interested in either or neither," her grandfather said.

"But if I don't like one or the other, then you'll just present me with a list of acceptable alternatives?" Kane asked. "It's not like I can just pick a person off the street to spend time with, can I?"

Kane swore she saw her grandfather's gaze flicker toward Gade as the bodyguard finally stepped inside from the balcony. But the Senator looked directly into Kane's eyes when he answered.

"No," he replied. "Not if you want to be a princess."

Did she? Did she want to limit the list of future suitors just to keep her crown? Was she willing to sacrifice possible true love to remain Princess of America? Maybe she would fall for Prince Richard. *Probably not*. Or perhaps Hashim happened to be the man of her dreams. *Maybe*. Wait and see, she decided. It wouldn't be a sacrifice if she found a wonderful man who also happened to be on her grandfather's list.

* * * *

The Prince of England was one wound-up royal.

Prince Richard fidgeted in his seat across from Kane, as if the court jester had sprinkled itching powder down his pants. His posture was as perfect as those guards with the fuzzy hats Kane saw on pictures from London, as if someone had stuffed a royal scepter up Richard's ass. His face featured funny expressions, as if he were perpetually flatulent and tried mightily to hold back a fart.

Richard wasn't unattractive. A professional had styled his ginger hair perfectly, and the copper coif appeared to be held in place with some sort of sturdy hair product. The reddish color of his hair made his freckles seem afire, like embers of glowing ash that cascaded onto his plump cheeks and sat there, softly illuminated. His green eyes made her think of Ireland. Kane didn't even know if Ireland was included in Prince Richard's kingdom.

They made small talk while sipping tea. The prince had asked if she was hungry, but Kane was frankly afraid to eat, sure cameras somewhere waited to catch her with food on her face or something stuck in her teeth. So, they had tea and tried to carry on a conversation for longer than five words. It seemed to become some sort of unsaid challenge after a dozen exchanges as to whether they could even keep the momentum of words going forward on any subject at all.

"You're nervous, aren't you?" Kane finally asked after they failed to sustain yet another discussion, this time on football, after Kane had realized she was talking about the NFL and Richard was speaking of soccer.

"I'm not very good as this," Richard confessed.

"I think you're just trying too hard. This isn't an interview for a job, Richie," Kane said. "Can I call you Richie?"

"No one calls me Richie," he said, more like it was a revelation than a response. Kane took that as a 'yes'.

"Why are you so nervous?" Kane asked. "You must talk to princesses all the time."

"My parents are getting very frustrated," Richie said. "I'm the heir to the throne and I've failed miserably at finding an acceptable wife. I've been potentially betrothed to six other royal representatives over the last five years. Every one of them has declined a second date. The last woman was the Duchess of Daughton, a widow who's eighty years old. She picked a dithering Duke from Romania over me."

Kane smiled. The prince had finally strung together more than five words. "Let's say that we'll have a second date, Richie. Right now. Guaranteed. Will that help alleviate some awkwardness?"

"Really?" the prince gushed, looking like he had been drowning for a long time and Kane had just offered him a lifeline.

"It wouldn't be very princess-like of me to tell a lie," Kane said.

The transformation was amazing. Richie loosened up, an entirely different guy once the pressure to impress was relieved. He told her a string of absolutely terrible jokes, but his delivery and accent made them quite funny. He gave a self-depreciating account of his family history and a revealing inside look at the royal family—scandalous affairs and petty politics, cold parents and a lonely childhood. It seemed that Kane's royal story wasn't the only one in the world that didn't read like a regular fairy tale.

In the end, by promising Richie a second date, Kane ensured that she actually wanted to see him again socially. When her grandfather had been pushing her to meet with these suitors, Kane had been reluctant. Resistant. Now she had already agreed to another date and was eager to spend more time with Richie.

"Hmm," she marveled as they said their *adieus*.

"What is it?" Richard asked.

"I actually had a fun time."

"Wonderful," Richard said with a winning smile. He kissed her hand just like one would see in the movies and he got into his chariot—a brand-new cherry-red Lamborghini.

Richie had entertained her at a posh Manhattan restaurant called Manchester Meats, and Hashim was scheduled to be her date for dessert. He met Kane at a place called The Sands, which featured an indoor desert with stretching dunes rolling in front of a massive television screen. The effect made the scene seem to stretch into infinity. It felt like Kane was standing at the edge of the Sahara.

"Dessert in the desert?" Kane smirked.

"Genius," he said, his voice like a melody.

Hashim had a blanket spread out over a flat spot in the sand. He sat down beside a basket that looked like the kind Yogi Bear would steal in Jellystone Park. He pulled out a fruit that appeared to be an apricot and pulled it open, handing Kane half.

"A date," Kane said, taking a bite of it, smiling. "While we're on a date."

"Is that what this is?" Hashim teased.

"You like your ironies, don't you?" Kane asked.

"Puns," Hashim answered, shrugging, like it explained his whole life.

Hashim was the opposite of Prince Richie. Charismatic and cool, he was easy to be around from the very first moment. His relaxed attitude was infectious.

"So what do princes and princesses talk about?" Kane asked.

"Well, you haven't been a princess long enough talk about palace intrigue or royal politics," Hashim teased. "So tell me about yourself. The Kane before she was pampered and powdered."

Kane found herself talking and talking, telling him all about what her life had been like before she'd found out about being royalty—before Gade and Dash and everything else. Hashim listened then he told her his own story. The conversation flowed so easily that she didn't even notice the fake sun set. Suddenly, stars scattered across the television-screen sky. The sand directly under them had been just an image on more screens underneath the floor. The dunes shifted away during dessert, and now the screen underneath her had turned from sand to stars. The stars above became the stars all around.

The blanket they sat on was the only thing besides the night that surrounded them, above and beneath and all around. It looked like a rug floating in the clear night sky.

Hashim was taking her on a magic carpet ride.

Somewhere unseen, a fan blew her hair in a manufactured breeze and made it feel like they were really sailing through the stars. The effect was so impressive that Kane felt like she was actually flying.

She wrapped her arms around Hashim and he held her as if she were actually in danger of falling off. She laughed so hard that tears flew from her eyes. It felt like a scene from *Aladdin*. Maybe her brand-new world was a real-life fairy tale.

Gade had been relegated to redundancy on her recent activities, the Prince of England and the Sultan's son both utilizing their own security personnel. If he watched her now, it was from afar, forced to abdicate primary responsibility for Kane's safety to the princes' patrols. Hashim accompanied her home in his own limo with his own driver, his royal guard in vehicles in front of and behind them. When Hashim dropped her off, she thanked the Sultan's son and waved his limo away.

Kane looked around and didn't see any sign of Gade's Camaro. The traffic was bumper to bumper. He might have been delayed in the Manhattan traffic. Gade would want her to wait for him. He was probably panicking right now, but Kane felt a certain freedom—like the leash was loosed. She started strolling into her hotel alone, feeling for the first time since she found out she was royalty that no one was watching her every move.

Jesus, was she wrong.

Paparazzi swarmed like a billionaire had just blown up his fat wallet and hundred dollar bills were raining down. Kane was the riches, and the right picture could be worth some serious cash. They swarmed, flashes, sounds, catcalls and questions swirling like angry bees. Freedom turned to fear in a split second. There were two dozen of them, cornering her in the lobby, pouncing like predators when they saw she was alone. "Was it love at first sight with the Sultan's son?" "What is the situation with Dillon Durfee?" "Your bodyguard is a total Costner." "Was that sparks we saw between you and Dash Dameron?"

Speaking of the suave devil. "I get the exclusive, gents." Dash appeared behind her, taking Kane by the elbow and sliding her into a service elevator that she hadn't even seen. The flashes from the cameras had blinded her. Dash held up his hand like Moses commanding the Red Sea and the paparazzi heeled like trained dogs, every flashbulb instantly going dark.

The elevator doors closed, leaving her alone with Dash. He had saved her.

Kane leaned against the back wall of the elevator car, issuing a long sigh that almost turned into a sob. She looked at her hands and they were shaking. The image of hordes coming at her like she was Frankenstein's monster remained vivid in her vision, the villagers surrounding her with pitchforks and burning torches. The entire moment had been so scary, and Kane had never in her life felt so terrified. Maybe Gade had been right all along to put such importance on her safety.

The elevator was moving and Dash leaned over, pressing the stop button between the third and fourth floors. The numbers on the board went all the way up to sixty-three. Kane was staying in the penthouse suite and the number at the top was the only button illuminated. Dash had a room keycard inserted into the console and Kane knew from her previous trips up and down that this overrode the system and would take the car all the way up to her room without stopping for more passengers. It locked out all exterior buttons, only stopping at the floors designated inside the elevator on this control panel. When Dash deselected the stop button, they could go all the way up to the top floor without another pause. But first, Kane needed a moment to get it together.

"Are you all right?" Dash asked.

"That was pretty intense," Kane said. "I felt like a little fish surrounded by big sharks."

Dash had his patented smile in place, but the expression didn't convey happiness today. It indicated concern. "They're hungry for a story—the biggest in a long time. It's like blood in the water, Kane."

Kane shivered. It had felt like they'd wanted to devour her—rend her limb from limb metaphorically… mostly. She had never felt so vulnerable—not when she had stood in all her naked glory in front of the city on her Manhattan balcony, not when she'd walked around the Royal Ball without underwear and not even when she had pleasured herself in the infinity pool where anyone could have walked in.

"You saved me," she said.

"Well, you probably would've saved yourself," Dash said. "You were backing up toward the elevator anyway. But thanks for making me look good. I always enjoy a good quip for the paparazzi."

She rubbed her arms. "I have goosebumps all over."

"All over?" Dash teased with a change in his grin, gradually growing from concern to coy.

Her whole body buzzed from the adrenaline rush. She felt attacked, but alive. She'd survived. Now she felt like she needed to celebrate. Kane was amped, like she had touched a live wire and ended up electrified.

Kane stepped a little closer to Dash. "I owe you for saving my ass."

"Your ass is always worth saving, Princess."

Her lips were closer and closer to his. "How can I pay you back?"

He took her by her arms. "Maybe there's something you can do. However, it's something more for you than for me. Although I assure you that I will get a little enjoyment out of it myself. It's something that might be…over the edge."

"It sounds dangerous," Kane purred, tingling all over.

"I suppose," Dash said. "You see, the really dangerous thing about those bastards invading your privacy is that there's the threat that you overreact—that you close yourself off and hide from them. But that's when they win, Kane. If you retreat into yourself, sneak around and start living like a hermit, then they've taken away your freedom. I've seen it too many times. It drives some celebrities nuts. So you can't let them win."

"That was crazy back there, Dash," Kane said, anxiety again at the edges.

"It'll be crazy again," Dash warned. "Will you run and hide every time?"

"It'll be different when Gade is near," Kane said.

"And you're comfortable depending on a big, strong man to make you feel safe?" Dash asked. "Sounds like the plot of some animated fairy tale and not the story of Kane Cambridge."

"My story is different now than it was yesterday," Kane said.

"It doesn't have to be," Dash said. "You can take charge of your privacy…own your own story."

"How?" Kane asked, still close enough to kiss him.

"I dare you," he said, his smile turning lascivious.

"Is this the time for games, Dash?"

"It's the time to stiffen your spine," he said. "And maybe some other things…"

"Just how will a dare go about that?"

"If you give in to your fear now, it'll only be easier the next time…and the next time. You can't just run and hide."

"So what do you have in mind?"

Dash leaned over and pushed three random buttons in addition to the glowing sixty-three. Fifteen, thirty-seven and fifty-one. The stop button still stalled the car. Dash looked Kane in the eyes. He was all confidence and charisma. He had saved her from the hordes. She wasn't going to say no. Besides, she already understood when he was suggesting.

"Completely?" she asked.

"Every last scrap."

"And you think this will help?"

"It's a test," Dash said. "Can you take back control of your story? Can you risk being revealed to the world? Or will you just hide forevermore?"

"Hmm-m," Kane murmured. Then she demurred. Her blouse fell to the elevator floor—then the skirt she'd worn on her dates with Richie and Hashim. Her underwear was black today. She glanced up at the camera in the elevator car, and Dash reached up and put his hand over it. Kane unclasped her bra and let it drop. Then her underwear came off as well.

She stood naked in the car. Nothing Dash hadn't seen before. She looked at him and his smile was appreciative and impressed. Kane nodded. With the hand not covering the camera, Dash turned off the emergency stop. The elevator started again.

Each floor gave off a sound, a quiet blip that counted down to the fifteenth floor. The car slowly stopped. The doors started to open. Kane had a chill. There could be anyone on the other side—anyone or no one. Her skin felt full of little sparks.

There was no one all the way down the hall along the fifteenth floor.

The doors slowly closed and Kane sighed. Her whole body revved with arousal. Dash stood right next to her, close enough to start a crazy, wild romp. But the elevator started moving and the thirty-seventh floor was getting closer and closer.

The elevator stopped. The doors started opening again. Kane stood in front of the sliding doors in all her natural glory, a naked princess presented to any awaiting eyes. The breeze of air-conditioning caressed her bared breasts. She wanted to touch herself between her legs, aching for either eyes or fingertips to settle on her soon. She planted her feet a little farther apart and put her arms over her head like a feline stretching, making her chest arch outward. The elevator doors revealed her to whatever potential audience.

Did she hope there would be no one or someone? Did she want a stranger to see? What if they recognized the new American royalty? She shuddered, on the very edge of orgasm.

The entire length of hotel hallway was vacant.

The doors closed again. One more floor. One last chance. She could probably get covered in the few seconds before they arrived at the fifty-first floor. But Kane stood still. Revealed. Her nipples ached, so hard and hungry for attention. Her nether regions were soaking, and Kane didn't move to conceal anything.

The last floor. The last chance. The doors seemed to open so very slowly. Finally, like a beautiful flower opening in the dawn, the length of hall was revealed. An old man stood twenty yards away, fumbling a keycard into his hotel room lock. He looked down the hall as the elevator opened. Kane looked him right in the eye, then his eyes roamed her naked figure. She stood like that for long seconds. When the door started to close, the old man just gave her a polite nod of thanks. Kane waved like a princess—a naked one.

The car started moving again. "You did it."

"God, I'm so turned on," Kane said.

"Confidence," Dash said. "I think you'll be fine, Kane Cambridge. Don't let the paparazzi or the press take away control of your privacy."

"Thanks, Dash," Kane said, leaning forward and giving him a kiss on the cheek. She wanted to push the stop button and pounce, but instead she let the elevator take her to the top floor. The doors opened again.

Gade was waiting. His eyes grew wide as he got an eyeful of naked Kane. She stood there for a long while and just let him get a good look. Then she walked by him, strutting toward her penthouse suite.

"It isn't anything you haven't seen before, Gade," Kane quipped as she disappeared into her room. "Now be a gentleman and gather my clothes, won't you?"

Chapter Eleven

Kane's dream was pleasant.

Gade rowed the boat while she reclined against the bow, going backward. The pond was pretty and placid, their wake the only movement in any direction. As they glided away from shore, they also moved back in time. Her memories erased like she was regressing to yesterday. She forgot about Richie and Hashim, then Dash, then even knowing she was a princess. Soon it was just Kane Liberty and a guy named Gade. Alone. He stopped rowing when they arrived at the very middle of the lake.

Kane stripped down under the blue sky and bright sun. It felt fantastic to be free and naked in the center of all this nature. Gade kissed her everywhere, licked her where she wanted, then slipped inside her when she was ready. Her mind felt like water, melting and becoming one with the pond. His hips thrust, driving his manhood so deep inside her, every piston pump making waves that radiated out from the rowboat in every direction – rhythmic concentric circles that pulsed again, again, again, again. Eventually, he brought her to a fantastic climax. A perfectly amazing happy ending.

Being awake was unpleasant.

She blinked, wondering if the shouting was coming from the next room or from her own subconscious. Then it came again, louder, certainly not only in her head. Kane sat up, wiping away the sleep from her eyes. Her phone said it was eight in the morning. The people fighting in the hallway outside her penthouse door had woken her up before the alarm.

Who in the hell was yelling outside the top floor suite in a premiere Manhattan hotel? And why hadn't they been bounced out onto the street already? Kane marched across the room in the Air Force Fighting Falcons T-shirt she'd stolen from Gade once upon a time, with super-comfy sweat pants cinched tightly around her waist. She slipped on some fuzzy slippers that she had requested especially from room service the night before to ward against the cold tile floors. Then Kane whipped open the door without regard to who was outside or how dangerous they might be. Gade was surely not far away. He wouldn't let her out of his sight again after he'd lost her the past night.

Two men were rolling around in the hall, engaged in what might have been the most embarrassing cockfight Kane had ever seen. It reminded her of a charity event in high school when her sister Mary had to mud-wrestle her gay frenemy Scott Bilko for free tickets to a Streisand concert. There was maybe more hair-pulling and scratching with the teenagers, but certainly no less slapping or name-calling.

Standing over the two men were Sora, Lani and some girl with a purple streak in her hair that Kane thought she recognized from her grandfather's entourage at the Royal Ball. At the end of the hall, standing back as if he worried that such utter wimpiness might be contagious, Gade watched with his wide arms crossed. After some quick math and the process of elimination, Kane realized that the two 'men' rolling around on the floor were Sora's slimy husband Sevin and Kane's own brother.

"Quit, Sevin," Sora cried, confirming the identity of one 'combatant'. "Just stop! Someone might get hurt."

"I really don't think anyone will get hurt," Lani smirked.

"What the hell is going on?" Kane asked.

The two grown men finally disentangled, getting to their feet, huffing and puffing. Mark had an extra twenty pounds on Sevin and looked like he hadn't exerted himself that much since the elevator to his third-floor apartment building had broken the past summer and he'd had to use the steps. Sevin had arms thinner than Kane's wrists and had the general appearance of product that had been pulled out of a taffy machine.

"He's a goddamn pervert," Sevin accused, pointing at Mark like Kane's brother had just cold-cocked Colonel Mustard with a candlestick.

"You're the one who posted naked pictures of your wife on the Internet, you son of a bitch. Keep them to yourself if you don't want anyone else looking."

"It wasn't for friends and family, you sicko."

"I'm a man. We look at naked women, especially hot naked women. And Sora is hotter'n hell, dude. She's had a million frickin' views already. What the hell is one more?"

Sevin raised an open hand like he was going to slap the shit out of Mark. Mark flinched like Sevin's hand was a wasp. The girl with the purple-streak looked mortified that she had chosen to be with a guy who flinched, who said 'frickin'' and who fought like a sissy. Sora stepped between the men, and Kane swore she saw Mark look at her best friend like he was picturing Sora naked. Lani noticed, too, a smirk still on her face.

"Don't you dare start fighting again," Sora warned.

"There isn't anyone on the planet that would call that fighting," Lani said.

"That's enough," Kane said, and it was done. Somehow, she had turned into Aunt Polly. Her word was law. Mark immediately surrendered. His sister, after all, was now royalty.

"I'm done," Sevin said, looking at Sora, who looked at the floor. Her tears dappled the carpet. "I can't do this—everyone looking at you, everyone who saw..."

"She did this for you, you selfish prick," Lani snapped.

"I did this," Sevin said. "I know."

But he still turned. Sevin still walked away. Gade stood aside and let him on the elevator. Everyone was so focused on Sora's reaction that no one noticed that the girl with the purple streak had slunk away with Sevin.

Sora had been voted Most Likely to Succeed in their senior class. She'd graduated valedictorian from an ivy league university. She had become CEO of her own company by twenty-five. Now she was most famous for an X-rated Internet video. Sora Chan crumpled. Lani caught her before her legs entirely gave way and rocked her as if Sora was her own child. Kane reached over and stroked Sora's fine, black hair.

Mark stared at the elevator where his girl with the purple streak had disappeared. Another bimbo gone.

"Shit," he mumbled. Gade just looked at the lot of them and shook his head.

Everything was a mess.

It was as if Kane's good fortune had affected everyone else inversely, her happiness making everyone else miserable.

Yet, how happy was she?

She wondered if American Princesses got happy endings like all the princesses in every other fairy tale.

* * * *

Kane entered her grandfather's suite after Abigail answered the door. The suite wasn't as traditionally grand as Kane's, but what it lacked in old-school charm it more than made up for in sheer opulence. This room actually took up more than one floor of the hotel, a spiral staircase in the center leading up to another level. Water contained in a clear plexiglass cylinder rose through the center of the spiral and contained brightly colored fish swimming up and down the column. The steps themselves were made of translucent acrylic lighted from underneath and the view was striking. Kane smiled as she followed a particularly enthusiastic clown fish up and up.

As Kane approached the top step that led to the study located on the next level, she paused. Two people were exchanging harsh words in the tone of an argument.

"—heard the last of this." A woman sounded tense.

Her grandfather replied in a terse tone, "You wouldn't dare."

Kane continued up the stairs. A young Asian woman with black hair in a pixie cut stood in front of her grandfather. She looked meek and small standing before the Senator. Sidney Cambridge loomed larger than life, like an object that overshadowed everything else in the vicinity. The woman was shaking. Kane's grandfather pointed his finger at the woman and wagged it, scolding her.

When she noticed Kane at the top of the spiral staircase, the woman escaped her grandfather's orbit like a rocket ship finally getting away from the gravitational pull of a planet and flying free. She didn't meet Kane's gaze as she skulked by, taking the steps two at a time as she descended and departed. The clown fish followed the woman down to the next level.

"What was that about?" Kane asked, walking across the room.

"A disgruntled employee," the Senator said. "She wanted more out of the deal than what we'd originally agreed to."

"That sounds like ambition."

"She reneged on an arrangement," her grandfather grumbled. "That is unacceptable. It will ruin her reputation in this town. She's done."

"That seems harsh."

"That's politics, my dear."

"Good thing being a princess isn't a political office."

Her grandfather scowled. "It's hardly a private enterprise, either, Kane—as I'm sure you've already realized. We serve at the mercy of popular opinion. Our station in society might've been granted by a secret amendment to the Constitution, but the royal titles are meaningless if our positions aren't recognized by the masses. That's why it's important for you to win the hearts of the men and women of America."

"Sounds a lot like a campaign."

"Popularity is power, my dear. They stop being interested in us, and we go away," her grandfather cautioned. "The British royals have remained relevant because the world loves a good fairy tale. You have to pique their interest. You have to keep them wanting more."

"Nothing like a good love story to keep our ratings up, Grandfather?" Kane quipped, walking among furniture made of more clear acrylic—a coffee table filled with water and sea life, a bar made out of a tank containing coral, an entire wall that featured more fish.

"I don't want you to pursue a relationship with someone who doesn't interest you, Kane. This is twenty-first-century America and not feudal Europe. There won't be an arranged marriage. Reality television has made everyone a relationship expert, so the public can smell a sham hook-up a hundred miles away," the Senator said. "But it would help the royal brand if you stayed in the public eye…with a popular prince on your arm, occasionally."

"Does that include the son of a Sultan?" Kane asked. "I'm meeting Hashim for football this afternoon at the new FC Stadium."

"Yes, I've heard. He rented out the entire arena and invited the media," the Senator said. "That will play well on the news feeds. And maybe even ESPN."

"Hashim seems to like the spotlight." Kane thought of the swarm of paparazzi that had attacked her yesterday like piranha and shuddered. "At least the media is invited this time. The cameras always seem to find me anyway."

Her grandfather nodded. He understood. He had been in politics for decades. Being in the public eye was second nature to him. Kane was still getting used to it.

"I'll be returning to Washington, D.C. today," her grandfather said. "Tomorrow, the Supreme Court is taking up the case of the constitutionality of the secret amendment initiating American royalty. I want to be present for the ruling. It will look good for the cameras."

"You think they'll affirm the legality of the amendment?" Kane asked.

"Of course," the Senator declared. "They have to. It's a historical document, fully authenticated. Just because something has been ignored for a long time doesn't mean you can still turn your back on it once it's publicized. A secret isn't the same as a lie. They have no choice but to allow it to stand."

"And that's it?" Kane asked. "Then we're official? American royalty, forever and ever?"

"Almost," Senator Cambridge said. "Once we are legitimized by the American judicial system, we must still be accepted into the World Court, the consortium of global monarchies. The rest of the world's royals must welcome us into their group. After America gives the stamp of approval, we'll travel to England to apply for authentication."

"London," Kane sighed.

"To Buckingham Palace," her grandfather said, "for a coronation."

* * * *

The stadium was something to see. Kane had been in big league parks before for concerts and sporting events. She had gone to a Beyonce concert with Lani and Sora a few years back that had featured a sold-out crowd, and Dillon had taken her to an NFL game the past year where the stadium was filled to capacity. But a place like this looked so much larger when Kane was the one standing on the field and the bleachers all around them were entirely empty.

Gade expressed concern about security at the stadium. "There are too many points of entrance and egress," he said. "Besides, the entire field is wide open. No ceiling. Danger could literally drop right out of the sky."

"I don't think danger just randomly falls out of the sky, Gade," Kane scolded. "And you won't be the only one in charge of security. Do you think that the son of the Sultan of Brunei is going to arrive alone?"

Sure enough, Hashim entered with an entourage, no less than twenty armed security, providing Gade with all the firepower he could want. Gade cooperated with the Brunei security detail and finally seemed to approve of the level of safety provided by Hashim's team.

Gade might have eventually been comfortable with her safety, and that made Kane relax a little, but she still felt exposed out on the soccer field. Twenty-five-thousand seats surrounded her, each empty chair representing someone who wanted to watch her. There were more than this many interested citizens around America right now, wanting to know Kane's every move. She felt like she was standing under a spotlight.

"You get used to it," Hashim said, noticing Kane fidgeting.

Kane looked at him, blinking, as if she'd just woken from a dream. She tilted her head and said, "Pardon?"

"The attention," Hashim said. "It becomes normal, like background noise you learn to tune out."

Kane nodded. He looked adorable in his custom jersey. It was bright yellow, with a black and a white stripe diagonal across his chest, representing the national flag of Brunei. On his back, he wore the number 2, signaling his position in the line of the crown. He held out a jersey for Kane with the same colors and a +1 as her number on the back.

She smirked. "Cute."

"Suit up."

Kane considered for a split second pulling off her blouse and donning the jersey right there on the middle of the field. The idea of standing in front of all those seats in just her pink bra made her tingle all the way down to her toes. Showing so much skin in the center of a *stadium...* But the jersey was oversized and just slipped on over the top of her shirt.

Hashim picked up a soccer ball and bounced it on his knee, off his foot, an elbow, bonking it up and down on his head. This apparently wasn't his first time. He was good.

"Back home, I practice every opportunity I get with our national soccer team. I'm better than most of the players," Hashim said. "But as a member of the Brunei monarchy, I'm not allowed to play the game. It was just one of the things sacrificed when you're the Sultan's son."

"It seems like we have to give up a lot to be royal."

"And we get a lot in return," Hashim said. "Now, you want to be shirts or skins?"

Kane smirked. She wanted to say 'skins' but there were a dozen eyes on her at any time, and the cameras would arrive at any second. The thought of being completely topless in this massive auditorium made her melt in all the right places—but she dismissed the idea.

"Shirts, I suppose," she said, sounding reluctant.

Hashim grinned and pulled off his jersey. He *obviously* trained frequently with the soccer team back home. He was fit, his stomach a rippling wonder of muscle. His chest was sculpted as if by a talented artist, a subtle scree of black hair in an arc over his pectorals. Defined biceps accented his lean arms. Hashim was easy to look at.

"I'd say you have an unfair advantage," Kane pointed out, waving her index finger at his half-naked figure. "That's nice work. Very distracting."

"Well, I plan on moving fast enough so that it will mostly be a blur," Hashim warned.

And he wasn't lying. Hashim played hard, without giving any consideration for her lack of skills. She chased him up and down the field, laughing as he expertly avoided her every attempt at defense and swiped the ball each time she started kicking it toward the goal. After an hour, the score was like six hundred to zero. Finally, Kane just picked up the ball. "This is how we play football in America," she said, and started sprinting downfield. Hashim feigned defense and she elbowed his rock-hard abs. He dramatically sprawled out on his back on the turf as she ran all the way downfield with the soccer ball tucked under her arm, stopping right between goalposts.

Kane pulled the yellow jersey over her head and whipped it around in a victory twirl, finally tossing it in a high arc like it was a penalty flag. Then she collapsed on the ground. Sweat shimmered over every exposed inch of her body. Her blouse stuck to her everywhere, turning the white material translucent. Kane's bright pink bra showed through the shirt. Hashim arrived, looking down and apparently appreciating the view, his eyes traveling from her head to her toes. He dropped beside her and rolled onto his back, like two stargazers looking up at the sky. It was still bright daylight, clouds chasing across a background of blue.

Kane hadn't felt so physically drained in a while—at least, not with her clothes on. Maybe she could move if she really wanted to, but she didn't. Her huffing and puffing eventually subsided and Kane just lay there. In the moment, she managed to ignore everything and everyone around her.

"The press is here," Hashim said.

Kane didn't even look. Of course they were. Of course they always would be.

"You ever just want to give them a totally bonkers story?" Kane asked. "Have you been out in public and surrounded and you just want to give them all the finger? Or start spray-painting your royal crest on everything like gangsta graffiti? Just start making out with some random old man? Maybe mooning the whole lot of them?"

Hashim rolled over, leaning on an elbow. He looked Kane over again. Her shirt had dried, the white returning to opaque. If Kane gave him the signal, he would kiss her.

"Sometimes," Hashim admitted. "Do you want to give them something to talk about, Princess Kane?"

"Sometimes," Kane said, sitting up with no little strain, "but not today."

There were enough stories this week—so many that it seemed as if some had happened to someone else. But it was Kane's new life and surely her adventures were not done yet.

Chapter Twelve

Kane woke and Dillon was standing over her.

At first, she thought it was a dream. A bad dream, so she choked back her scream instead of letting one rip. She sat up, her body creaking and groaning from the exercise the day before on the soccer field. Dilly didn't fade away. So, this wasn't a dream.

"What the hell are you doing in my room, Dillon?" she demanded, suddenly a little afraid of the man she had so recently called her fiancé. Now, Dilly seemed dangerous.

"You said I didn't have a chance, Kane. But *you* do. You can choose to turn your back on this. Maybe I'm not worthy of a royal relationship, but you can still renounce your title. I saw the interview on *DamTime,* Candy Kane. You said your father relinquished his role because he was in love. He gave up all this and followed his heart. You can do the same, baby."

Dillon looked terrible. He apparently hadn't slept in some time, his eyes red and bloodshot. Had he shaved since he'd arrived in Manhattan? Dillon never could grow facial hair, so brown fuzz grew in sporadic patches on his cheeks and chin. Pimples swelled in the creases of his nose and under his jawline. The smell coming off him suggested he hadn't showered in days. Where was he staying in New York? Was he sleeping on the streets? He wore the same outfit he'd had on three days before when he'd been stalking her at the Ball. Dillon fidgeted like he might be either drunk or high. Kane felt like she was in danger.

"I told you that it's over, Dillon."

"Call me Dilly."

"Not anymore," Kane said. "The only thing I'm going to call is for security."

"You don't want to do that," Dillon said. Was it a warning? He had his hands in his pockets. Did he have a weapon on him? Kane had known Dillon Durfee better than anyone in the whole world for the last three years, but now he looked like an unhinged stalker that was no more predictable than a desperate heroin junkie.

"My father gave this up for the woman of his dreams, Dillon. But look at us. This isn't any dream. This is a nightmare."

"This isn't real either, Kane. Do you think this life is what you really want? It's a fairy tale—a romcom that will only last so long. The credits are going to roll eventually, baby. And when the movie's over, who'll be there? The audience is going to be gone. The room will go dark. Then what happens? Who's left? That cocky son of a Sultan? The puffy little British Prince? Your bodyguard? Who will be there when it all ends and reality sets in, Kane?"

"*You* weren't there, Dillon. You were gone before it ever began. When this all happened, you were shacking up with some other woman. Why would I think that you could be there at the end when you were gone from the beginning?"

"I made a mistake, Kane. I loved you when you weren't a princess. Which of these other guys could ever say that? Which of them would still love you if you didn't have that ridiculous tiara?"

Kane knew then that he was delusional. Her tiara was certainly *not* ridiculous.

"I warned you before," Kane said softly. She felt a little sorry for him. He was taking this hard. And she knew how it felt to take a breakup hard. A week and a half ago, she'd tried to drown her sorrows in alcohol. But that was the right way to do it—not stalking someone. Dillon diverged from proper protocol. He was being a bitch about it. "Don't come back again, Dilly."

Gade entered. He had given Kane a panic button after he had lost her in traffic after her first date with Hashim, when she'd had the episode with the paparazzi. It was the size of a dime and applied anywhere with an adhesive, like one of those round little Band-Aids that covered up a small puncture. Kane stuck it to the hem of her underwear and she was relieved for the second night in a row that she hadn't slept in the nude. Kane had pressed her thumbprint to activate it shortly after she'd realized Dillon was delusional and maybe dangerous.

Gade charged like a prized bull. More than a mere man, he moved like a mobile mountain. Dillon still had one hand in his pocket, but Kane was no longer afraid. Gade would never let Dillon hurt her. Kane trusted

Gade to keep her safe. She knew that if it came down to it, her royal guard would take a bullet for her. She prayed it didn't come down to that.

Dillon moved his hand in his pocket, as if he was going to pull something out. Gade noticed. Kane's bodyguard shot her ex-boyfriend. The taser struck the target in the chest and Dillon danced, a twitching jig that wasn't really so different from the jerking movements he managed back when they would go out dancing and Dilly had insisted on grooving to Rihanna. Then Dillon's legs went to jelly and he flopped and flipped on the floor like a fish out of water. Gade made sure he was unconscious before he turned away from the target.

"Are you okay, Princess?" Gade asked.

Her royal bodyguard and former lover had just tased her ex. There was a lot not okay about that. But Dillon was the one making bad choices. She couldn't take responsibility for his asinine actions, so she nodded.

"How did he get in?" Kane asked.

"He must have come from outside," Gade said, checking the open door to the balcony off her suite. "I told you to lock it."

"I like the sounds of the city," she said. "Besides, we're sixty-three floors up."

"He managed it somehow," Gade said. "Probably dropped down from the roof. It won't happen again."

"What did he have in his pocket?" Kane asked, peeking over the bed at her unconscious ex.

Gade pulled his hand out of Dillon's pocket. He held up a roll of Rolos, Kane's favorite candy. That was it. *Just chocolate*. It was almost sweet.

"Damn," Kane sighed.

Kane Cambridge tried to live free and move forward, but there was everyone and everything around her trying to hold her back. She reached for the future while so many people around her remained stuck in the past.

* * * *

Kane had her second date with Prince Richie scheduled for later. Gade had Dillon packed up and removed like rubbish by the time breakfast was served. She had all day to waste before she had to be escorted again by her royal guard. Kane didn't want to go anywhere that needed any protection from overzealous exes or Nazi paparazzi. Her list of choices for a companion in relaxation mostly included people with a lot of problems.

She went down her list, texting her entourage one at a time. Lani was with Scatch, meeting with a recording exec downtown. Mark declined, currently accompanying another one of Senator Cambridge's busty assistants to D.C. Sora didn't answer her texts—or her phone, or the door. Kane sighed after knocking for five minutes. She huffed and turned.

"Aw, damn," Kane muttered.

Mary was walking Abigail to her room at the end of the hall. They conspired like teen lovers, giggling like kids. Abby leaned on the wall like the jock trying to impress the cheerleader. Mary looked at her feet with a smile, twirling the toe of her shoe against the hotel carpet. Kane stood too far away to hear what they were saying, but Abby stopped mid-sentence when she noticed Kane. Then Mary finally looked up, turning her dark skin an even darker blush. Abigail excused herself and Mary walked toward Kane.

"If you're looking for Sora, she's out," Mary said. "She didn't want to stay in this hotel anymore. She got a room at the Hilton and warned me last night she planned on taking enough Nytol that she shouldn't wake up until dinnertime."

"What are you up to this afternoon?" Kane asked, looking down the hall in the direction Abigail had disappeared. "I'm looking for some company."

"Uh, I just had to run some errands," Mary said in a way that meant Kane had certainly interrupted illicit plans.

"Where's Larry?"

"At the airport," Mary said, and Kane worried that Mary had made a mistake and confessed to her husband. "He's picking up the kids. He decided he wanted to fly them out here and bring them along to the coronation. He thinks seeing England is more educational than staying home and being in school."

Kane thought there was another reason. Larry suspected something. He wanted the family together in full force to avoid Mary sabotaging their entire future. Did he think she wouldn't have the guts to leave him if Artie and Agnes were around? Kane thought about what Lani had done to her family and the lengths Sora had been willing to go for the man she loved. Then she considered Mark and his many Manhattan mistresses, who were certainly milking him for much money. Kane wasn't so sure Mary could avoid Abby, even for the sake of her children.

"Well then, whatever errands you have can be canceled. I don't feel like being swarmed by paparazzi and I don't want to mope around my hotel room alone."

"So you expect me to entertain you?" Mary snapped. "Now that you're a princess, you think you can just boss me around?"

"I think I'm doing you a favor by making you do what I want instead of what you want, Mary."

Mary bit her lip. She knew Kane knew. This was the moment Kane worried about. Would she step back from the edge or would she jump over with abandon? Did the allure of Abigail override her feelings for her family?

Mary nodded.

So she was not *hopelessly* in love. Not yet, anyway.

"So what do we do for an afternoon in a posh Manhattan hotel?" Mary asked.

"My grandfather is going to appear before the Supreme Court when they hear arguments on the validity of the secret amendment to the Constitution that grants us our royal status," Kane said. "Their decision will affect the course of our future."

"Well, let's see if you're still a princess or back to just being a royal pain in my ass," Mary said.

They went to Mary's room. Gade hovered at the end of the hall, Kane always within a distance he could cover with a short sprint. He stayed outside while she went in. Mary's room was much smaller than Kane's, yet still richer than any room they'd ever stayed in while they were growing up. Aunt Polly and Uncle John had never been rich. Now Kane realized they had never even been happy. They had endured for the sake of the kids.

Now that was what she wanted for Mary? Was it the right thing to wish for? Kane didn't know anymore.

Mary turned on the television. The Court had already announced the verdict, moments before. They'd unanimously affirmed the veracity of the document—the amendment making it official that an American royalty was constitutional. It could be undone only by proposing another amendment to the original Constitution that would repeal the Royalty clause, which would have to be affirmed by three-fourths of the states.

Senator Cambridge stopped for an interview by none other than Dash Dameron on the steps of the Supreme Court. Her grandfather singled him out among all the reporters, a friendly face among the antagonistic press. Dash looked dazzling, the sun glinting off his white smile like some kind of a special hologram effect.

"Senator Cambridge, a question," Dash set up. "This has turned out to be a momentous day for the royal Cambridges."

"Mr. Dameron," Senator Cambridge said with a smug smile. He had just been legally declared the King of United States. "While my family has always believed in the authenticity of the documents in our possession, it's with great pride that our claims have been affirmed by the highest court in the land."

"I may be biased, Senator, but I've always believed that there's a higher tier of judge than even the members of the Supreme Court," Dash said. "Of course, I speak of the court of public opinion."

"Indeed," Kane's grandfather conceded with a flourish, like an actor onstage preparing for the big soliloquy. "And the good people of this great nation have welcomed my granddaughter into the public eye with graciousness and generosity. Certainly, the ratings from your interview can attest to that."

The swarm of piranha paparazzi indicated instincts that were other than being generous or anything graceful.

"How do you think the court of public opinion will react to the allegations against you, Senator?" Dash asked Kane's grandfather. "How do you answer the six women who have filed a joint lawsuit against you alleging multiple counts of sexual harassment?"

Senator Cambridge blinked. Dash had led him into a trap—Dash, who had been her grandfather's confidante and his choice to reveal Princess Kane Cambridge to the world—Dash, who had watched said princess pleasure herself in a rooftop pool. It was a 'gotcha' question.

And for the first time since Kane had met Sidney Cambridge, the Senator was speechless.

Kane tried to call her grandfather repeatedly after he had ended the interview with Dash Dameron and retreated with his posse of political apostles. He hadn't answered the first four tries Kane attempted throughout the afternoon, but on the fifth, Abigail answered. It had been two hours since the interview had exploded. Dash Dameron's bombshell was dissected and discussed ad nauseam on cable news. Kane wondered how the hell Abigail had gotten from Manhattan to D.C. so damn quickly. The whole team must have scrambled into emergency response mode.

"What the hell happened, Abby?"

"Lies," Abigail said. "A vindictive group of former employees and associates want to take down a powerful man. They're trying to overthrow a king."

"Insurgency via #MeToo?"

"Whenever there are those who make a reputation for themselves, there are always people who seek to tear it down. It's a tale as old as seeking a grand adventure or a princess in peril. The public just loves the story of a fall from grace."

On television, every channel presented evidence of Senator Sidney Cambridge's many transgressions. Six women with six stories. The details remained mostly confidential, but both fact and fiction were argued and debated between a steady stream of professional pundits. The same talking heads that praised Princess Kane's poise at the Royal Ball now eviscerated her grandfather for his pervy indiscretions.

The six accusers would get time in the spotlight to tell their stories that night on *DamTime*, hours away yet, but that didn't stop a steady stream of acquaintances of the accusers and every other legal eagle in America from offering a five-minute evaluation of Senator Cambridge and his life, his career, his psychology, his morality and the fate of his eternal soul. Most agreed he was fucked, any way one looked at it. As an old veteran of the news industry put it, "A reputation, once besmirched, is forevermore tarnished, no matter how much you polish it ever after."

"There seems to be a lot of evidence against him," Kane told Abby, watching the mother of one of the accusers give a credible account of Senator Cambridge making untoward advances on her daughter.

"He's your grandfather, your grace," Abigail said. "Will you believe the King of America or a bunch of babbling bimbos?"

Kane thought about Mark and his steady stream of the Senator's assistants. Those women used her brother for his money and his reputation then tossed him aside.

There had been four or five different girls in just a week. They were ambitious and ruthless. Kane didn't feel so sorry for Mark. He was getting something out of the deal. The young women were all ten years his junior and far more attractive than any woman Mark had ever dated before Kane had become famous. Could she see six of this group of women using her grandfather to further their fame? Sure she could. But the evidence against him…

"I don't know him well enough to say one way or another," Kane confessed.

"Well, you better figure it out fast, Princess," Abby suddenly snapped, certainly not addressing Kane like Abby was her royal subject. "This scandal could bring you down, too. Your fast rise to fame could end just as quickly. The press won't leave it alone. You will have to answer questions. You will have to take a side."

Kane disconnected before Abby's belligerence earned the assistant a sharp rebuke and caused Kane to get her fired. Then Mary would hold it against her. Kane wanted Abby out of the picture—but that wasn't the way to do it. The way things were, at least Kane had some influence over what Abby was doing and with whom she did it. And Kane wanted to make sure she wasn't doing it with Mary.

"This looks bad, Kane," Mary said, watching a promo for *DamTime* that promised an in-depth exposé on the day's events on a special report later in the evening with Dash. Abby had wanted Kane to believe her grandfather was innocent, but Kane had known Dash better than she knew Sidney Cambridge. How could she choose between the two sides?

Kane recalled the argument between her grandfather and the young Asian woman with the black pixie hair in his hotel suite. The conversation had been tense. The Senator had appeared domineering and threatening. What had he said? *"You wouldn't dare."* Had he been talking about the woman going public about some accusation?

Kane dialed Dash. She didn't expect him to answer. His exposé was set to air in just a few hours. He was surely fielding calls from everyone with a microphone. This was the biggest story of the moment, and moments meant everything in a twenty-four seven news cycle. Yet Dash answered on the first ring.

"I'm sorry that this is going to blow back and get some on you, Kane," Dash said.

"Are you sure you want to run with this, Dash?"

"I have to. These women need to be heard. Their story is important."

"Do you have enough evidence to justify bringing ruin to my family? To the career of a respected politician that's been putting America first for decades? Are you really sure that he is what they're saying he is?"

"It's up to me to tell the story. It's up to everyone else to decide what it means."

"You're going to ruin a legendary career based on stories, Dash."

"Just listen to what they have to say. Then you can draw your own conclusions."

"This will be the end of my fairy tale, too, won't it?"

"It doesn't have to be," Dash said. "Snow White wasn't defined by the Evil Queen. Cinderella wasn't persecuted because of her Wicked Stepmother. Just make sure you stand on the right side of the story, Kane. Because otherwise, your grandfather will surely take you down with him."

****

Everyone in America knew about Central Park, but there was a less legendary place known to locals that was just as magical. Officially known as the Esther Evelyn Hammersmythe-Ratched Memorial Conservation and Appreciation Park—or the E.E.H.R.M.C.A.P.—everyone on the Upper East Side just called it 'The Enchanted Forest'. Smaller than the nearly fifty acres of the much more famous Central Park, it looked just as idyllic and much less congested than its touristy alternative. Set in the middle of acres of tarmac, this plot of land had been left to nature, lush vegetation thriving without the competition of urban development. A pond stocked with coy featured a mermaid-shaped sculpture acting as a fountain in its center, spouting a stream of water out of her tail and cascading back down over seashell breasts. Trees along the winding path blocked out the looming Manhattan skyline, transporting Kane and Richie to another world.

Richie had texted Kane late in the afternoon as the news story about her grandfather dominated every channel. He offered to cancel their date, as if he had always expected as much. But Kane wanted to be distracted and she was damn well not going to let her grandfather's fucking antics affect her social life. She had to move on as if there might still be some future left in this princess thing.

You're not getting out of this date that easily, Kane had texted back.

Richie had replied with a 'happy face' emoji, seemingly custom created with a silver crown.

So here they were, walking through The Enchanted Forest like life was just a story in a book and Kane was only just another distressed damsel. Richie couldn't save her from this peril—nor could any other prince. This was a crisis of Kingly creation and Kane suspected there was nothing that could salvage her grandfather's ruined reputation.

He had greeted her with a pink rose. "I heard these were your favorite."

Kane smiled. He was sweet. "Pretty and pink. It's my Molly Ringwald jam."

Richie smiled politely, not understanding the reference, and showed her the way. They started along the path, Kane twirling the pretty pink rose in her hand.

"Do you think the accusations are true?" Richie asked as they walked side by side among towering pines, majestic oaks, elms that overhung the path and made shadows of the way forward.

Kane pictured the argument she'd witnessed between the Senator and his assistant. "I don't know."

"What will you say when the press asks you about it? Do you take your grandfather's side?"

"Does royalty mean loyalty?" Kane asked. "Does family stick together, no matter what?"

Kane thought about her father renouncing his legacy for the woman he loved. He had stood up against Kane's grandfather because Sidney Cambridge had disapproved of his choice of wife. He'd given up his name and his title because he'd wanted something different out of life than the direction the Senator had tried to move him in. Maybe Kane could learn more from a man she didn't remember than the grandfather she hardly knew.

"I have a cousin who took his studies at seminary very seriously," Richie said. "The Church is an important part of the legend of the British royals, so participation and education is *de rigueur*. My cousin took some of the studies too much to heart and developed a seething prejudice against anyone with a differing sexual identity. His ire included the Duchess of Somerset, who you might've heard about when she transitioned from the *Duke* of Somerset. My zealot of a cousin's inflammatory comments caused him to be banished from the royal family. Hate is never tolerated over heritage."

Kane nodded. They walked in silence for a bit. It was nice, being there with Richie. He wasn't a distraction, like Hashim and his alluring aura. He didn't create an awkward air like Gade, even now looming somewhere unseen in the shadows of The Enchanted Forest. There wasn't some complicated history between them like she had with Dash. Things were simple with Richie. But after a while, 'simple' and 'nice' weren't enough to divert her thoughts from considering her troubles. Kane grew weary of worrying. She needed something else to think about.

"So what's your story, Richie? You came all the way to New York City to woo the new American Princess. But I don't see romance in the cards between us, do you?" Richie shook his head. "So where does your fairy tale go from here?"

Richie shrugged. "I think my family thought this was probably my last chance for romance."

"Maybe we aren't destined to be together as a couple, but I think we make great friends," Kane said. "And I want to help you find your happily ever after."

"It might be too late for that," Richie mumbled. "I think I blew my chance with her already."

"So there's someone who has already stolen your heart, Prince Richard?"

Richie paused. The thick copse of trees bordered both sides of the path, casting them in deep shadows. He looked around for his own royal guard, as if he were afraid of being overheard. "There's a young queen in Egypt. Her name is Nefertari. We met last year, but I wasn't able to string two words together without stuttering like a blathering fool. She's an absolute goddess."

"You just lack confidence. Do you ever just throw caution to the wind and do the one thing that's the last thing you *should* do? Jump off the cliff instead of always standing at the edge?"

The prince looked terrified by the possibility. "I never jump," Richie said.

Kane thought about Dash and his lesson in the elevator. She had stood naked before the world, possibly to be caught at any moment. As the car stopped at each floor, the sound of the bell announced that the doors were about to open, Kane entirely exposed to anyone waiting on the other side. Every time, the worry of being seen had faded a bit, and confidence filled in the void when she conquered her anxiety...her *fear*. She had taken back the power over her own person. If she hadn't, she might have given in to being afraid ever after. She would have left the power over her privacy to the paparazzi and the public. Instead, Kane had snatched it back.

Kane said, "Today, we're going to jump, Richie."

They rounded a tight bend in the trees. Gade probably watched from somewhere in the woods, concealed behind a tree or two, but Richie's royal guard was less precise and more perfunctory. Their royal charge wasn't so prone to the princess dashing off and disappearing. They weren't paying enough attention to notice as Kane grabbed Richie by the lapel and tugged him into a thick copse of woods. She led him off the path and they sprinted deeper into the forest, alone—or *almost* alone. Gade certainly still monitored them, even if Richie's royal guard was instantly lost. Richie had surely never given them trouble before.

"What are we doing?" Richie whispered nervously.

Kane put a finger to her lips. Her mouth was a smile. Richie nodded.

She made sure they were far enough from the path that Richie's royal guard wouldn't find them too quickly. She stopped and faced the Prince. Kane still wore that naughty little smile. Richie looked nervous and excited.

"You want to jump off a cliff with me, Richie?" Kane asked.

Richie shifted from foot to foot. "I'm afraid of heights, Kane."

"It's metaphorical."

"I'm afraid of metaphorical heights, too."

"Take off your clothes," Kane commanded.

Richie didn't move. He didn't blink or breathe. "Are we going to…?"

"We're going to streak through these woods." Kane placed the pink rose by her feet. "Right now. You and me."

"N-n-naked?" the prince stuttered.

"Otherwise it would just be called 'walking' instead of 'streaking'," Kane said.

"I don't know if I can do th—" Kane pulled up her top, her sports bra coming off with her shirt in one smooth action.

She stood topless in front of Richie under the thick canopy of The Enchanted Forest. Light and shadow played across her brown skin and her smile was hopefully persuasive. "You're next."

Richie stared for a long while. Kane wasn't sure he could do it. But then he moved. He jumped off the cliff. *Shirt. Pants.* He stood before her in boxers tented out so far that the navy blue cotton almost touched her. She hooked her finger into the waistband of her yoga pants, under the hem of her underwear. Richie grabbed each side of his boxers in his trembling fists.

"Let's do it together. On three," Kane said. "One… Two…"

And she dropped trou. So did Richie. They faced each other, naked. He was pudgy and soft, pale with ginger fluff over his breasts and down his belly, a thatch of orange around his penis. He had extra pounds, but he wasn't unattractive. The prince was sort of adorable out of his clothes.

"C'mon," Kane said and started walking. She didn't know if Richie would follow her, but when she turned around after a few feet, he was right behind her. And his eyes were on her ass. His erection bobbed like it danced to a beat. They left their clothes behind in piles and marched through the undergrowth.

They reentered the path at a different point from where they'd exited it. Richie's royal guard was still hopelessly lost along the bends and switchbacks of the route. Kane stood naked in the middle of the path as Richie crouched behind a tree. A slight breeze stirred her black locks, tickled her bared breasts and felt fresh on her uncovered undercarriage. No one was around, although certainly Gade had eyes on her. She was showing nothing he hadn't seen so often before.

"Jump with me, Richie. Come out here. After this, you can do anything. You can ask your Queen Nefertari out on a date," Kane said.

Richie didn't move for a moment. Then he stepped out…exposed along the path. Anyone could come around the corner at any moment. Kane reached out to him and Richie took her hand. She started to walk forward. He walked beside her. Out in the open, under the trees, both as bare as the moment they were birthed. One bend. Another. Two joggers passed them by, neither slowing, although both men looked back and appraised Richie's impressive erection. A woman on a bench looked up from her book as they walked by, a naughty little smirk curling the corners of her mouth. Richie passed her proudly, like a King wielding his scepter.

Kane felt like electricity crackled along her exposed body. She imagined taking a left and walking out of the woods, into the city, hundreds of eyes all over her. She could feel herself getting wet down there. The idea of being naked on the streets of Manhattan pushed her pleasure to the very edge. If she got any more aroused, she might mount Richie right there in the middle of the path, unconcerned by the endless mobile devices that could record her inevitable orgasm—and damn the viral video that would flood the Internet. She had to get dressed before she ended up royally fucked.

After a euphoric few minutes, Kane and Richie finally ducked off the path. They doubled back to where they'd left their clothes. As they pulled on their pants, Richie smiled across at her. "You aren't quite like any princess I've ever met, Kane Cambridge."

"Well, I'm sort of one-of-a-kind," Kane said.

Just one. All by herself.

She knew what she had to do about Sidney Cambridge.

Chapter Thirteen

Kane woke up late. She inspected the pinhole on her big toe. She had stepped on a pine needle while walking naked through The Enchanted Forest the previous day. She thought about the story of Sleeping Beauty and how she'd pricked her finger on a sewing needle and fallen into a long slumber. Kane checked the date on her phone. She had overslept by just hours, not years.

What was fresh news? Kane sat up in bed and turned on the television. It was closer to noon than dawn, yet her grandfather remained the hot topic of gossip. The women of the morning trash-talk shows opined indignantly at the nature of men in particular and the patriarchy in general. Scholars sniffed and sniped about the culture of the penis and what drove men in power to commit sexual harassment. The regular mouthpieces of the #MeToo movement made appearances on every station to channel their ire at yet another instance of masculine abuse. A preview for the evening's episode of *DamTime* aired every ten minutes, Dash promising to disclose more exclusive details about the salacious allegations against Senator Sidney Cambridge.

Abigail entered at approximately eleven. Instead of some fancy silver platter with expensive silverware and food off a menu mostly in French, she carried a paper bag with a cartoon pig on the side that said simply, 'Bob's'. Kane hadn't eaten anything by a 'Bob' in a while. She'd been having a 'Robert' couple of weeks. She craved her some plain-ole *Bob*. The bag contained a breakfast burrito, eggs and sausage wrapped in a tortilla shell with some hot sauce that might have been harvested in Heaven. Kane moaned as she took her first bite, and it was the best thing that had happened in this bed since she'd arrived in Manhattan.

"You're going to have to make a statement about your grandfather today, Kane," Abigail said. "The press is crucifying him."

"A king isn't crucified," Kane mumbled around meat and eggs. "That's for saviors. Kings are toppled…or overthrown."

"The coverage is savage. Dash Dameron is as much a Judas as there ever was. He just turned on your grandfather for ratings rather than pieces of silver."

"I got the impression from our…interactions that Dash seemed to appreciate getting at the story behind the sensationalism," Kane said. "He always treated me fairly."

"No offense, your grace, but your grandfather doesn't have a perfect set of tits," Abigail answered.

Did Abby know about her rooftop rub-off? Abigail probably knew everything about Kane. Did she know about Gade? Did she even know what Kane had done in The Enchanted Forest with Richie? Or in the elevator with Dash?

"You think Dash compromised his ethics to get ratings by promoting propaganda against my grandfather, but he kept quiet about any salacious details of the new American Princess just because he's seen me naked?"

"Exactly," Abigail agreed.

"Why in the hell would he make major career decisions based on what was happening below his belt?"

"Because he's a man. They all think with their dicks. Simple story. Old as time."

"All those women accusing my grandfather of sexual harassment… Are you saying that the allegations against the Senator are *true*?"

Kane considered once again the tense verbal exchange she had witnessed between Sidney and one of his assistants. Was that woman just one more example of someone victimized by the Senator? Was Kane's grandfather arguing with his assistant about the truth coming out—or was he trying to stop a series of lies?

"Those women are lying," Abby dismissed. "As long as men have been ruled by their libido, there have been conniving women taking advantage of it."

"And you want me to make a statement to the press to that effect?"

"What else could you say? Senator Cambridge is the reason you're the most famous face in the world right now. While the accomplishments of his entire career are being dragged through the mud, you've remained relatively unscathed. Every pundit mentions how you'll survive without tarnish since you've been estranged from your grandfather your whole life. He saved you from obscurity and now you need to rescue him from ruin. You need to use your stellar reputation to support the Senator."

Abigail retreated after arranging Kane's outfit for the day, something that would make her look pretty and plaintive...a pastel pink skirt and suit coat that appeared entirely inoffensive, a hat that looked more suited to someone octogenarian. Hadn't Kane seen this outfit on the elderly Queen of England at some royal wedding?

Abigail expected Kane to address the controversy by afternoon. What would she do? Would she defend her grandfather, even if she didn't know if he were innocent or guilty? Whose fault was it that she hadn't known the Senator long enough to be confident in his innocence? Sidney Cambridge let his own son disown him because Kane's dad loved someone who Sidney didn't approve of. What else was the Senator capable of? It was her grandfather's own damn fault that he was a complete stranger to Kane. Kane finished her breakfast and headed for the shower.

Mark was waiting when she emerged a half hour later. He sat on her bed, watching cable news. The same motormouths expelled the same vitriol as earlier, as they had yesterday and they probably would again tomorrow. The press loved to tear down even more than they loved to build up. The fall of an American King was the juiciest political story since they'd brought down the President of the United States.

"They want me to make a statement," Kane told her brother.

"What're you going to say?" Mark asked. He looked like he hadn't slept. Nowadays, Kane wasn't sure if that meant he was having good times or bad.

"I don't know what to believe."

Mark looked away from the screen and into her eyes. Kane saw that there was no fun in his recent past, nor in his near future. Mark looked used and abused. The parade of women these last several days had exacted a toll. He looked spent.

"The women I've been with this week," he said. "My, uh...dates. They didn't have anything good to say about the Senator."

"So you think the accusations against my grandfather are true?"

Mark shrugged. "They all had a story, Kane. Your grandfather expected certain things from certain women in exchange for certain privileges."

"Sexual favors?" Kane asked.

Mark shrugged. "Look at the women he surrounds himself with—beautiful and ambitious."

"So he offered them incentives in exchange for sleeping with him? Why would he risk fifty years of accomplishments for sex?"

Mark shrugged. "That's the whole history of powerful men, Kane. The list is endless."

"He could lose everything."

"Do you think Dash Dameron is wrong?" Mark asked.

Dash wouldn't be spreading unfounded rumors. He had to have concrete proof. He had moved against Senator Cambridge because it was the right thing to do.

Would she be strong enough to do the right thing, too?

Kane had considered a call to Dash Dameron. How would that play out? Could she offer him another exclusive and arrange a private sit-down with Dash? Or would her illicit escapades under his tutelage come to light and taint his altruistic reporting? In the end, Kane had decided to steer clear of Dash and the danger of two supercharged superstars crossing paths once again. She worried a little bit about what Dash would dare her to do next and if she would be able to resist a naughty challenge.

Kane opened the door of her suite. Gade stood right outside, standing guard across the corridor, his arms crossed, his wide muscles flexed right over his heart, as if he could keep it under control with a bear-hug. His eyes were dark and intense, and when Gade looked at her as she opened the door, Kane felt like a bright star being pulled in by a black hole. His gaze had its own gravitational force.

"I need to get out of here without Abigail Morgan being any the wiser as to my whereabouts," Kane said. "Will you help me or rat me out?"

"I work for you, Princess, not Abigail Morgan."

"You know a back door we can sneak out?"

Gade nodded. "But a royal limousine is out of the question. Abigail is sure to find out if we take an official vehicle. We'll have to take my car."

"A sweet red Camaro instead of a stodgy old Cadillac? You don't have to twist my arm."

As in the beginning, Kane and Gade were sneaking around alone. He took her hand and led her through a door that read 'Employees Only' and down a staff elevator. Gade had prepared extensively and memorized the blueprints of the building, as expert on the layout of the hotel as anyone since the original architects. They took a shortcut through the kitchen, weaving through the laundry room and down a stairwell that circumvented any public hallways. The route led to a long corridor that ended in an inconspicuous exit. Gade stopped at the bottom of the stairwell before entering the hall.

"Shit," Gade said, ducking around a corner and pulling Kane with him.

"What?"

"The parking garage where I left the Camaro is right through there, just past the VIP sauna. But there are three paparazzo staking out the exit."

Kane peeked carefully around the corner. A trio of portly pimpled photogs mulled around at the end of the corridor, just inside the exit door. They leaned against the wall with cameras dangling against breasts almost as big as Kane's. The three men talked among themselves, their hands twitching at their sides, all of them ready to snap a picture of the American Princess.

"Can we go around them?"

"If there are three here, there are more anywhere else," Gade estimated. "This is our best bet."

"I can't get my picture posted all over online before I finish what I started with this," Kane said. "Abigail and my grandfather will try to stop me if they read posts about me sneaking out of the hotel."

Gade surveilled the hallway, roaming his gaze like a raptor scanning for ways to snap up its prey. His features were chiseled as if from stone, expression neutral and focused. His muscles were tensed, biceps bulged and the tendons of his neck acted like steel cables holding his manliness together. Gade's shaved head resisted shine, the dark color of his skin like smooth leather that just needed to be touched.

"You really need to do this?" Gade double-checked.

"Senator Cambridge is a sleaze, Gade."

"So you think he did it?"

"Do you?" Kane countered.

"I think sex has brought more men ruin than misfortune or malfeasance."

"I believe those women," Kane said. "I need to show support for truth instead of standing up for my grandfather's bullshit."

"You're an amazing woman, Princess."

"How do you do it?"

"Do it?"

"Men all around me give in to lust. They are seduced by power. They use their position and influence to get sex. But you refuse to compromise your nobility. Men like my grandfather throw away their entire careers to get what I'd give you freely."

"That's a weakness of the flesh, Princess. Your grandfather and others like him never resist their desires. That's giving control over to your biological urges. I've worked hard to be physically strong my entire life. I don't give in to lust. But no matter how hard I train or how much I hone my body, I cannot harden my heart. It takes everything I have to stop my feelings for you."

"Then stop stopping, Gade."

"I can't, because it would betray everything I believe in," Gade whispered. "I can't love you, because it will make me hate myself."

"While other men are ruining their careers for love, you're ruining your love for duty."

"What your grandfather is accused of is not love," Gade said. "Now tell me, is your heart true? Is this thing you're trying to do *true*?"

"Yes," Kane simply answered.

"I'm sworn to protect you, Princess. That means I'll stand in front of a speeding bullet or push you out of the way of a powerful locomotive. I will always guard your life with mine. But protecting you means more than just making sure you're not physically harmed. I also need to protect your reputation. I won't allow your grandfather to ruin your good name. So, today, I must leave you unguarded to best protect you."

"What are you talking about?"

Gade handed her a set of keys. "The Camaro is at the end of the second row. Treat her gently. Watch out on the streets of Manhattan. Traffic's terrible."

"You're letting me go out there alone?" Kane asked.

"I'll distract the paparazzo," he said, peering around the corner and down the hall.

"How the hell will you manage that?"

"You gave me the idea, actually. I'm going to give them a show," Gade said, his face expressionless. "Give me a minute."

Gade went around the corner while Kane waited. He entered the VIP sauna. She counted to thirty in her head. Gade emerged in just a small white towel, his muscles bulging from everywhere, his skin already shiny and slick from the steam. Instead of returning to Kane, he turned the opposite way and walked right toward the paparazzo crowded by the exit. The trio of chubby, scuzzy men stared as the beefcake in the little towel strode toward them. Gade stopped right in front of them.

"Ain't this the Princess's 'roided bodyguard?" one quipped.

"What the fuck you want, Schwarzenegger?" another asked.

"The princess isn't coming out today. Sorry to disappoint," Gade said. "But you fellas want another story? Something sensational for your blogs?"

Gade walked down the hall away from the exit, where the corridor led away from the sauna in an L shape. Before he turned the corner and Kane could no longer see him, he dropped the white towel. She caught a glimpse of perfect ass cheeks disappearing around the bend. All three paparazzo began flashing bulbs and trailing behind the spectacular specimen of naked man striding down a public corridor. His hulking form would be as popular online as any unauthorized photograph of the American Princess.

The piranhas distracted, Kane was able to sneak down the hallway and out of the exit, into the parking garage. She rushed to the Camaro and slipped inside. She thought of Gade and how he had walked naked down the hall, in public, letting the photogs snap a thousand pictures. He had done it for her. That was so damn *hot*.

The Camaro moved through Manhattan traffic like magic, as precise as a needle weaving rags into a gown fit for Cinderella. Already aroused by Gade's flashy, assy distraction, Kane became doubly turned on by the revving horsepower of the machine growling under her as she shifted and slipped through the noon-hour rush. Manhattan traffic *was* terrible, so many people all around her. So many eyes…

She wanted to unbutton her blouse and take off her bra, bare her chest and drive through traffic topless. The thought made her body abuzz from top to bottom.

Maybe someday. Just not today.

Kane pulled into the studio lot of the network rival to the channel that aired *DamTime*. Dash was big dog on Network A, while Whitney VanderWahl was big dog on Network B. The 'B' stood for Bitch, according to Dash. It was one of many insider stories he had shared with Kane in their hours together. Whitney was his mortal enemy.

Kane parked the sweet red Camaro in a spot in the front row reserved for 'Special Guest'. Being a princess should probably qualify as special. She took a deep breath to tamp her urges. Finally, she felt in control enough to exit the car and marched right in. A tall, broad woman who looked like she might be a match for even Gade Williams met Kane before she'd managed to make it to the receptionist desk. Maybe she did need her big bodyguard after all. The she-hulk introduced herself as a producer for the network.

"Then you know who I am?" Kane asked.

"Everyone knows who you are, Princess Kane."

"Tell Whitney she gets the exclusive," Kane said.

The big woman looked her up and down. Kane wore a white blouse that failed to concealed her lacy lavender bra. Her tight hole-y jeans had embroidered hearts on the pockets hugging each cheek of her ass. "I'll tell wardrobe to get ready for you."

"No wardrobe," Kane said, and suddenly she thought about walking naked through the woods with Richie or riding topless through traffic in Gade's red Camaro. *Is it warm in here?* "I'm not here to be a pretty princess."

The broad-shouldered producer just nodded and led Kane along the hallways. The next hour was a whirlwind—introductions, prep, staging, makeup. Then Kane sat across from Whitney VanderWahl, the most famous interviewer who wasn't someone that had seen Kane naked. The legendary newswoman asked Kane her first question, launched like a straight arrow, leaving no room to wiggle out of a direct answer. Kane didn't plan on wiggling anything.

Whitney asked, "Tell me, Kane… Does the Princess of America obey her king?"

"I am a princess, authorized by the Constitution of the United States of America," Kane said. "My duty is to my constituents. To the people. So I stand with my sisters and seek to discover the truth. No person should have to suffer the abuse of anyone in a powerful position. As American royalty, our role ought to be to serve and not to rule. I want to be an example of what you can *be*, not what you can get away with. No king should ever be above the laws of the land…so let justice be done."

* * * *

He was waiting for her as she exited the studio after the interview with Whitney VanderWahl. Gade Williams had a great deal more articles of clothing on now than when she had last seen him. Kane didn't ask how he had known where to find her because she knew Gade was better prepared now than when she had disappeared on purpose with Dash Dameron or when the paparazzi had accosted her after her date with Hashim.

"I'm not ready to face Abigail and all the other enablers," Kane said as the Camaro exited the news studio's secret lot.

"Where to?" Gade asked, driving through grimy streets. He always looked tortured lately to be in her close proximity. She remembered there had been a time when she had been irresistible, bringing a grin to her face, rather than a grimace.

"Do you know a place where we can escape? Somewhere that the paparazzi won't find us and I might not get bombarded by a bunch of requests for selfies?"

Gade smiled for the first time in a long time. The expression was a welcome departure from his doom and gloom attitude ever since he had decided not to pursue their romance. *He* had decided. If Gade asked right now, Kane would let him whisk her away to some private island for the foreseeable future, skipping the coronation and her princess-ever-after.

But Gade didn't ask. He just said he knew such a place and made the next turn.

The place was called Patriots and had nothing to do with a Boston football team. The American flag fluttered on the front marquee. A line of Harley-Davidsons leaned in perfect symmetry in a long row across the front parking places. The rest of the vehicles lining the street were mostly big trucks and large SUVs. Bumper stickers supported every military branch, the commander-in-chief and the Second Amendment.

Inside, country music played on the radio. Not any of those current douchebag country singers either—it was Jackson and McGraw, Strait and McEntire. Kane only knew them because Dillon Durfee had always listened to country music from the nineties. He said it reminded him of his mother. This honky-tonk bar didn't remind Kane of *anyone's* mother.

Inside was dimly lit and smoke lingered in a haze, despite New York City's strict anti-cigarette laws. The guys and gals in this place didn't abide by rules that limited their freedom. They had fought for this country, bled red for the nation and had friends who'd died doing their duty, so if one of them felt like smoking a Marlboro while having a beer, Jesus help the poor progressive asshole who tried to take either out of his hand.

Kane generated no more than a cursory glance. Anywhere else in this city, she would've been the center of attention. She could tell by the way they looked at her that they knew damn well who she was, but they didn't seem to much care if she was a princess or the Pope himself.

"I feel almost anonymous," Kane said as Gade pulled out a stool for her and saddled up on the next seat.

A thin man with a prosthetic arm worked the bar. His face was grizzled and his eyes were haunted. His smile seemed less warming and more warning. He wore a shirt that reminded Kane of the T-shirt she'd swiped from Gade's place, a bald eagle with spread wings over faded letters that read 'Air Force Academy'. The remaining arm still made of flesh sported a tattoo in Latin—*Prosequor Alis.*

"This place is filled with soldiers who've seen some pretty awful shit, Princess," the bartender said. "They tend not to react to much of anything that isn't trying to kill them. And no offense, but you look pretty harmless." Then he added with a charming wink, "Emphasis on the pretty."

Gade had a warm twinkle in his eye. "Princess Kane, I'd like you to meet Blast. He owns this place."

"I like it," Kane said. "I feel safe. And everyone just minds their own business, huh?"

"Yeah, you won't get anyone asking for an autograph in here. None of those pussy paparazzi, either," Blast promised. "I guarantee there would be about fifty fucking guns out if anyone tried to accost a lady inside these walls."

Blast slid Gade a beer and Kane held up one finger. He nodded and brought her a tall one. Kane looked around at the men and women in the bar. Some argued politics, although they seemed to be in agreement and just debating with some anonymous snowflake academic in-absentia. A group of old soldiers reminisced about the days when battles were fought by men instead of drones. Two women talked about their kids. The mothers were inked up and down each arm and featured bulges on their hips that indicated pistols and not extra pounds.

"How did a beautiful bird like yourself end up with a bodyguard like grumpy Renegade Williams here?" Blast asked after making the rounds and serving several thirsty patrons.

"He worked for my grandfather," Kane said. "Now he works for me."

"Must be difficult," Blast teased, "keeping an eye on such a lovely subject all day, every day."

"She makes it difficult most of the time," Gade agreed.

"It isn't my fault that I attract trouble everywhere I go."

"You won't get any trouble in here, young lady," Blast said. "No offense, but the only royal highness we pledge fidelity to is Lady Liberty. I've been married four times now and the only mistress I can manage to stay faithful to is Miss America."

"Wasn't your second wife Miss America?" Gade taunted.

"Yep," Blast bragged, "from Florida. She won the pageant in 1984."

"And the marriage didn't last past 1986," Gade pointed out.

Blast grinned. "Wife number three came along."

Gade shook his head. "Your heart switches gears more than my Camaro."

"Then you're not driving it right," Blast said. "Love is a wonderful thing, but it's temporary, so enjoy it while it lasts. The best love stories burn brightest and fade fastest—like stars. Eventually they burn out and streak one last time across the sky."

Gade shook his head. Blast made his rounds again, but Kane just thought about what Blast had said. *Love that burns brightest fades fastest*. She thought about Uncle John and Aunt Polly, about Mary and Larry, Lani and Chase, Sora and Sevin, Mark and his many Manhattan mistresses. Kane thought about Gade and Dillon and Dash and Hashim.

She thought about her parents, who had died before their love had started to wane. Maybe true love *was* short-lived. Perhaps the best love stories were the ones that ended before love started to fade. Was *real* romance only the Romeo and Juliet kind?

She looked at Gade. Gade looked at Kane. Then she looked away. If Blast was right, she didn't want that kind of love.

Chapter Fourteen

Kane was up at dawn. She stood on the balcony, looking out at the city. She wore a robe to cover up, as there were certainly cameras on her somewhere out there and she wore nothing underneath. Manhattan was alive with eyes, people watching from any window or out across the rooftops. She felt a rush being in front of everyone, the morning breeze blowing the thin material over her body, making the silk robe hug every part of her. She felt perfectly on the verge—both in the public eye and yet the essential part of her just hidden away from eager eyes.

"Your grandfather would like a word with you," came a voice from behind her.

Kane turned around. "How in the hell do you get into my room whenever you damn well please?"

Abigail held up a keycard. "I arranged the rooms. I have an extra key."

"I'll have to remedy that," Kane said. "Does that mean you have a key to my sister's room as well?"

"The time I spend with Mary isn't any of your damn business, you traitor."

"Traitor?" Kane snapped, coming inside and striding across the room, letting her robe fall away without a thought of Abby watching her disappear naked into her bedroom. She wouldn't have done that just a few weeks ago. "Senator Cambridge sexually harassed at least a half dozen women. He's a pig who doesn't deserve loyalty."

"Those women got something in return for their services," Abigail said. "It was to the benefit of all parties involved."

"It was a selfish display of power without regard to anyone else's wellbeing," Kane countered. "Just like your relationship with my sister."

Abigail followed Kane into the bedroom. Kane stood naked in front of her closet, looking for something that Abby hadn't picked out for her to wear. She hardly had anything besides what the woman had purchased. Kane finally settled on the Air Force Fighting Falcons T-shirt that was kicked into one corner. She rummaged around in her suitcase for a pair of jeans and pulled them on without bothering with underwear. Abigail looked flustered when Kane finally turned and confronted her.

"Just because you're a princess doesn't mean you need to judge everyone else on their actions, Kane," Abigail said. "I don't know if you want the world knowing about your predilection for exhibitionism."

Kane paused. She stared at Abby, meeting her eyes. Abigail thought she would get a reaction, but Kane had learned a lot about herself over the course of the last couple of weeks. She wasn't weak. She wasn't ashamed. Kane was figuring out what it meant to be a princess and how to deal with having eyes on her always. This was just another facet of her newfound fame.

"Where is *grampa*?" Kane sneered. She was so done with Abigail Morgan.

Abby pointed out of the front door of the hotel room. Kane marched out and down the hall. Her grandfather occupied the same room he had earlier in the week. Opulence wasn't sacrificed just because he had been accused of being a creepy bastard. Apparently, Sidney Cambridge wasn't feeling penitent.

But he *was* looking old…ancient. Sitting in the center of the main living quarters of the room, the cylinder of water reaching up through the spiral staircase behind him, Kane's grandfather looked like he was a hundred. His face was gaunt, as if the turn of recent events had drained the vigor from his very flesh. His hair, formerly silvery and vibrant, had become flat and gray, hoary and mussed. His eyes had dulled, the sparkle of pomposity due to his kingly station now brought low. He looked at Kane through steepled hands where his fingers barely touched, as if in prayer, his glare piercing through the gap between his palms.

"You turned against me," he accused, no less antagonistic than Caesar to Brutus.

"You made your bed," Kane said. "Maybe you should have slept in it alone once in a while."

"Those…*bitches*," the Senator spat. "They each and every one benefited from my bed. They're calling me an abuser…a user, some sort of pervert who used my power to sleep with beautiful women. There was a time when that was known as just 'being a man'."

"These are different times," Kane said softly. "You used your power to solicit sex. Those women felt powerless to say no."

Senator Cambridge balled his hands into fists. "I never forced any one of them to have sex with me."

"Look at you," Kane said. "You're a grandfather. Some of those girls are younger than I am. Do you really think they were racing each other to get into your bed?"

He scowled. Her grandfather looked like a bitter old man who had spent his entire life alone instead of enjoying a steady parade of paramours who were less than half his age. He turned away. There was clearly nothing he could do about his situation. He was impotent after decades of abusing his virility.

Would he retaliate against Kane for her betrayal? Reveal her secrets if he knew what Abigail knew? No. His only remaining legacy was the Cambridge name and his royal line. Kane was all he had left.

"Was it worth it?" Kane asked. "All those women? You risked everything for sex, and now you've lost it all. Were those little moments between the sheets really worth it?"

"Get out," he mumbled.

"Why couldn't you just be my grandfather? Just a sweet old man who doled out wise advice and was inherently asexual...like Yoda."

"Because Yoda was a goddamn puppet," the Senator said. "And I am a man."

Sidney Cambridge stared at the fish swimming up and down the column of water between the two floors. He apparently couldn't look at Kane anymore.

Kane turned and exited. The King was felled. She was the last of the family line. Kane Cambridge was now the sole hope for a royal future. Her grandfather could be no part of it. She was now truly, completely solitary.

* * * *

Just because Kane was now alone didn't mean she was lonely. She might be solo, but she was not brought so low. Kane took lunch in the same five-star restaurant in the lobby of the Royal Palace Hotel where she had first met her grandfather, regal eats now once again spread out before her. Then, she'd been a novice potentate navigating a new world of fame. Today Kane was the last US royal standing, the descendant ascended to sit solely on the throne. Things had come full circle.

"Does this make you Queen Kane?" Lani quipped on Kane's left, efficiently eating up expensive lemon tagliolini without bothering to pause and savor a single bite.

"No," Kane answered. "My grandfather will technically be considered 'in exile'. As long as he's alive, I'll be ranked as a princess. He won't be acknowledged as king at the coronation at Buckingham Palace in London, so I'll be the only US royalty recognized by the World Association of Monarchs."

"W.A.M.," Mark abbreviated, sniggering from across the table. He had a smear of sauce across his chin. He was alone again. Kane sighed. She was tired of people and their bad choices.

"La, is Sora coming to London?" Kane asked. Sora had been missing-in-action ever since she and Sevin had separated.

"Yes," Lani answered without hesitation. "I told her she had one last day to get her shit together. I know the situation with her dickwad husband is devastating and everything, but she can only wallow in self-pity for so long. She's better off without that douchebag anyway. Besides, what better way to escape American Internet infamy than to flee to another country? So, she will be there even if I have to drag her sulking ass across the pond." Lani affected the worst British accent in history to say that last part.

Kane nodded. Maybe things were getting sorted out for the best. Mark didn't have another gold-digger joining them this afternoon. Sora would be at the coronation, thanks to Lani. Lani herself didn't have Scatch tagging along scarfing tagliolini, and Kane had fired Abigail as soon as she was done with her grandfather.

Sex and love—two things inextricably connected and yet entirely opposite. Whoever first equated the two and tangled them together? Love was bright and beautiful. It filled the heart and could elevate paupers to princesses. It made for 'once upon a times' and 'happily ever afters'. But sex was the evil opponent, as wicked as any witch and more dangerous than a hundred villainous stepmothers. Sex could bring down the most powerful rulers. It could tempt the most pious preachers. It was a weapon more destructive than an atomic bomb. More important figures had been brought to ruin by sex than by any other enemy.

Kane's grandfather was just the latest in a long list of infamous figures to fall from grace.

The restaurant wasn't as empty as when the Senator had rented it out. Kane was heir to a great fortune amassed by her secretly royal family, but legal entanglements restricted the resources of her vast estate. Now, her grandfather's current legal conundrums would further delay her assuming access to the Cambridge wealth. She didn't have the money to rent out the entire restaurant, especially since Manhattan socialites had learned that this was where the American royals dined. The place had been packed all week.

Gade stood sentry at the perimeter of their dining area. Plenty of gawkers milled about the main lobby of the restaurant, but they were Manhattan socialites proper enough to resist approaching Kane and asking to take a selfie. If the urge occurred in any of the other patrons, surely the presence of the massive bodyguard between them and her highness dissuaded any attempts. Kane enjoyed her tagliolini in relative peace.

Mary sat on Kane's right, her face in her phone. Her kids were both around the table, picking at the pasta like it was garnished roadkill. Larry sat on the other side of the table, opposite his wife. Kane could see the estrangement in this marriage, but maybe it had a chance to survive without Abigail in the way anymore.

"You see this?" Mary asked, holding out her phone, showing her sister the screen.

Mary was watching the *DamTime* exposé from the previous night online. The six accusers appeared briefly but said very little because of the upcoming court case. Dash, however, summarized the affronts perpetrated by Senator Cambridge and the effects on the six former employees. He listed accusations of improper fondling, offensive comments, unwarranted sexual advances and erotic expectations in exchange for advanced positions in the Senator's employ. The last part was where Kane's grandfather could end up in legal hot water as the women accused him of solicitation of prostitution, since he had essentially offered them positions of higher salary in exchange for sexual favors.

Dash had been gracious about Kane's place in the salacious story, making it a point that the allegations against Senator Cambridge in no way reflected upon the honor of his estranged granddaughter. Kane appreciated the effort.

"I saw it," Kane said.

Mary continued to watch the full hour-long special, and Kane wondered as her finger tapped her screen every once in a while if she used the episode of *DamTime* as an excuse to stare at her screen and reply when Abby texted her. Kane couldn't wait to get to England and leave Abby and Sevin and Mark's consorts and the Senator all behind.

"Who are you bringing as your date to the coronation, Kane?" Lani asked, finished with her tagliolini and already on her second glass of red wine.

Kane glanced at Gade. He stood at the entrance of the restaurant, guarding against any anti-royal terrorists, unhinged exes or socialites with selfie syndrome. She wanted to attend with Gade, but he would say no. He would be there anyway, just not on Kane's arm. She would have to officially attend with someone else.

Kane considered Hashim. Prince Richie. Even Dash Dameron. She sighed, just staring at her knight in a three-piece suit. There was the problem. She didn't want anyone else.

Chapter Fifteen

Kane was in the sky on a private jet, on her way to London. The flight was long. Gade had left for England the previous night on a redeye to Heathrow. He needed to finish coordinating security with the British for the princess's stay, insisting he scope out the lay of the land in advance of her arrival. Lani and Mary and Mark had all offered to accompany her on the flight to London, but she booked them first class tickets out of New York instead. Kane had been in the spotlight for a while and would be the center of attention for the foreseeable future, so she just wanted a little time to herself.

Kane had stared out of the window for the last hour, watching shapes in the clouds, wondering if the world was trying to send her a message.

"Can I get you anything, your highness?"

The young woman who'd asked her the question was named Rachel. She was polite and professional, but there was a hint of concern in her eyes. *What is she thinking?* Rachel was probably wondering why a princess was flying solo on the way to her coronation. *Because I have to find my own way on her own terms.*

"Thank you," Kane told Rachel. "I'm fine."

Am I? Hashim had offered to escort her to the coronation but Kane had declined. She didn't want to attend the ceremony with Hashim. Her grandfather wanted her betrothed to another royal, but she couldn't pledge her heart to the Sultan's son. Besides, her grandfather's opinions were nullified by his nocturnal activities.

Prince Richard called as they made their final approach to London. He wanted to finalize some of the arrangements for hosting the events surrounding Kane's coronation.

"Who's the lucky man you've chosen as your escort?" Richie asked after a bit of business. "Hashim of Brunei seemed eager to be your 'plus one'."

"I didn't choose anyone," Kane replied.

There was silence on the other end of the line. "I can attend with you, Princess," Richie offered. He sounded reluctant but resigned to duty. Kane realized Richie must have already made other plans. So had she.

"I'm not going to ask anyone," Kane declared. "I'm going alone."

"You truly are an American Princess," Richie sighed.

"Why do you say that?" Kane asked.

"Any other princess would feel bound by history and tradition—attending such an important event without an escort? Unthinkable for the British or the Danes or anyone else, really…but not for an American," Richie said. "Your country has always been the maverick. Nonconformist adventurers carving your own path in this world. Why would the expectations of a crown be any different?"

"A maverick?" Kane asked wistfully. "You mean, like a renegade?" The word in her mouth had made her think of Gade. Renegade Williams…big and strong and making her feel like she'd never felt before.

"Like an outlaw princess."

Kane grinned. She liked that.

"I don't want to follow rules someone wrote centuries ago, Richie. I want to be something new. I'm determined to make my own happy endings."

"Americans… You have grown up on spunky Disney royalty drawing their own destinies," Richie teased. "You really think there's true love and happily ever afters, Princess?"

"My brother says the only kind of love that is really true is the kind that ends before it sours—like Romeo and Juliet, like my mom and dad."

"That's a distressing idea," Richie said.

"But Mark doesn't know how those stories would end because they never lasted long enough to find out," Kane replied. "My dad turned his back on all this for my mom. He felt something so strong that he chose love over legacy—a tale of heart and honor. How would it have ended if they'd more time?"

More time, she thought as she hung up with Richie. She would have more time than her dad ever had. Kane was eager to get her own 'ever after' started.

The plane started its descent into London. Gade would already be there. The rest of her screwed up family and friends would arrive shortly. She would deal with the lying and cheating and bad decisions, because she was Princess Kane and she had to stay above it. The scandal of Senator Cambridge couldn't touch her. Whatever sexual shenanigans her entourage had recently engaged in weren't her issues. Kane had wallowed in their problems for too long. It was time to concentrate on her own story.

Kane came back down to earth. The plane touched down and she felt a certain peace. A Cambridge was back in Great Britain, the home of an ancestor who had left so long ago. The prodigal daughter returned. She sat up straight in her seat and watched as they taxied along the tarmac. For the first time since she'd found out that she came from royal blood, Kane felt like she was truly a princess.

Her evolution felt complete. The daring trials that Dash Dameron had put her through had started her on the path to becoming. Skinny dipping in the infinity pool had baptized her. Her experience of peekaboo on the elevator had conquered her fears. The naked stroll through The Enchanted Forest with Prince Richie had been another initiation. Kane had come into herself, transformed to the woman she needed to be, self-consciousness shed and confidence complete.

Princess Kane descended the steps where her entourage awaited—a world of paparazzi pictures, the press barking questions, legitimate dignitaries waiting to greet her and guards protecting her every flank. All eyes were on her. She was immersed in attention. Gade stood at the end, her unwavering protector.

Kane smiled. She was finally ready to wear the crown.

* * * *

The coronation was a two-day event. A formal crowning was scheduled to take place in the evening, which made Kane think of a woman giving birth. Perhaps that wasn't such a mismatched metaphor as she was being born into the global community as a new royal member. But at five-ten in heels with a dress that plumed out eighteen inches on either side of her, heaven help the vagina that had to spawn Princess Kane Cambridge.

Kane met the elders before the ceremony to present her petition of recognition to the World Association of Monarchs. These were the Kings and Queens from the reigning regions all around the world. Some wore regional headdresses and fantastic robes from their kingdoms in Africa, as others displayed European family crests with ornate patterns. Some royal houses from the Middle East were represented, monarchs with expansive turbans featuring the family gemstones. All the women wore jewelry that was elegant and expensive. Two very old men sported swords at their hip, so heavy that each stood slightly askew.

When they asked Kane who would be attending with her, she puzzled the royal court by responding, "I'll be arriving at the coronation alone. What happens at the afterparty, however, I cannot say." Kane gave the stuffy line of kings and queens a wink, but not one of the elders cracked a smile. She missed Hashim and Richie, her royals with less starch in their undershorts.

"The coronation is a social event that is intended to act as a platform for an entire royal line," said one British bloke so stiff that Kane wondered if Excalibur had been inserted into his ass instead of stuck in stone.

"Americans were never much for strict arrangements," Kane said. "We like to do things differently."

"You are definitely something different, Kane Cambridge," complimented one elder royal from Turkey, showing some signs of loveliness under the veneer of stoic stone. "This is your coronation. It seems only fitting that an American eschews previous tradition."

So it was an accompaniment of strings playing the soundtrack to a Disney Princess movie that ushered Kane down the aisle at the coronation.

The gala took place outdoors along the Thames, a stiff-lipped British affair that would benefit from the loose American style of the newest member of the world's royalty. The opening event was the coronation of Princess Kane. In the British tradition, royals were crowned by the Archbishop of the Church of England in Westminster Abby. But American royalty didn't get power from the pulpit but from the United States Constitution. The American government had already authenticated Kane's stature. The ceremony in England was a formality that simply welcomed Kane into the arms of the global elite. No foreign church was necessary to give Kane Cambridge its approval.

Kane felt like she was getting married. She wore a dress more resplendent than whatever she would have worn to walk down the aisle in an alternate universe where she had never become a Princess and had ended up marrying Dilly Durfee. The trio of cellists played her chosen selection as she walked along a green path toward the site of her coronation. Chairs lined the veranda on either side of the aisle, attendees watching like she was marching toward a groom.

The guests each wore a pink rose boutonnière, pinned on a lapel or the breath of a gown, every attendee sporting the honorific symbol of the bright and engaging flower. Hundreds, a massive bouquet, were spread across the entire ballroom. A smile touched Kane's lips. This was all for her.

Her family was all here, just like she was being wed. Sora and Lani stood along the aisle, both grinning brightly as she passed by. It was heartening to see Sora smile again. She attended alone, and being away from the follies of home had apparently freed Sora from her shame. Lani had brought Scatch—the deejay in a cap that featured a rapper's name and was turned sideways, Lani in a dress straight out of an enchanted movie. Mark and Mary flanked the aisle near the end, Mark's plus-one a busty blonde who was yet another intern who had been on her grandfather's team. Mary stood with Larry and her two children, Abigail nowhere in sight. Aunt Polly and Uncle John were in the front row, both of them looking at her like she had just won the Miss America pageant. The Duke of Richmond had been purposely placed between them, the elderly, uppity royal acting as an awkward buffer between the divorced couple.

Among the attendees also along the front rows were British officials, including the Prime Minister of the United Kingdom. She recognized other heads of states set like chess pieces positioned by a premier player. Kane believed Mark's opportunistic date stood right next to the Queen of Katchikstan. The Senator from Kane's home state was in attendance, wedged between the Duchess of Windsor and one of the wee British princes.

Prince Richard, Kane's Richie, represented the world's royal community. He stood like a priest awaiting the bride at the head of the gathering, cradling a crown ringed by a fantastic circle of gemstones in every color, an eclectic band of rubies, sapphires, diamonds and opals that made her rainbow tiara something different from any that had come before. Kane Cambridge was something new.

Behind Richie stood the line of stuffy royals she had petitioned earlier. They all looked at Kane in the same way, no matter what color or country. She was the upstart who'd crashed their royal party. No matter from Europe or Africa or Asia, man or woman, elegant outfits or stuffy suits, all their expressions were alike—like statues cut from stone, cold and unanimated.

And Gade. He stood sentry at the flanks, like a groom waiting in the wings for his betrothed. He wore a black suit that would have looked perfect on any potential husband, but Gade wasn't there for a full commitment of vows. His purpose was to honor and protect her—that he loved her was just a bonus.

She knelt before Prince Richie and he smiled warmly. They were cousins so far removed that Kane was probably more related to Oprah than the royal before her, yet he gave her a look of approval that could only be passed between kin. She was family...royal family. He placed the crown upon her head then spoke a few words in a voice more confident than he had been when they'd first met. Kane stood, a full member of the global royal society. Regal. Poised. Then she pulled Richie into a warm embrace...unscripted.

"Now," Kane announced, turning toward the crowd, "let's dance."

* * * *

Kane cataloged her partners. There was an old man who could barely walk but could talk faster than a hyperactive bullshitter, who feigned frailty and leaned heavily on the princess as they waltzed around the outdoor travertine dance floor, his face conveniently placed directly in Kane's bosom. The Prime Minister of Uzbekistan had two left feet and stepped on Kane's pinky toe no less than five times. Sir Willard of Rutherford was polite, exceedingly handsome and obviously oblivious to her plunging neckline, more eager to find romance with some fancy prince than with Kane Cambridge. Mr. Mumford was Chancellor of the Duchy of Lancaster, a lengthy title for a small man. He repeatedly alluding to the 'fact' that although he barely came up to Kane's shoulders, he was no slouch in size when it came to other parts of his body—more like the Chancellor of Douche-y.

Kane mentally cataloged her *other* kind of partners over the course of the fifteen years since she had lost her virginity. Henry Lowry had been first, when she had been sixteen. It had happened unexpectedly, and it was over before she'd known it. He had promised to call her and never had. In between, she'd had a steady boyfriend in high school, a guy for a while from college, then Dilly. Dilly was supposed to have been the last. But then Dilly had turned out to be an asshole.

Dash Dameron was in attendance, passing near her just once the entire night. He had smiled that dashing smile and said, "You look like you have this princess thing figured out."

Kane had nodded and given him a grateful grin. "Confidence. I'm ready for people to see me as I am…all of me."

Dash had returned a playful wink and moved on, a trail of ladies trying to get his attention. He hadn't seemed interested in a single one of them. He was clearly intoxicated by Kane.

As Hashim had been.

And all these princes.

Then there was Gade. He was the one her thoughts and her heart circled back to again and again. He was the partner she wanted to dance with until the music stopped playing. She didn't care who was looking, who was watching, who judged her choice of companion. Kane was ready for the world to see her with Gade Williams.

Gade watched her as she changed partners from those with esteemed airs to acquaintances with suspicious life choices. Kane danced with Lani, who was trying to look ten years younger than she was and like she had three kids less than she had. Her dress looked more fitting for someone nearer twenty than past thirty. Her boobs were practically squeezed out the top and the cheeks of her ass peeked out below her high hemline whenever she moved the wrong way.

"What exactly are you doing, La?" Kane asked as Lani tried some move she must have thought was sexy and instead she stumbled over Kane's shoe. "Scatch isn't even looking this way."

"There are too many little goddamn debutantes around trying to woo him away," Lani pouted.

"They can only lure those who are hungry for something else."

"He doesn't need anything else," Lani said tersely. "He's got what he needs right here."

"Good lord, La, just take a minute and think about what you're doing with your life," Kane begged. "You left your kids. You left your husband. What's this all about?"

Lani wasn't even listening. Her eyes glided across the crowd, searching. She detached, stalking away in a rush. Her lover had disappeared—likely with one of the 'goddamn debutantes'. Lani had left Kane alone on the dance floor.

Richie, ever the attentive prince, swooped in more gracefully than his pudgy persona suggested probable. His wide, smiling face made the mess of Lani Travers evaporate. He danced exquisitely, certainly trained by the best in all England.

"I see you're not alone," Kane said, glancing at the beautiful Egyptian woman sitting beside the empty chair that Richie had just vacated.

"I took your advice and invited her to the coronation," Richie proudly announced. "Queen Nefertari accepted my invitation…eagerly."

"She's a lucky woman," Kane said. "Perhaps you can take her for a lovely stroll in the real Sherwood Forest while she's here in Britain. A walk in the woods can be liberating and *so* illuminating."

Richie grinned mischievously.

Then Mark tapped Richie on the shoulder and Kane was suddenly dancing with her brother. "Have you seen Mary?" Mark asked.

"She was here earlier," Kane said. "She was with Larry and the kids at the coronation."

"She disappeared shortly after the dancing began," Mark worried. "Larry hasn't been able to reach her on her cell."

Kane looked around. There was a sea of faces. One was the bimbo who Mark had brought from her grandfather's entourage. Sora. Lani. Aunt Polly and Uncle John.

"Have you seen Abigail Morgan?" Kane asked.

Mark frowned. "What does she have to do with Mary?" Kane just looked at her brother. She didn't have to say. Mark knew Mary as well as Kane did. He swore. Then he took off, chasing after his twin—and probably too late.

Sora didn't seek Kane out on the dance floor, so Kane politely declined an eager earl from a small fiefdom that Kane had never heard of. He was old enough to be her dad if her dad hadn't died when he was younger than Kane was now. The princess parted the crowd like she was a celeb strolling the red carpet. Sora stood near a member of the waitstaff, the young man eagerly attending Kane's best friend's bottomless thirst. Kane pulled Sora out onto the ballroom floor.

Sora was tipsy but not drunk. "Maybe inebriated is the only way I can come out in public anymore," Sora said.

"Sevin didn't come?" Kane asked and regretted the question…obviously.

Sora shook her head. "No," she answered. "It's over."

But there were no tears. Half the men that glided past on the dance floor looked at Sora like they were undressing her with their eyes, and Sora ignored them all. She was already growing numb to the attention. Kane had masturbated in a public pool, played strip peek-a-boo on an elevator and hiked through woods in the buff. She understood the idea of getting used to overt sexuality and the attention it brought.

"You're going to be okay," Kane said.

Mark showed up. He shook his head. No Mary.

"She made her choice, Mark."

"We all make our own choices," Sora slurred. She wobbled and Kane caught her elbow before Sora tipped over.

"I've got her, Kane," Mark offered, taking Sora by the arm.

"What about your…date?" Kane asked.

Mark shrugged. "Sora needs me more than she does."

Kane nodded. Mark and Sora wouldn't be good for each other for very long, but maybe they were what they each needed right now.

So many bad decisions. Kane was tired of poor choices. Someone had to make a good one.

The master of ceremonies announced the last dance in a lilting British accent. Kane stood alone a moment. She saw a dozen eyes on her, each ready to pounce. A princess without a date to coronation was as alluring a prize as any of these royals had seen in a generation. What fresh fondler would be next to try to woo her?

She turned her back on them all. Kane Cambridge strode alone across the dance floor, making a direct line to the man standing at the opposite side. Everyone's eyes were on Princess Kane as she eschewed the tradition of men courting women. She had suffered one eager beau after another, and she was interested romantically in none of them. Kane wasn't going to wait for another to try his hand.

"So, are you going to dance with me or not?"

"Is it a command or a request?"

"Does it matter?" Kane asked.

Gade stood professionally, unbending, silent. Everyone's eyes were on them.

"Are you going to embarrass me by turning down a princess in front of a roomful of dignitaries?"

"No," he answered.

He took her hand. They glided along the floor like they were floating. Kane's heart soared, as if she had finally found a real-life magic carpet ride. This was what she wanted. This was everything that mattered.

"They're all watching," Gade warned.

"It doesn't matter," Kane said with a smile. "I don't care if everyone watches."

Gade grinned. "You're not the same young woman I met a few weeks ago."

"No," Kane answered.

"You're making your own decisions," Gade said. "And you accept any consequences."

"I know what I'm getting into," Kane said. "I didn't before. I do now."

"You do," he agreed, grinning.

His smile felt like the sun coming out after a cloudy spell that had lasted too long. She embraced her role as a princess and she knew what it meant to pursue Gade. She had tasted the life, seen the sights, worn the jewels and been wooed by the rich and powerful. After being offered the world, she chose Gade. That was apparently what he'd been waiting for.

Gade spun her around, lifting her off her feet. He leaned in and whispered in Kane's ear, "And I'm not wearing any underwear."

* * * *

Gade secured a secret escape from the coronation. He was head of her security and could arrange a surreptitious disappearance as spectacular as any magic trick. Kane wanted to exit the gala without encountering pestering paparazzi, fawning fans or endless angsty acquaintances. Gade paid one of the caterers to smuggle just the two of them out in the back of a bakery delivery van.

"Not exactly a limousine," Kane said as she looked about at her current accommodations.

"We avoided about a hundred requests for selfies, as well as all your friends and family. Everyone else's problems are now someone else's concerns—at least for one night," Gade said. "And no paparazzi."

"Just lots of paprika," Kane said with a smirk, gazing at rows and rows of spices lining one wall of the box truck.

And flour. Bags and bags of flour were stacked along the opposite wall of the truck, in large clear plastic bags that could be molded into comfortable furniture, like white-powdered sofas situated for seating. Gade made her a comfy seat. Kane reclined in a throne made of ground grains.

"Not exactly executive arrangements," Gade said.

"I'm not looking for the royal treatment, Gade. I'd rather be riding in the back of a bakery van with you than as part of some regal motorcade without you."

"You deserve only the best, Princess, but this is what you get with me."

"I've been courted by kings and dukes and sons of sultans, Renegade Williams, and I've found not one of them any more princely than you," Kane said, touching his chiseled chin with the tips of her fingers. "You're as worthy as any knight who ever defended Camelot, and I wish to choose Sir Lancelot as my consort rather than King Arthur. Perhaps chivalry should count as much as social status in considering the worthiness of a royal suitor. Maybe the world should start looking less at pedigree and more at merit. We've always done thing differently in America, Gade. We are the rebel state, after all—so let's rebel."

Instead of answering her with more words, Gade gave in. He pulled her into his arms and kissed her. It had seemingly been too damn long since he had given in to his passions. Like a dam holding his longing at bay, his lust for her suddenly burst through all barriers, flooding forth. He wrapped his strong arms around her like iron bands that could protect from any attack. His chest was a bulletproof barricade that could repel any enemy fire. Easily, he scooped her into his arms and held her, propping her neck with one hand while he cradled her back with the other.

Somehow, he managed to unzip her dress and the outfit valued at almost a million dollars was tossed on a small hill of corn starch. Her tiara was worth more than her Uncle John's pension plan after forty-five years working for the city, and it ended up dangling from a tray filled with boxes of cream of tartar. Kane kicked off her shoes onto a sack of granulated sugar.

They tore holes in their mattress of flour bags, Kane's writhing making small incisions with her sharp gemstone accessories. Flour started sifting through the slits. White dust gathered in small drifts in the shape of their bodies. The fine powder stuck to Kane's and Gade's skin like they were pieces of meat prepped for simmering.

Kane felt like she was sizzling. Her skin was on fire, and she was kicked into overdrive. Gade seemed to have his hands everywhere already, but she wanted more—more than everywhere…against, over, on, inside.

She didn't even feel him unclasp her brassiere, but she was suddenly bare, her breasts covered in handprints made of flour. Kane leaned back and sighed as he traveled his lips across her chest. She held his shaved head against her as thoughts washed away and consciousness seemed to float outside her body. They were fooling around in the back of a bakery truck. This was confection perfection.

Kane started to undress Gade. Her hands were covered with flour, and she left white powdered fingerprints on his impressive pectorals. The effect decorated his detailed muscularity, making accents of every curl and curve of his chest. There wasn't a part of him that wasn't perfect, and he looked just right against her. Their skin seemed to be made to be shared, hers against his, like the duet of two perfect song-makers.

Then she was completely naked and he was completely naked. Kane took a moment to measure Gade's impressive proportions. There were many physical specimens out in the world, and she had seen a few of them in the past few weeks, but emotions enchanted her appreciation, and her feelings for Gade made him the superior subject.

Gade took his time. Before, they'd been unable to resist each other, their hunger for physical pleasure overriding any restraint they might have otherwise had. And Gade had put her on a pedestal at the beginning, so was unable to long delay his thirst for her perfection. But their abstinence had given them an appreciation for pace. Gade had seen her flaws and wasn't desperate to delve into her perfection. Kane's exhibitionist escapades had given her confidence. She would get what she wanted whenever she wanted it. So she could slow down and wait, instead of grabbing it quick before it slipped away. Gade wasn't going anywhere.

Then Gade paused, holding her face in his hands. Both she and Gade were messy and hot and naked and ready. Yet Gade just stared into her eyes for long seconds.

"I love you, Princess," Gade said. "I have from the first moment I saw you."

"And I love you, Gade. I'm so ready to tell the whole world."

"But not right now," he said.

Kane nodded and smiled. "Not right this minute."

Then they were one. There were no more words. They made love in the back of a bakery van in a hill of sifted flour, white clouds moving in patterns associated with their undulating bodies, like two angels finding each other in the heavens.

Chapter Sixteen

Kane woke up. She lay in bed looking up at the ceiling—another hotel, a different city, one new experience after another. The tiara she had worn at the previous night's coronation rested on the bedside table. She could see her gown hanging in the walk-in closet across the room through the open door. She was alone in the bedroom, but she hadn't been alone last night before she'd fallen asleep.

Kane slipped out of bed. She didn't know where her underwear had ended up. Maybe it had become some princess prize for a baker when he cleaned up the sifted, sexed mess in the back of his bakery van. Kane had paid the baker handsomely for his troubles, and the young man had seemed amused by and appreciative of her efforts to apologize and compensate. He would fetch an impressive price for her coronation bra if he tried to sell it online.

The smell of breakfast wafted from the kitchenette in Kane's suite. She padded out in bare feet, barely awake, bared to the world and hungry as a bear. It may be someone other than Gade making her an early morning omelet—perhaps a chef had been arranged to make her fresh breakfast or maybe Mark was trying to make up for making a mess of his life. Yet Kane didn't hesitate on walking naked into the main living room of the suite. She just knew it was Gade. This time, he wasn't leaving. He wasn't hiding anymore.

Gade smiled, working at a small cooking area behind a peninsula. He looked even more massive in relation to the single-burner kitchenette cooktop. The wisps of steam rising off the breakfast created a mist that made Gade seem like a dream. His rippling biceps flexed as he flipped the omelet. His chest glistened as the steam condensed on the wide surface. She could only see him from the waist up, but she was certain Gade remained as naked as she was.

"That smells divine," Kane said.

"You look divine," Gade replied.

"Food first," Kane scolded playfully. "Flirting later."

Kane started eating. Gade leaned on the counter, smiling, watching. His gaze seemed to soak her up. The man's stamina was impressive. He had performed three times for her since her coronation. Gade hadn't been kidding when he'd whispered in her ear that he wanted to make up for lost time after the second occasion they had made love, right on the handwoven cotton rug outside the bedroom of her pristine Princess suite.

"Aren't you going to eat?" she asked.

"I would rather watch you than be distracted by breakfast," he said.

"Did you put cheese on the omelets—or just your corny come-ons?"

"Time is too sweet to waste on anything besides you."

"Saying things like that could spoil a girl," Kane warned.

"A princess should be spoiled," Gade replied.

"I need a shower," Kane said. "If you're looking to spoil me, you could scrub my back."

"Your wish is my command, m'lady," Gade answered.

The shower went on for an hour. Gade lasted just long enough for Kane to be satisfied…again. A new record. She could get used to this kind of attention. After attempting to avoid the paparazzi and popularity for the last couple of weeks, she finally wanted to be seen, to be obsessed over. No more hiding. No more standing in the shadows. No more sneaking through the woods. She wanted to stand in the sun and be seen.

"Are you coming with me today?" Kane asked.

Kane had a press junket scheduled for the afternoon, and it was nearly lunch time. Her breakfast and her fabulous dessert in the shower had wiled away the morning. Mark had texted her ten times by the time she checked her phone, repeatedly reminding her of her commitments. Kane texted her brother back and started to get ready.

She could understand if Gade needed to sleep. After the physical performance that he'd accomplished both last night and this morning, he might need rejuvenation. Every man had his limits. Kane would give him the day off for good behavior if he wanted it.

"I'm with you wherever you go, Princess. I'm not going to let you out of my sight."

"I don't think it's supposed to be dangerous, Gade. It's just a photo op—something staged along the

English countryside with hot air balloons and a lot of photographers. Mostly boring, I'm sure. Although I've never been in a hot air balloon before."

"I won't be there as just your royal guard."

"No," she agreed with a smile, "you won't."

Kane pulled on the Air Force T-shirt she had stolen from Gade's apartment so long ago now that it seemed like it had been someone else's life. In a way, she supposed it had been. The Kane that pulled the shirt on now wasn't the same one who had done so the first time. Now she was a princess—and wearing this shirt meant something very different.

"I think they might want you wearing something more appropriate to your stature, Princess," Gade said.

"You're right. They might want me to wear some sort of flowing gown or riding chaps or whatever princesses wear around here. But I'm not from around here. I'm an American Princess. I don't have a tradition. Everything is brand new. And I can't think of anything more appropriate than a shirt advertising the United States Armed Forces."

"It means more than that, Kane."

"It does," Kane said with a wink. Then she walked out wearing his shirt—and Gade followed.

On the way over, Gade rode in a separate vehicle and made final security preparations in coordination with the British officials. Kane was left alone with Mark in the back of a limo that stretched as long end to end as her old apartment. Lani was running late after sleeping off a blimey bender with Scatch that had lasted until well after sunrise, she'd reported. Sora said she'd get her own ride, avoiding the spotlight that centered always on Kane. The brutal British tabloids had been unsympathetic to Sora's wish to put the sex-tape incident behind her. The rumor-sections of the local rags featured blurred screen-captures accompanying Sora's personal biography. Mary remained missing as of lunchtime, Mark fearing the worst involving his sister and Abigail Morgan. Would she really throw away everything for an illicit affair with Abby? Would it be any different from what Lani had done to her life?

Kane didn't want to talk about any of the gossip.

"You don't look like a princess prepared for the press, Kane," Mark said.

"This is me," Kane answered, looking down at her Air Force T-shirt. "They get the real American deal."

"Authenticity," Mark said. "They won't know what to do with that."

Outside the limousine window, the English countryside opened up and a wide field stretched on for miles in every direction. Kane could see a collection of cars in the distance. In the pastureland behind the spontaneous lot, a large balloon made up of bright reds, cerulean blues and stark whites floated a few feet off the field, like something out of a fairy tale. Against the blue sky with puffed clouds, it was as magical a montage as anything Kane had encountered these last amazing days.

"Things just keep getting more unbelievable," Mark said. "Like your life is a series of bedtime stories."

"I don't know if I'll ever get used to it."

"Well, just take it day by day, sis. It can always end at any moment. Enjoy it while it lasts."

"I prefer to be a little more optimistic than that," Kane said. "I make my own future, Mark. I'm not going to let anyone else dictate tomorrow for me."

"But some things are out of your control. Do you think that Sora wanted her sordid story played out in vicious online blogs and terrible tabloids? Do you believe that Lani even realizes what she's doing to her family and her future? Mary is making a mess and she can't help herself. Your grandfather risked all his accomplishments and aspirations for a string of sexcapades. It doesn't matter what you plan. Your heart always manages to get in the way."

"It isn't like that. Gade is amazing."

Mark shrugged. "That's what I thought about Brooke—and Kelli, and Martina, and Chelsea and Rose. But they were all just temporary, Kane."

"Do you really think any of that was love, Mark?" Kane asked, picturing the parade of different women he had been with these last couple of weeks.

"It was for me. At least for a little bit," Mark answered. "Love is like the wind. It can blow in unexpectedly, last for a while and make a mess out of everything. It can storm something fierce for a spell, but eventually it puffs out...stills. Sometimes it's a lull so stifling that you cannot even breathe. It grows so stale you feel like you're suffocating."

"That's dismal, Mark. You've just had a string of sucky relationships."

"I've seen the truth. The best love is the kind that ends before it starts to sour."

"The Romeo and Juliet scenario again?" Kane asked. "Don't bring my parents into this. That was an accident, Mark. It wasn't damn Shakespeare."

"Like the flower pressed and preserved before it had a chance to wither and turn black."

"What about Sora?" Kane asked, trying to change the subject. Mark had escorted her to her hotel last night after the coronation.

Mark smiled. "It was nice. She's nice. Being with her isn't a storm. It's more of a soft breeze. Maybe that's a better speed. Maybe it will last a little longer that way."

"You are depressing me. Why can't you just believe in a little romance?"

"Like Mom and Dad?" Mark retorted.

Polly and John had just been faking it for years to keep the family unit together. Were they better people than Lani or Mary? Or just sadder? Maybe life was too short to weather the lulls? Maybe you had to set sail whenever the breeze blew? Did that mean that her affair with Gade wouldn't be happily ever after? According to Mark, the only ever-afters that ended happily also ended too soon.

"I have to believe in more than that, Mark."

"Mary believes in more than that, so she chases Abigail. But Abby is just the next Larry. Scatch is just the next Chase. I'm the next Sevin, although I'll treat Sora a hell of a lot better than that son of a bitch did. And Sora is just my next next—better than the last and probably whatever comes after, but who knows if it's even love? If it is love, it isn't love forever. It never is."

"I really wish I would have called a cab," Kane said. "You're unbelievably dreary."

"I've learned just one thing with all these girls coming and going, Kane. Hearts port in a temporary station. Love lasts only so long."

"So you think there's no such thing as true love? No one ever gets the fairy-tale ending?"

"There's a reason that movies are only an hour and a half long or why romance novels have a finite number of Chapters," Mark said. "What happens after 'The End'?"

Kane sat in silence as the large red, white and blue balloon loomed in her near future. What would tomorrow hold? She had told Mark that she was the captain of her own destiny, but what she thought and what she felt might be two different things—too different to sustain, like a Princess and her royal guard. Perhaps Gade was just momentary, like every other affair she had witnessed. Maybe love could only be sustained so long?

The limo pulled into the lot. Kane exited and the photographers became instantly obsessed with her look. The Air Force Fighting Falcons T-shirt and tight blue jeans was a unique ensemble…all-American. The reporters shouted questions about her attire, but Kane was disinterested in fashion. Her gaze found Gade. He stood across the field, consulting with security. He noticed her looking and smiled at her. And Kane hoped that she would never face the moment where that look no longer set her heart aflutter. She believed in a brighter future than Mark prophesied.

* * * *

Kane felt like Dorothy at the end of *The Wizard of Oz*. The balloon awaited her and there was a crowd gathered that included everyone imaginable, except maybe a complement of munchkins. *Reporters and dignitaries and celebrities, oh my!* Instead of a fairy godmother in attendance, she had a horny grandfather, not so much a good witch as a son of a bitch. Standing near the Senator was Sora, who had recently lost her mind and done desperate deeds to try to save her marriage. Lani was there, who had given away her heart to some string-bean idiot who looked more like a scarecrow than a lothario. And Mark, the man who had mustered enough courage to ask out girls ten times hotter than he was and had gotten burned over and over and over again. Mary had managed to reemerge, glowing like a schoolgirl with a crush. Abby attended, sucking up to Dash Dameron in the press pool, trying to spin a redemption storyline for Senator Cambridge.

Dash indecorously dismissed Abby as soon as Kane approached. Maybe he knew nothing at all about the situation with Kane's sister and her sapphic indiscretions, but it seemed like Dash knew something about everything. In any case, the host of *DamTime* making small talk with a former power player whose sponsor had lost all their clout seemed a waste of 'damn time'. He walked away from Abigail mid-sentence. It was rude, and Kane loved him for it.

Dash looked at Kane's T-shirt and smirked. He followed her eyes to the mountain of a guard standing among the other security officials. Dash nodded approvingly.

"You found your way," he said, "with true Kane Cambridge style."

"All new American ingenuity with a smattering of old-school royalty," Kane quipped, beaming ear to ear.

"He's a lucky man."

"What does luck have to do with love, Dash Dameron?"

"Everything," Dash said, his signature smile finally faltering. His eyes were entirely serious. For the first time since Kane had met him, Dash became entirely somber. "Happenstance works against true love. Fortune favors fleeting feelings, and such emotions fade as quickly as they bloom. Love can occur any night, any moment, for just a while or maybe for a little longer. But *true* love is precious and rare, Kane."

"Mark believes there's no such thing as true love. He thinks love that lasts forever is just a fairy tale," Kane said. "He told me that the most beautiful love stories end in tragedy, preserved before they have a chance to fade—like my parents or Romeo and Juliet."

"That sounds positively dreary. I'm much too optimistic for such Shakespearean bullshit," Dash confessed, his dazzling smile returning. "However, I've never been in a relationship that lasted longer than a weekend, so who am I to quibble?"

Kane looked at the hot air balloon. It was majestic and photogenic, a perfect punctuation mark to her English expedition. American colors rendered brightly against the evergreen British countryside. And there was Kane, in worn blue jeans that looked as authentically Americana as Springsteen, with an Air Force emblem across her chest. How many reporters in attendance would frame their story historically and how many sartorially?

"What's your angle on this story, Dash?" Kane asked before she started toward the balloon.

"Personal," Dash said, his smile winking in the bright British sun. "As always, Princess."

Kane walked across the open field. Gade intersected with her halfway between the front lines of the press and her destination. The photographers lit up the field, their flashes competing with the shining sun. None of them had confirmed the story just yet, but they had all seen Kane dance with her royal guard the night before. They wouldn't be reporters if they hadn't suspected the truth about Kane and Gade at the coronation ball. Now here were Kane and Gade again, together, reunited in the English countryside like two lovers out of a Jane Austen story.

Mark's voice whispered in her head—*"That's why romance novels have a finite number of Chapters."*

"Local authorities have assured me of proper protocol," Gade said. "I would've preferred to have had a more personal hand in arranging security for this event."

"Your personal hands were all over me this morning instead," Kane reminded him.

Gade smiled, that way of being both shy and sly at the same time.

"If anything happens, there's a plane fueled and ready for takeoff. I can be in the air in seconds," Gade said. "I'm on standby."

"Nothing is going to happen."

"I like to be prepared, just in case."

"And what will you do in an airplane that can help me in a hot air balloon, Renegade Williams?"

"I'm sure I can think of something."

Kane smiled. It was so easy with Gade. She knew right then and there that Mark was wrong. This feeling wouldn't end. If they lived to be a hundred, their love would survive that long inside them. Without a second thought or hesitation, Kane leaned forward and kissed Gade fully on the lips. The cameras took a million pictures, preserved for all eternity—as long as their love would last.

Kane strode across the rest of the field. British security surrounded the basket of the balloon. More royal dignitaries were in attendance, including Prince Richie. Kane smiled and the prince grinned back. Richie helped her aboard the hot air balloon. The idea was to float her up and away, the parting shot for her British adventure—something just for the press. She would land over the hills and be whisked away to a private airport, then home. Back to America.

The hot air balloon rose into the bright sky, soon just a red-white-and-blue American inflatable against big, puffy clouds. Kane waved like a princess in a parade, afloat instead of in a float. A hundred lenses reflected the shining sun, all a-twinkle below in the field like scattered shimmering diamonds. Kane watched as Lani and Sora and Mary and Mark grew smaller and smaller. She saw Gade sticking out in the crowd, tall and broad, looking up. Watching over her as always.

The only other person in the basket with her was the pilot. He wore a hat that looked like the Wizard's at the end of *Oz*, something of the sort that Abe Lincoln might approve of. Kane had paid the pilot little attention other than that the hat fit right in with her blue-jean-and-Air-Force American theme. The brim concealed his face as the pilot busied himself with the workings of the balloon. Kane hadn't recognized him…until he spoke.

"The easy part is getting these things airborne, you know. I had to Google that shit after I disposed of the real pilot. Easy peasy. Right there online. Now landing it might be a bitch, Candy Kane."

The pilot was Dillon. And he looked like he had gone quite mad.

The red, white and blue balloon continued rising higher and higher. All the people Kane loved were just small dots along the landscape, too tiny to tell who was who. She couldn't tell if Gade was staring up, wondering how high she was supposed to go, maybe realizing something was wrong. Would it be too late? What could he do about it anyway? What did he say before she left him? *"I'm sure I can think of something."*

"What the hell are you doing, Dillon?"

"This is what had to be done, Kane. I love you. It's the only way to make you see."

"By kidnapping me? Do you even know how to fly this thing?"

"Going up is simple enough. Just turned the valve," Dillion said. The look in his eyes was worrisome, like he wasn't quite *there*.

"Did you learn how to get down?"

"I needed to see you," he said. "Spend time with you…alone."

That didn't answer the question.

"In a balloon that you don't know how to land?"

"It'll land on its own, Candy Kane," Dillon said dismissively. He looked terrible. His eyes were red. His face featured a scrim of stubble. Dilly had gone nuts. How had security missed this madman? "We can float for a while, just you and me…into the sunset, Kane. That's a cool ending, right? Like out of a fairy tale?"

Kane pulled out her phone. "I'm calling for help."

Dillon backhanded her device with a violent swing of his arm. The phone flew out of her grip, spinning over the edge of the basket. The gloss of the screen caught the rays of sun, so that it looked like a twinkling star falling, falling, falling.

"Dillon, this is crazy! We're going to *die*."

"I just want you to listen, Kane," Dillon snapped. He paused…sighed. Dillon pulled a folded piece of paper from his pocket. A dozen petals from a pink rose pulled free with the paper, scattering across the bottom of the balloon's basket. The wad of paper was a wrinkled receipt from a liquor store, words written on the back in smudged black ink. "'*With love's light wings did I o'erperch these walls, for stony limits cannot hold love out.*'"

"This isn't a damn love story. This is an abduction."

"Princess, just shut up," Dillon muttered, "and enjoy the view."

He sounded like he was drunk, slurring words. He looked like he hadn't slept in days. Maybe she could fight him and take over somehow. But he was unpredictable and wired. He could flip her over the side of the wicker basket too easily. A wrestling match at two thousand feet seemed foolish.

So Kane shut up. Gade was down there, somewhere. He said he would find a way to save her if things went wrong. Well, things couldn't be wronger. But what could a man in an airplane do to save a woman in a balloon? The two things went together like a dart and a dirigible.

Kane worried she wouldn't survive this. Dillon didn't know how to get them down. They would most certainly crash. She could only hope that the air ran out gradually and they glided to a nice, soft landing. That seemed more like a fairy-tale ending than real-life results.

What had Mark said? The only true love stories are one that end in a timely fashion? Like her parents dying in a terrible car accident. Like Romeo and Juliet. Dead before their love could wither and fade. Maybe Mark was right after all.

"I just wanted some time with you, without you running away or your fucking body guard interrupting us," Dillon said. "Quality time, Kane. To help you remember the love we had."

"You really think we can have a second chance, Dilly?" she asked, keeping sarcasm out of her voice. She didn't want to provoke him.

"From up here, it looks like the whole world is ours. We can have whatever we want."

"I want to land safely," Kane said. "Let's make sure we live through today, then we can discuss tomorrow."

Dillon looked at the apparatus that breathed the fire into the belly of the balloon. He squinted against the heat of the flames—as if considering the mechanics, trying to figure out how the damn thing worked.

"I'm glad you're starting to see things my way," he said. "Let's enjoy the view for a little while longer."

Dillon reached out with his hand and Kane let him take it. They stood in silence for a while, looking out at the world around them. The early afternoon started to turn. Things passed beneath them, changing landscapes turning from prairie to lake to forest to a rocky cliffside that extended along a beautiful valley. Kane thought it would be a perfect setting for some love story…just not this one.

"Just let me go, Dillon," Kane finally pleaded, tears rolling down her face. She couldn't play this game anymore. "I don't love you anymore. This isn't some demented romance where everything is going to turn out all right."

Dillon blinked, as if waking from a bad dream. He let go of Kane's hand. He looked over the edge of the wicker basket, straight down, for a long while. Then he turned toward Kane. A light flickered behind his eyes, like he'd just figured something out. Like he'd seen the truth after believing a lie for too long.

"Just take us back, Dilly."

"I can't, Candy Kane," Dillon said. "I don't know how."

Then she saw *him*. Gade. He was parachuting through the sky like some superhero arriving to save the day. Dillon had his back to the direction where Gade was floating in. Gade was descending at a fast pace, aimed directly at the wicker basket. He had said there was a plane prepped and waiting, and now here he was. He had found a way to rescue her.

Gade crashed into the side of the wicker basket and released his parachute before a gust pulled him away again, the gossamer sheet floating down like a maiden's discarded kerchief. He climbed over the side as Dillon turned, Dilly's eyes becoming portals into madness. Dillon seemed unable to comprehend what was happening. He backed into the opposite corner of the basket as Kane fell into Gade's large, strong arms.

"You can land this thing?" Kane asked.

"If it's in the sky, I can get it to the ground safely," Gade said.

"No!" Dillon screamed.

His eyes were crazy. His face was something that Kane had never seen before. How could someone be so different from what she'd always thought? Then she considered Lani—everything thrown away for a tryst. And Mary with Abby… Mark and his temporary conquests… Sora's sordid video stunt… Aunt Polly and Uncle John living a lie for years and years… Her grandfather's legacy in ruin over sex… Now Dillon gone crazy because he couldn't have Kane.

"Let's get on the ground and we can discuss this like gentlemen," Gade said.

"I'm writing this ending," Dillon sneered, "not you."

Dillon grabbed one of the propane tanks strapped to the side of the wicker basket and Gade moved as fast as he could. But he twisted his trajectory as soon as Dillon's hand touched the valve. Gade was too late.

Dillon had become too desperate. Instead of running toward Dillon, Gade spun around in a pirouette, pulling Kane with him. Dillon lifted the propane tank up into the flame as Gade tumbled over the side. Gade hugged Kane in a protective embrace as the tank exploded above them.

The basket was between them and the bang, protecting them from a fierce fireball. The balloon went up in flames. Kane watched over Gade's shoulder as the whole airship became consumed by fire. Dillon was certainly dead. Gade had saved her from his crazy for a few seconds. Now they plunged toward the ground thousands of feet down.

"Gade," she said as the wind whipped her words away.

"I love you," he replied, his baritone voice sounding over the rushing air.

He held her in a tight embrace, his back to the wind. She felt safe. She felt protected. It was a good way to go…better than being blown up, better than a crash landing. But there was no friendly dragon that would come out of nowhere to catch her, no magic genie to save the day. She didn't expect a Pegasus to snatch her from certain death. This was real life.

Then they hit. Together. And Kane only knew darkness.

Chapter Seventeen

Kane dreamed.

Gade was a prince. He rode in on a white horse. Kane was asleep, under the spell of some evil queen. He possessed a shining sword and slew the monsters who guarded her. Then Prince Gade leaned over and woke her with a kiss.

Kane's eyes fluttered open. Everything was all right. It had just been a dream—and dreams had happy endings. But she was no longer dreaming and real life didn't always have a happy ending. She thought about her dad, the exiled prince. He'd died with her mother, too soon. And her grandfather, the king? His reputation was in ruin. Could there be a happily ever after in the story of the House of Cambridge?

Kane had survived. Gade had saved her. He had taken the brunt of impact and saved Kane's life. He was her royal guard…to the end.

Renegade Williams, her Air Force hero. He said if it was in the sky, he could get her to the ground safely. Well, she had been in the sky, plunging toward the ground like a falling star. And he had gotten her to the ground, safely.

Mark sat in a chair at her bedside. He looked like he'd been there all night. There was another chair beside him, a frumpy pillow hanging over the arm. Kane didn't have to ask. It was Mary's. Her brother and sister hadn't left her side.

"Mom and Dad are on their way," Mark said. "They were here earlier. Both of them went back to the hotel to get a little sleep."

"And Mary?" Kane asked.

"She stepped out to make a call," Mark said. "She didn't know when you would be waking."

"A call?" Kane asked, trying to distract her discordant thoughts. "To Larry? Or to Abigail?"

"I didn't ask," Mark said.

I don't want to know was what he meant.

"You two need a break. Why don't you head back to the hotel?"

Mark stood and stretched, his joints popping angrily. "If a king can sleep all night in a chair, I think I should be able to manage it."

"My grandfather?" Kane asked, surprised. "He's here?"

"He wouldn't leave," Mark said. "The British royal family offered him a guest room at Buckingham Palace. Fucking *Buckingham Palace*! But he stayed here instead, sleeping on a chair in the waiting room." Mark shook his head, as if that was the most unbelievable part of this whole story.

"He stayed?"

"He's worried sick about you, Kane. He lost his son too soon. He isn't ready to lose his granddaughter."

Kane thought about Dillon, who had once-upon-a-time been her one-and-only, then just lonely, then looney. She remembered wondering how a person could know someone so well and not know them at all. The same could be said for all her friends and family lately. Her grandfather had started out as her fairy godfather, turning Kane from mundane to majestic. Then he had showed his true colors, the evil old antagonist that liked pretty, perky flesh. Finally, Sidney Cambridge revealed his human heart, still beating within the beast.

"And you?" Kane asked. "Are you here alone?"

"Sora is in the waiting room," Mark answered, "with Lani."

"Waiting," Kane sighed. "I'm done waiting. I want to see him."

"Maybe you're not ready yet," Mark said.

"Ready?" Kane asked. "What do I need to get ready for? I'm not going to be putting on a princess dress before I leave this room. I want to see him, Mark."

"I just want to make sure you're strong enough, Kane. Everyone is pulling for you."

"Everyone?"

Mark turned on the television. Coverage of the kidnaping consumed every channel. Someone caught the balloon on camera at the end. One of the dozens of paparazzi chasing Kane around all day had filmed the footage of a lifetime. Kane could see her shadow falling with Gade, dark wraiths against the blue sky. The balloon exploded, the basket engulfed in bright yellow flames. A black husk trailed Gade and Kane on a different trajectory, the charred remains of Dillon Durfee. Kane watched until the falling shapes disappeared behind the tree line. Then the newscaster cut away to a live shot of the front of the hospital where Kane was right now. Flowers placed by well-wishers covered the grassy boulevard out front.

Pink roses…thousands.

"Help me up," Kane told her brother.

"You're not supposed to. The doctors told you to—"

"The doctors don't tell me shit," Kane snapped. "I'm a damn princess."

So Mark took her under the arm not in a cast and helped Kane get to her feet. He brought her IV stand as tubes trailed from her fingers. Kane shuffled beside her brother, down the hall, into another wing. A doctor tried to stop her, but she gave him such a withering glare that he balked and scurried away like a timid fawn.

She found the right room. Mark waited outside and Kane went in. Gade was there, flat on his back, a thin sheet draped over his big chest, looking so still and still perfect. He had smashed into the world like a comet careening from space, Kane curled protectively in his massive arms. He'd saved her life. He was the hero she needed…always. He had crashed into a planet and he still looked so handsome.

"Oh, Gade," Kane whispered softly.

He fluttered his eyelids open and he looked at her and smiled. "Princess."

* * * *

Gade would make a full recovery, eventually. The path to getting patched up would be prickly, but Kane didn't know anyone stronger than Renegade Williams. He had a broken fibula, cracked ribs and a snapped collar bone. Bruises purpled his brown skin. All in all, he was in good shape for a man who had plummeted a half mile out of the sky.

It was a miracle they weren't both dead.

Kane had been told that as they'd fallen, Gade had maximized drag by using his big body and his flapping coat, his arms spread like a man making a snow angel with Kane curled against him and holding on tightly. Gade could affect the direction of descent just a little...just enough. A line of resort hotels overlooked the valley beneath where the hot air balloon had floated just moments before. He'd aimed, and his aim had been true. Gade had hit the glass ceiling of a posh hotel at about a hundred miles an hour. They'd crashed through, landing unconscious in an Olympic-sized pool in a rain of shattered panes and pain. Bystanders had pulled them out and called for help. The sheet of glass and the water below had absorbed enough kinetic energy to save Gade's life—and Gade had saved Kane's.

"I'm alive," Kane said, sitting beside him, her hand in his.

"I promised," he said.

"So it wasn't *Romeo and Juliet* after all."

"More like a fairy-tale ending," Gade said.

"The hero saved the princess." Kane sighed. "How cliché."

"Sometimes the old stories are the best ones."

"The story of the American Princess was supposed to be a little more modern," Kane said. "Yet here I am, saved by the big, brave man at the end."

"Oh, Princess, that isn't how it really ends," said Gade. "I'm the one who needed saving."

"You're strong and fearless, Gade. You survived falling from the sky. No one needs to save you."

"My mother told me something when I was very young. I was always so tough, so big, strong ever since I can remember—protecting the littler kids and standing up to bullies a lot older than I was. I defended those that couldn't defend themselves."

"A hero from the very beginning, huh?"

Gade shrugged humbly and continued. "Mother said to me once that I was her valiant knight. But like a knight, clad in armor impervious to attack, there was still a man inside the suit, a heart that beat beneath the iron flesh. Mother said my heart was soft and vulnerable. That was my weakness. I was strong on the outside but vulnerable on the inside. That's why I resisted you so long, Kane. I wasn't strong enough to let you in. But you didn't give up on me. You see, *you* saved *me*, Princess. You're *my* hero."

Kane smiled, her eyes spilling over. "I see," she said through happy tears. "Well, I guess that makes us even."

"Even," Gade echoed. "We saved each other."

"Always," Kane agreed.

Mark stepped into the room. "He'd like to see you," Mark said.

Kane nodded. She kissed Gade on the lips and whispered in his ear, "I'll be right back."

Mark escorted her down the hall. The office at the end was assigned to no less than the hospital's administrator. Even fallen from grace, Kane's grandfather still had impressive influence. He could commandeer the best office in any building. Mark waited outside as Kane went in.

Sidney Cambridge sat behind an opulent desk, sipping fancy liquor alone in the large room. He looked tired and weathered. Back home, he was being investigated over ethics fraud. There were growing calls for him to resign. Certainly, his reign as king was over. Yet here he was, imbibing an expensive drink and reclining in an expansive office. At least a fall from grace could happen with style.

"I was surprised you stayed."

"I came to England in case you needed me for the coronation," Senator Cambridge said. "I never expected you would need me for this,"

"I should've seen it coming." Kane said angrily. "There were signs for weeks. Dillon was unstable. He thought he could get me back. And when he couldn't..."

"Love drove him over the edge."

"Love?" Kane asked. "Oh, I don't know if it was love—maybe obsession or something wrong in his head. What makes a person just snap like that?"

"Passion is the most powerful of potions," Sidney Cambridge said, swirling the swill in his glass.

"Gade was able to resist it," Kane said. "He put his duty over his desires. He waited until I was ready before he gave in to his feelings for me. I needed to become royalty on my own terms. He gave me space. He loved me, and he let me be free. Once I embraced my royal status, he knew I was ready to make my own decision. Instead of doing the easy thing, Gade did the *right* thing."

"He's a good man, Kane," her grandfather said. "He reminds me of your father."

Her mother and father had died in the full bloom of their love. It was eternal, existing beyond the reach of the normal decay of such passions. Now Kane's love for Gade would be something else—something new, like an American Princess. She would write a new ending to an old story. Her 'ever after' would be 'forever and ever'.

"I want to leave, but I'm not going without Gade. I don't think the doctors will sign off on his release."

Senator Cambridge nodded. "I can pull some strings. It's not *who* you know, it's *what* you know. I know a lot of secrets about a lot of people who owe me favors."

Sidney Cambridge had power. The Senator might be disgraced, but he still wielded great influence. Her grandfather would use it—and Kane would let him. She was done with England, and Dilly and coronations. She just wanted to go home.

* * * *

New York City. They landed late. The first stop was a posh hospital experienced in dealing discreetly with the rich and famous. Kane reluctantly departed after an extended exit, last kisses that would have made even a harlot blush. Gade smirked as she finally made it to the door of his hospital room. He looked all smug, despite an IV, beeping heart monitor and a cast peeking out of a thin blanket. Gade could make even a simple hospital gown sexy as hell.

"One more," Kane said, and rushed back for another kiss.

He smiled under her lips after more than just one. "There's will always be one more, Princess."

Kane had almost lost Gade. Just when they had finally grabbed hold of each other, they had been nearly torn apart.

"I love you, Kane," Gade said. "Forever."

"I love you, too," she replied. "But let's leave it at 'till tomorrow'. 'Forever' seems a little ominous."

"As you wish, your royal highness," Gade said, giving her a mimicked bow from his hospital bed.

"My wish," she sighed, "has already been granted."

Moments after, inside a limo, three strangers sat across from her. They all featured stony expressions carved into hard faces, like gargoyles upon the parapet. Kane's royal guard. It took three of them and they still weren't equal to one Gade.

The limousine arrived at a red-brick three-story residence in the middle of Manhattan. Kane looked it up and down. It was the grandest place she'd seen this side of a five-star hotel. A wrought-iron fence surrounded the perimeter, large gates standing open that allowed the limo entry. The front door looked like it was hammered from solid gold and trimmed with authentic silver. It even had turrets in the four corners. All it lacked was a moat. It looked like something right out of a fairy tale. Standing on the front stoop was Abigail Morgan.

"What is this?" Kane asked Abby as she exited the limo. Kane's trio of guards took up positions around the perimeter of the building.

"A princess needs a palace," Abby said.

"This is *my* place?"

"If you want it," Abby said. "The owners offered a one-night trial."

"Impressive."

"Does this mean I'm not fired anymore?"

"I can tell you to stay away from my sister if you work for me."

"You can," Abby said. "But will you?"

Kane considered Mary and Larry. Could she shut this down right here and now? If she commanded Abby to stay away from Mary, would that extinguish their feelings? Had Kane stopped thinking about Gade when he'd told her it was over? Mary had to find her own path, even if it left the devastation of her family in its wake. It was Mary's life to live, not Kane's.

"No," Kane whispered.

Abby nodded. "Stay the night. We can put in an offer tomorrow."

Abby left. Kane watched her walk away, wondering if she was the Romeo in Mary's story. What tragedy awaited the two of them? Or maybe Abby wasn't Romeo or Juliet. She was the poison that would end someone else's romance.

Kane went inside her castle. In the entryway awaited Lani, Sora, Mark and Mary. They were there to say goodbye. It was time to leave the princess to her palace—time to let Kane face her future.

Lani was first. She gave Kane a hug.

"Going home?" Kane asked.

"Going on tour," Lani bragged. "Scatch is promoting it as the 'Royal Escapade'. Deejay to the American Princess."

"That sounds like copyright infringement, La," Kane said.

Lani shrugged. "Your kingdom enjoys capitalism. It's not a monarchy, Kane."

Kane gave Lani a kiss on the cheek. Lani had her own story. Kane didn't foresee a happy ending in the magic mirror of probable futures. Lani rushed out the front door and down the marble steps as Scatch pulled around in a red Ferrari. Kane watched her go. Lani was riding high, like a surfer who'd caught a wave and stayed on top until it broke on the shores. Then Lani would catch another, then another, a series of crests and troughs, until she was too old to worry about such excitements. Kane would be there for her when she finally tired of the ups and downs.

Mary stepped forward and tried to give Kane a quick embrace. "I have to get to the airport, Kane. Larry booked us a flight home."

Kane held her, afraid that if she let her go, Mary would make a terrible mistake. "Take my limo."

Mary let her go and turned away, unable to meet her gaze. "I already have a ride."

Abby had pulled up to the front of the castle in a BMW and was waiting. Mary descended the steps before Kane could say anything. She climbed into the passenger seat. Her sister gave Kane a quick wave, then they were gone. Kane wondered if she would get a call from Larry before long, wondering why Mary was late for their flight.

Mark and Sora were the last ones left. "We can stay awhile, Kane. This is a big place to spend the night alone."

"I won't be alone," Kane said with a smile, hand on her heart. "My Romeo is right here."

Mark smiled and nodded. His hand was entwined with Sora's. Kane could tell they were eager to explore whatever was kindling between them.

"We'll be in town a few days," Sora said, looking sideways at Mark.

"Maybe you were right, Kane," Mark said, giving her a hug. "Maybe there can be happy endings."

Mark was saying what she wanted to hear, but he didn't believe it. He doubted. Mark and Sora were still looking for something that they weren't going to find in each other, like Kane and Gade had been in the beginning. Kane had to find herself on her own first. She found her happy ending after completing a series of challenges. More like a knight on a quest than a princess rescued from a tower, Kane had found her true self.

Kane hugged them both. They used her limo and disappeared.

Kane stood alone in the front entryway of the castle but she didn't feel alone. She felt protected. Gade was with her. Even apart, they were *together*.

Romeo and Juliet. Their love story had endured more than four hundred years. How long would the story of Kane and Gade last?

Sora, Mark, Mary, Lani, Dillon, Uncle John and Aunt Polly, her grandfather… They'd all had romance that had ended, but Kane loved Gade as much at the end as she had at the beginning. This was *her* love story.

Once upon a time, there was an American princess. And she lived happily, forever and ever after.

Want to see more like this?
Here's a taster for you to enjoy!

Sag Harbor:
The Billionaire and the Princess
Katherine E. Hunt

Excerpt

There is no excuse for this kind of behavior. I've promised, sworn and vowed never to fall for a bad guy again. *Take some time out,* I told myself, *learn the real Caitlyn, love yourself before you love others.* Why, oh why, then, am I half-naked in an airplane bathroom with a frickin' drunken, horny cowboy? Why indeed? He's hot, there's that, like *six-foot-two* hot. *You know what I'm talking about. The type of guy that makes you catch your breath when he brushes past you, hair a little unkempt, jaw a little too sharp.*

In my defense, I've had a very strange year and, frankly, life's gotten really, *really* complicated. Then there's the free alcohol, first time in Business Class... It's all gone to my head. I might be forgiven for getting carried away. *But still, no excuse, Caitlyn, no excuse.*

He traces a solitary finger down the outside of my thigh—my leggings hang off one ankle, dragging on the floor. My other foot, placed firmly on the closed toilet seat, is the only thing holding me up.

I lift my hair, curl it up on my head with my hands, soft lips brush against my neck. "You're so freaking hot," he slurs.

At first, I'd thought he had a Texan drawl until he'd confessed, giggling as the words came out, that he'd stolen the cowboy hat from the guy in the next seat down.

He's not Southern—he's just drunk off his head.

He brushes his fingers up my spine, circling the crux of my neck before gliding over my breasts, past the tips of my nipples, until they stop at the slick gusset of my undies. *Fuck.* For a man who smells like a brewery and has lost the capacity for coherent speech, he's pretty deft with his hands.

Pressing tightly onto my pussy, like it's the only thing holding us up, he fumbles with his trousers, pulling at his belt.

"Do you have a condom?" I ask.

"Uh…shi-it. Maybe?" He tries to grab his wallet with his one free hand and we rock back and forth as he tugs at his pocket.

Is this really happening? It was all going smoothly. Steamy, unexpected, drunken smooch in the corridor, unilateral decision to glide into the bathroom. Semi-naked foreplay.

It's all so serious, all of a sudden. Sex with a stranger. That's a sobering thought. *Is this how I want to start my new life?* It isn't part of the plan, that's for sure.

I've never done anything like this. I'm not an angel, but I've always been the *wait a few days, get to know the guy* kind of girl. Admittedly, they'd all turned out to be Mr. Emotionally Unavailable, Mr. Terrified of Commitment or Mr. Sleeps with Your Friends Plural Behind Your Back, but hey, I'd always kept my side of the bargain.

His fumbles prove fruitless. He takes his hand off me to grab his wallet, falls backward, slams hard into the door and slides to the ground. Turns out I *was* holding him up after all.

I spin around. "You okay?" He doesn't have any visible injuries, but he's a tall man in a small space and his knees are around his ears. He still looks cute though. *God, I need to get laid.* My horny is showing.

"Oh shit!" He says it way too loud. *Fuck, he's going to get us caught.* I'm not sure what the punishment is for kinky stuff in airplane bathrooms, but I know I don't want to start my brand-new life in America in an orange jumpsuit.

"Shh," I whisper, placing my finger over my lips.

"Shh. Hee-hee." That giggle again. He's wasted-like, actually out of it. This is rapidly turning into a very bad idea, not that at any point sneaking around with a man I've just met had been a solid choice. Kissing him? That had been fun, but now it feels a little like taking advantage.

He flicks through his wallet, still sat, half on the floor, legs splayed either side of me. "Shit. I got nothing."

I lean down and put my arms around him. He nuzzles into my neck. *God, he smells delicious.* Whoever he is when he isn't half-naked and hammered, he has incredible taste in aftershave. "Let's get you up."

"Wheeee!" With one hefty yank, he's on his feet. The effort sends my back crashing against the toilet roll dispenser. It's like getting a devastatingly handsome, six-foot-two, curly haired, horny octopus to stand to attention. *Impossible.*

Stepping back to steady myself, I hear a crack. *Shit.* Hopefully, his phone isn't super important because it has just smashed into a million pieces under my foot. I kick it out of sight, sit him down on the toilet seat and pull my leggings back up. My libido is fading. Fast.

I pull up my leggings and put my top back on. "You don't wanna do it anymore?" he drawls, his face downcast.

"I don't think that's a very good idea, do you?" He can't even stand up for a start. God knows whether he can get anything else up.

"You're hot." He snakes his hands up my sweatshirt.

"Thank you. You're very, very drunk." I fasten his belt for him, inciting more giggles, and hand him his wallet, which had flown into the sink. "I think I'm going to go back to my seat. It was very nice meeting you, cowboy. Maybe we'll meet again someday in better circumstances." I might sound like I'm fobbing him off, but some part of me sort of wishes it's true. I most definitely shouldn't. The type of guy who allows himself to get in this much of a state is not boyfriend material. Not for me, anyway. But he's a sweetie, and he's cute when he giggles.

Oh, Caitlyn, you're such a damn pushover.

* * * *

The old lady in the seat next to mine looks very concerned. "Did you hear all that noise in the toilet?"

"Yes. Apparently, some drunk guy fell over."

"Oh dear." She cringes. "Some people do get carried away with the free drinks on these flights. I hope he's all right." She's been reading a guidebook on New York for the last four hours and hasn't even acknowledged my presence, but now that I've got gossip, she's all ears.

"I'm sure he's fine. So where are you flying to today?"

She closes her book and looks at me. "New York." Her eyes widen with excitement. Bless her. She has to be at the very least in her seventies. I see a little of myself in her, always excited by new experiences, no matter how old I get. That's the only way to live.

"Well, yes. I meant for business or pleasure."

"I'm going to see my son. He's got a fancy job in Manhattan, going to show me the sights." She curls her lips into the biggest grin.

"Oh, that's lovely."

Something loud crashes behind us. "Oh dear," she mutters. "What now?"

A flash of white comes racing past our seats. A butt. A very naked butt attached to a very handsome, drunken, giggly cowboy.

"Shit," I whisper under my breath. Maybe I shouldn't have left him to his own devices after all. He turns and waves his not-insignificant appendage at a room full of dozing passengers before a hand reaches through the curtain behind him and pulls his drunken, naked butt into First Class.

"Good lord," she says, raising an eyebrow. "I haven't seen one like that since my Henry was alive."

I turn to her and smile, hiding my deep regret at my rash decision not to get cowboy's number before I'd left him. "Lucky you," I reply.

Sign up for our newsletter and find out about all our romance book releases, eBook sales and promotions, sneak peeks and FREE romance books!

About the Author

Romance author, traveler of the continental US, beachcomber, free spirit.

Antonia loves to hear from readers. You can find her contact information, website details and author profile page at https://www.totallybound.com

www.ingramcontent.com/pod-product-compliance
Lightning Source LLC
LaVergne TN
LVHW091023080826
845145LV00002B/335

* 9 7 8 1 8 3 9 4 3 7 4 2 7 *